ISBN: 979-8-9877273-4-8
Printed in the United States of America

Cover design by Manisha Holm

https://www.manishaholmauthor.com

REMEMBRANCE

DEDICATION

To Mary Stewart, who ignited my teenaged mind with a love of words and the stories they could weave. An adventure/mystery author who first introduced me to the astounding possibility of independent, intelligent, admirable women, in an era of widespread enforced pretense and repression. You changed my world view and life trajectory, Ms. Stewart.

QUOTE

My eyes are enthralled, O Father,
with the beauty of the flowers,
the passing scenes of life,
and the sailing, silent clouds.
Open that eye in me
which sees nothing but Thee.
With that gaze—
above, beneath, around, within, or without,
may I behold Thee.
Teach me to see in all things
nothing but Thee.
Open in me that eye
which beholds in all beauty
only Thy reigning beauty!

Whispers from Eternity
by Paramhansa Yogananda

Remembrance

A Journey of
Awakening

MANISHA HOLM

CONTENTS

AUTHOR'S NOTE

Whenever we visit another planet, we can become bewildered by unfamiliar names and terminology. In an effort to ease the bewilderment, you will find a glossary of names, places, and terminology at the end of the book. I hope this helps keep the Aironians in context, allowing their story to unfold in your imagination.

Best of luck!

Manisha

~ 1 ~

TWILIGHT

The Narsis wound their way along Stream, making their daily pilgrimage to Overlook.

The Eglans drifted on evening updrafts, relishing scents wafted from vast Forest with its towering trees.

Ava and Michael finished their nightly discussion of tomorrow's plans, rolled their screens, nodded goodnight. Ava turned to her favorite chair, deep and brilliantly yellow, fabric for a new skirt ready for her night's attention. Michael strolled along the Green, breathed in the twilit air, turned at the path that led to his front door. Harper looked up from her weaving as he entered, welcomed him with a brilliant smile.

Narsis flowed over mossy boulders, perched along Overlook, raised contented chests, and turned their gaze toward Sun as it touched a misted ridge.

Eglans swooped on silent wings, alighted, interspersed amongst stilled Narsis. Ancient partners shared events of their days, Above blended with Below. A twilight partnering, since all remembrance.

Scarlett doused the final glow of a final light, closed the wide door of her lab, shaded her eyes against the low sun that silhouetted the forest bordering Home Base, watched a turquoise cloud drift overhead.

Olivia smoothed her palm along the stainless-steel counter, a critical eye scanning the immaculate kitchen. She breathed in the fading aromas of dinner and laughter, drooped her shoulders, and bent her head; another meal survived.

Chatan and Aadhya curled into each other's warmth, watched the glimmers of Pond's surface, soared with the Eglans, skimmed the forest's heights with turquoise wings, felt the spray of the waves of Broad Sea, tasted the song of Lone Tree.

The turquoise cloud flowed, alighted on Lone Tree, first one, then five, then one thousand, dribbling down branches that sang the essence of Airon, since all remembrance.

Lone Tree sings of last light, caresses Burrow and Nest, Pond and Stream. Lone Tree holds Airon in its every fiber, holds Airon as she sleeps and dreams.

Final rays caught the Narsis as they wound their way along Overlook and Stream, filed lovingly toward Burrow, toward earned repose. Eglans rose and banked, watched Narsis wend, soared! to Nest, to their own earned repose.

Home Base sank into the night, white curves dimmed, silent, sheltered.

Airon sweeps along her ancient orbit, around her golden sun, dozing, dreaming, waking, cherishing, along her remembered path.

~ 2 ~

DAWN

As always, VaSoDeLa paused upon catching his first glimpse of the immense valley that spread below Overlook. Sun shone faint as dawn slipped into day, like a secret, filled with promise, whispered from one friend to another. He lowered his long body to lay in the morning shade and sent his awareness to flow across the void below him, awed by the day's grandeur.

The dawn Overlook soothed VaSoDeLa, an oasis of peace and simplicity. Vargad's meldmates, Sorgad, Dergad, and Largad each followed his lead and retreated to their own oases of peace and simplicity, relishing the delight and quiet shared across the far reaches that separated their lives and burrows.

VaSoDeLa watched a turquoise cloud of birdlings clear the treetops that crowded the brink of Overlook to cascade into the valley below, splash across a meadow, and skim a distant forest. Fresh joy brimmed VaSoDeLa's heart.

As Sun rose higher, a wedge of warmth lit VaSoDeLa's flank, crept, until it sprawled along his entire length. He slept. SoDeLa relaxed their vigilance, and all four meldmates drifted into dreams of splashing streams, swaying garlands, and frolicking younglings.

At the image of younglings, VaSoDeLa startled awake, raised his nose, and breathed the scents rising beyond Overlook's brink. Flowers. The sea. Birdlings. Many scents caressed VaSoDeLa's nose, but not the one he sought. He lowered his head, the gleam of the morning dusted with a longing he could hardly bear.

After a few final breaths, he rose and turned toward Burrow, carrying the hidden sadness he could not quell. His disquiet burdened him, a disquiet that he had learned to hide from his meldmates. The disquiet colored his thoughts and dimmed his Heading. Oblivious, his meldmates yawned, stretched, shook their pelts into tidy readiness.

The Arbans sing to the sky, and the Shosens listen. The Arbans sway in the wind, and the Shosens cavort, weaving patterns to shift the air and scent the wind. The Shosens sing courage and strength across grassy plains to twirl around Lone Tree, silhouetted against the dawn sky.

Lone Tree shimmers and stretches feathery branches toward the brightening air. Lone Tree sings of joy, awakening hope. Lone Tree turns its energy toward Overlook and breathes its song along its way. The song brushes VaSoDeLa's ears, sending hope along his spine.

Day is born.

~ 3 ~

EGLANS

In deep forest glade
branches woven
together woven
Nest embraces.
Twigs and tendrils
growing in and out
over and beneath
aflutter with dancing leaves.

Eglans are percussion
sturdy bills and strong feet
clacking and stomping
rhythms cascading through air
queues of gossamer wings
jingling harmony.

Eglans cherish Sky
Imagination soars!
ripples of wings
threads of air.

Narsis cherish Soil
solid knowing
queues of feet
threads of scent.

Partnership blending
bright Above
rich Below
lacing the world
making it whole.

Overlook dusked
evenings cherished
since all remembrance
as Sun meets far Mountain
fire sinking through Sky
to be quenched
quenched in twilit ridge.

Nest awakening
Sun climbing
Sky beckoning
Forest embracing
soar!
Eglans soar!
Soar! into day.

~ 4 ~

SECURITY

"We need to step up security."

"Oh!" Ava blinked. "What kind of security do we have now?"

"None! That's the problem."

Logan faced Ava across the slender table that held the center of her sitting area. She watched his face, waiting for clues about the seriousness of the conversation. "But why is it a problem? Has something happened?"

"Not yet. But we're just asking for problems if we don't do something."

Ava frowned. "Logan, forgive me, but I'm completely lost. What are we talking about here?"

"We know that the aliens are everywhere, all around us. We've known for weeks. We thought we had the whole place to ourselves, but now the forest is crawling with unknown...creatures...and they could be any size or shape. We have to protect ourselves."

Logan's lips pressed into a thin, straight line; sweat beaded on his forehead. Was she playing a game with him? Why did she have to question every single idea he proposed? He struggled to keep his thoughts ordered, dreading the manipulation that might ensnare him. Why couldn't he just go ahead with things? He hated this kind of song-and-dance routine.

Ava squinted, lining up her thoughts. "I want to correct you: They are natives; *we* are the aliens. It's an important distinction that we need to get right in our own minds. Moving beyond that...technicality...I don't feel any threat. Has something happened that made you feel threatened?"

"The Narsis are huge!" He held his arms out from his sides in a wide arc. "We don't know how fast they can move, but with all those legs, I bet they can really get going. We could be overrun in the blink of an eye. I think we need a wall. And I think we all need to carry protection."

"Guns? You're talking about guns, right?"

"Yes, ma'am! And a good strong wall. Something smooth so the Narsis can't crawl up over it and take us by surprise." As he described it, the obvious possibility took shape in his mind and the menace became even more real; imminent. He had to keep these people safe! They were too...naïve to think about these things themselves.

Ava's companion recognized a discussion of plans for a needed structure and tools. It relayed the information to the ship. The ship sensed the discord in the conversation and the wrongness of the proposed wall and the destructive purpose of the guns. The ship stilled its creation front in the recycling bay, deciding to remain unresponsive.

Ava patted the air in front of her with a stiff hand, marshaling her patience. "I'm being slow on the uptake, I think. Can I tell you what

I think you're saying and then you tell me if I'm understanding you correctly?"

Logan nodded, elbows askew, hands pressing down on his thighs. He swayed slightly from side to side, restless, but paying close attention. He waited for a trap, a way that she might turn the tables on him.

"We set up the settlement with the possibility that we were all alone on this planet, or at least on this part of the planet. We've met intelligent natives because the Narsis showed themselves to us and started a conversation with us. They're large creatures, and we know very little about their ways." Logan nodded as she paused.

Ava counted more facts on her fingers. "You're concerned that we don't know very much about them. We should prepare for the eventuality that they aren't as kind and gentle as they appear to be. We need to take precautions, mainly by establishing a perimeter wall that would keep them outside; one that would keep *all* creatures outside. And you're saying that we should carry weapons with us just in case they mount an attack and take us unawares."

"Yes, ma'am." He nodded curtly, satisfied that she understood the threat but suspicious that she would brush it aside.

Ava leaned forward, arms resting on her lap. "Have you seen anything specific that gives you a sense of alarm?"

"No." He shook his head emphatically. "I'm talking about prevention here, not getting even or...or reacting to anything. Simple prevention is all."

Ava nodded. "Have you talked to others about this? Are other people feeling alarmed?"

"Here and there. I'm too busy to talk to everyone." He shifted nervously. The ringing started in his ears. She was probably going to edge her way around him after all. He decided to broaden the scope of the threat. "It's not only to protect us, but also our stores. We have limited supplies, which we need to manage very carefully..." He lifted a forefinger to emphasize his point. "We need to take action. We need to be ready."

"You do an excellent job of managing the supplies," she said immediately. "You're the perfect person for the job."

Logan nodded absently. She was sweet-talking him, that was obvious. "Thank you." He paused, deciding to press the advantage. "But we really can't afford to have things go missing. They could just walk in and carry away everything in a single night, while we're all asleep."

"Has anything gone missing?"

"No." Logan took a deep breath, huffed. His frustration ratcheted up a notch. "Like I said, I'm talking prevention, not reacting to anything specific. We need to be prepared."

Ava sat back in her chair. "Okay. Thank you, Logan. I think I understand what you're telling me." She made sure her voice was calm, "But I'd like to suggest that separating ourselves from our surroundings would send the wrong message. I don't think we should fear the worst from the Narsis or from any other creature that might be wandering around in our forest. In their forest."

She continued. "The natives have shown us courtesy, kindness, respect, curiosity...They've let us go about our business of setting up Home Base, which must seem very perplexing to them, and throughout it all, they've displayed nothing but gentle kindness. I think it would be...well, *traitorous* of us to go on the defensive. I think it's safe to assume the best, and I think the right thing to do *is* to assume the best."

Logan sweated under her focused scrutiny, her commanding tone. Blood pounded in his ears, and the ringing threatened to drown out Ava's voice. He blurted, "I think we're just setting ourselves up for a disaster that could end up wiping us out."

Ava lifted her hands, perplexed. "But why in the world would you think that? I can see no indication that the natives are a threat. They've displayed no aggressive or even mildly negative behavior."

"Because we don't know anything about them. Who knows what they're doing out there without us knowing it?" He flung up his hands in frustration. She was doing it again. Now he was so confused, he couldn't think straight. He fumed that he'd lost the battle; just like with his sister. Every time. Why did Ava have to make this so difficult? Why did she always make it a point to out-think him? Why wouldn't she take this seriously?

She regarded him mildly. "So, we should fear them because they're unknown?"

"Because we might not be safe." He glared back.

Ava waited a moment and took a deep breath, careful not to show her frustration. "Well, it's true; we might not be safe." She raised her palm to forestall his words. "But I sincerely believe that if something were amiss, we would have sensed danger by now. Any of us who have interacted with the Narsis would have felt that something was a bit off. But we've all experienced the opposite. Every encounter has been delightful. No one has voiced any concerns. Not in the slightest."

She could feel his alarm, his frustration, and tried her best to assuage him. "Fear is not a trustworthy guidepost. If your concerns are based wholly on fear of what might happen without any indication that it's true, then it's *blind* fear. We can't be guided by blind fear. We can't let ourselves go down that road. It will take us somewhere we don't want to go."

He had heard her talk about things like this before, and he wasn't entirely sure he agreed with her or even understood her, but he continued to listen closely, giving himself a cover while he fought to calm down. "We have our guideposts that have proven trustworthy for eons: love, wisdom, calmness, joy, power..."

"Building a wall would show our power."

"I think it would show our fear."

They sat motionless in the quiet room. Logan thought of Ava's robotic movements in the shell of the gathering hall long ago and could think of nothing more to say. He drooped. It was useless. She had wrapped her crazy logic around his simple warning and outtalked him. He couldn't think as fast as she could, so he had lost. He sank into despair.

Ava relented. "I can see that you're still unsettled about this. Would you consider sitting down with Chatan and talking this over with him? He knows so much more about behaviors and interspecies signals than I could ever hope to convey. Plus, he has more direct knowledge of the Narsis than anyone else. He might be able to give you some certainty that will reassure you. Will you talk with him?"

"I don't know him very good." Logan liked Chatan well enough. Maybe he could explain himself better to Chatan. Man to man. Then they could convince Ava together; a joining of forces. The ringing in his ears softened, and his pounding ears dimmed.

Ava smiled reassuringly. "That's okay. I'll tell him you're going to come see him, and I'll briefly outline the situation. I think he might be able to put your concerns to rest."

She reached out and touched his arm. Logan wasn't used to being touched, but he managed not to flinch. "This is important, Logan," she said solemnly. "I absolutely do not want you to have to carry around this fear. Fear is an awful place to be stuck, and I'm sure Chatan can help you shift your worries into something that makes sense to you and gives you peace of mind. Will you talk to him? I really don't want this anxiety to go on longer if we can avoid it."

Logan heaved a deep sigh and patted his palms gently on the tops of his thighs, deflated. This conversation had not gone well, which did not surprise him. He just wanted to leave and go about his business. Waste of time.

He covered his disgruntlement and told Ava what she wanted to hear. "Yes. I will talk to him. But then," he shot at her, "we'll want to come back and talk to you, because we'll both know this is important."

"Fair enough. I'm completely open to further discussion. Do you want to walk over to dinner with me? They're about ready to serve."

"No." He just wanted to be gone. "I still have a lot of work to get done. I want to see where we are for the rest of the year."

They both stood up and moved toward the door. Ava touched his arm again. "Logan, I appreciate all the hard work you do. You've kept the community on an even keel with your firm management of our resources. You help me feel safe by letting me know we're not going to run out of anything crucial, because you're completely on top of the situation. Your work is vital to our success." She sensed that his dissatisfaction persisted.

She patted his arm. "We'll get this security thing worked out, so everyone feels confident on that front, too. I appreciate you bringing this to me so we could talk it through together. With Chatan's help, we'll make sense of everything."

"Yeah." Logan summoned his patience and waited while Ava sorted through her shoes, producing a matched pair. They walked along the path together and paused at the edge of the Green.

Ava turned to face him. "Thanks, Logan. I'll let Chatan know you'll be getting ahold of him."

Logan gave a low wave and walked away, head down, around the curve of the path. He turned back and called to her retreating figure, "Do we know anything about the plants yet?"

"Not yet," Ava called over her shoulder. "I'll let everyone know when Scarlett has results."

"And why is *that* still taking so long?" muttered Logan under his breath. He turned and clumped back to his shelter, where his screen awaited him with its stacked files of graphs and familiar columns of figures. He didn't like the way the meeting had gone at all. Waste of time.

Logan prickled at Ava's condescension. She always treated him like he was stupid. Maybe he didn't have some fancy degree like she did. Sure, he hadn't traveled all over the place like she used to, but that didn't mean she was better than him.

His scowl kept him company the entire evening.

$$\sim 5 \sim$$

GATHERING

"Shall we begin in stillness?"

The chatter quieted. Everyone scooted around to face the large window along the front of the gathering hall. Many people sat in chairs; others were cross-legged on the floor. Some propped themselves up on sturdy cushions.

The room fell completely quiet. Almost all eyes were closed, but Tom gazed out the window, smiling to himself. He had finished organizing his tools in his reconfigured workroom, adding new ones from the recycle bay. It had been a good day. He felt a sense of endless possibilities; new ideas popped into his head for extending the network of synthetic pathways throughout Home Base to eliminate the need for shoes. The weather was consistently pleasant; it seemed pointless to have to wear shoes. The shoe/no-shoe controversy remained fiery. People could keep to the paths to avoid blending; going in and out of shelters would be easier...

He sent the thought away and concentrated on his breath, watched it flow up his nostrils and down his spine, again, and then again. A favorite chant played in his mind, lifting him into bliss.

"Peace."

The room rustled slightly as people adjusted their positions, took off wraps, stretched a leg. Harper got up and moved to where Michael sat unrolling his screen in preparation for taking notes. She smiled as she sank to the floor next to him. "Hey," they said simultaneously.

"Well." Ava's voice carried across the room. "How was your day?"

Susan raised her hand immediately. "I've set up a new cistern for catching rainwater. We could use it for bathing and cleaning, until we install a filtering system for drinking water." Her sharing prompted an extended discussion, with other people suggesting additional water sources discovered during wanderings. Others asked questions about locating central washing facilities near the cistern. Should the cistern be nearer to the kitchen?

As the topic exhausted itself, Caleb spoke up. "I have new tools and equipment from the recycle bay, and I'm open for expanded business. Send me a message if you need help with maintenance or adjusting your shelter or workshop."

"Any interesting discoveries?" Ava asked the gathering at large.

"Henry and I wandered west this afternoon," Dylan said from the back of the room. "I climbed that shallow rise all the way to the top and found a wide vista beyond the rise. I could see a lake just over the next ridge. It might be a good water source. I saw plenty of flat land on one end of the lake. Might be nice for a permanent settlement."

"I thought this one was supposed to be permanent," grumbled Logan under his breath.

Sabri had been researching star maps gathered during their planetary approach as well as progressions of night skies as seen from Home Base. Anyone interested could easily download the files.

Study of weather patterns was ongoing. Some of the new food textures were well received (scattered applause here). Olivia implored people to arrive on time for their kitchen shifts and suggested instituting progressive consequences for those who failed to show up for an assigned shift. This topic ushered in a short, heated debate over commitments and overwhelm. It blew itself out, with everyone once again agreeing to accept greater responsibility for showing up when scheduled and to give kitchen assignments priority over individual projects.

At the end of the hour, Michael spoke up. "Any last comments?"

Nobody spoke for several breaths. "Okay, then," concluded Michael. "Shall we end in stillness?" People rustled into silence.

After a few breaths, Michael brought the gathering to a close. "That's it for today. See you all tomorrow and have a restful night."

Conversation rose on all sides as people gathered belongings and slowly filed through the doors, stopping for shoes and to finalize evening plans. People appeared animated and cheerful.

Everyone except Logan, who waited impatiently to retrieve his shoes. He was behind in his inventory updates and felt peevish about further delay. He had no time for everyone's nonsense. He struggled to hide his impatience, but his scowl showed his frustration.

The gathering ebbed outdoors, following the pathway toward the Green, dissipating into shelters and the dining hall. The twilight thickened. For the most part, 107 Earthens felt that it had been a good day.

~ 6 ~

VASODELA

Vargad moved through Burrow overcome with disuiet. He had lingered after the last Caretake-er had carried the last birthling from their sleeping niche. The last threads of Dawn Wisdom had drifted away, a faint fragrance floating in the birthling's wake.

Vargad pondered his yearning for Dawn Wisdom. His burrowmates treasured these moments with the birthlings as much as he did. Dawn Wisdom carried the strongest connection with Source when the birthlings were at their freshest, newly arrived in Burrow. But his burrowmates were content to then go about their days, wandering away from the sleeping niche with a sense of purpose and enthusiasm for a day with Sun, wandering through Forest, drinking from Stream.

Vargad enjoyed these activities, too, but always he carried with him an emptiness that he did not see haunting other eyes. Vargad pondered.

He moved through fragrant tunnels, rich with the teeming life that was Below. He ran his holderlings along walls, listened for songs from the trees growing above. He paused at a junction to appreciate the scents wafting from tunnels burrowed under other trees, heard their songs. Vargad immersed himself in the chorus that made up

Below, a choir of joy and purpose, a complex community threading through and around every particle of Soil, connecting all that is.

Vargad drew in another breath, quenched his disquiet as best he could, and continued his winding journey through Burrow, the scents of Above quickening the air before him. He paused at the threshold, eyes adjusting to bright sunlight, waited several breaths while Sun brightened his heart, and sent meld threads to sail across vastness in search of his meldmates.

He found them easily, the meld threads that searched for him, the three that sang the sweetest song, rang with the richest colors, that entwined with his threads. For a breath, two, they were back in their own long-ago birthling niche, surrounded by littermates, rousing themselves amidst the glow of Source, holderlings tremoring with the glorious cadence of the newly born.

Vargad held the remembrance in his heart, treasured it; treasured his meldmates. He opened his eyes, breathed deeply, and moved gently onto the nurturing families to doze peacefully, holding his meldmates in an entwined embrace. The nurturing families, stretched upward to meet Vargad's warm skin and pressed themselves into thin discs, a fragile synapse connecting Narsi with Below.

Nutrients flowed from leaf through skin, flowed upward from the wealth of Below, given with joy, since all remembrance. As Vargad's doze deepened, his nose lowered until it nuzzled amongst the Nurture-ers, giving them the gift of breath. The Nurture-ers captured his breath and spread it outward, sharing with all the richness of Narsi breath.

Time passed.

Sun rose fully and spread radiance across Meadow and the resting Narsis. Dew melted away and Meadow sang of warmth and light, a brilliance that danced each morning, in all remembrance.

Vargad yawned, gifted a final breath, and gathered his holderlings beneath him. He rose and brightened the threads that melded him to Sorgad, Dergad, and Largad. The four meldmates rose as one, VaSoDeLa stretching his nose, in unison with his meldmates' noses, reaching to greet a vividly blue Sky.

VaSoDeLa moved across Meadow, allowing time for his burrow-mates to stir from their rest, and watched as Caretake-ers lifted drowsy birthlings onto backs to carry them back to Burrow, their morning nourishment complete. Younglings scampered and tumbled, a covey of tumbling joy, rolling and chortling, filled with energy and delight.

As the family gathered to wander Forest and Stream, VaSoDeLa discussed Burrow matters with his meldmates, sharing news amongst the four, far-flung Narsi families. Dergad, Show-er, led a group of younglings to River. The younglings often splashed through Stream, and Dergad thought it time for them to understand the might of River, its power.

Sorgad, Caretake-er, sang of caution and concern. Largad, Find-er, sang of discovery and awe. Sorgad, Caretake-er, sang of caution! and concern! Vargad, Head-er, sang of confidence and courage. Vargad, Head-er, sang of trust and knowledge, in Dergad and his younglings, in all breaths shared.

Largad, Find-er, led her younglings to a distant burrow, to explore matings and meldings, a possible life burrow for one her younglings, a whiff of promise. Sorgad, Caretake-er sang of sorrow and separation. VaSoDeLa sang comfort and succor, sang of stages of life, the strength of new connections, blossoming awareness, growth.

VaSoDeLa smothered the sadness in his heart and followed his family along Stream. Younglings scampered across boulders and danced in the bright splashings of Stream. Turquoise birdlings swept over the family, and the Narsis paused to raise noses, caught the scent of treetops and vistas, waves and mist, glimpsed the distant sea. Onward the birdlings flew, to sweep across other Narsi families, who in turn lifted noses, catching the same scents, connecting all that is.

~ 7 ~

BLENDING

Harper threaded her way past enormous trunks and lacy ferns, Andy, her companion, drifting behind her. Zoe and Claudia traced her path, keeping Harper just in sight. Harper paused and breathed deeply, tasting the afternoon air. Blending was effortless when she wandered alone. Bringing others made her second guess and doubt herself, making her more cautious.

One place was probably as good as any other.

She turned and waited for Zoe and Claudia to catch up. The three women stood for several breaths, enchanted by the myriad colors and scents wafting through the forest.

"Ready?" Harper asked.

Zoe and Claudia nodded.

"Good. Me, too. I'll watch while you blend. Wander as much as you want, wherever you want. I'll follow Zoe," she lifted one hand to palm Zoe's arm, "and Andy will follow Claudia." she lifted the other hand to Claudia. "We'll keep you both perfectly safe; no need to worry about anything." She nodded to each in turn and dropped her hands from their arms. "We have hours to blend, if that's what happens. You can let yourselves be completely free."

Zoe and Claudia toed off their shoes, bouncy with enthusiasm. They turned, faced a random direction, and stood quietly. Harper moved to watch their faces, to see their eyes brighten, lose focus.

After many breaths, Zoe moved to a nearby tree and ran her palms along its smooth, white trunk. She stayed with the tree for quite some time, touching her forehead against the trunk, spreading her arms to encircle the girth as far as she could reach, bending her head to peer up along its height, holding still. Her movements were slow, loving.

Harper knew, without knowing how she knew, that the love flowed in both directions. Zoe poured love into the tree while the tree drenched Zoe with rapturous love. Harper spread a small sitting cloth some distance from Zoe and her tree and settled in to wait.

She saw Andy hovering, a silent white orb, a thoughtful distance from Claudia, who was running her hands slowly through tall ferns studded with gleaming crystals, soft lavender against dusky green. Harper could feel the wonder on Claudia's face, even at this distance.

Zoe backed from her tree, lifted a final hand from the glowing trunk, and drifted away, placing her hand on another trunk, another, lingering for a few breaths, then wandering farther. Harper scooped up the sitting cloth, settled it easily across her shoulders, and with a final glance toward Andy and Claudia, she followed Zoe in her random wander.

Zoe followed a brook, paused where it widened into a shallow pond, watched it tumble through a short cascade to fall into a second pond, smaller yet deeper than the first. Zoe sat on a poolside boulder and dipped her feet into the still water. She gazed up through overhanging branches, watched the sunlight glimmer on the ripples sent out from her swaying feet, and breathed in the silent air.

Languidly, Zoe placed her hands to either side on the boulder, lifted her weight slightly, and slid into the pool.

The water came up to her waist. Her thin shorts and top were no hindrance. She leaned forward and with two strokes reached the center of the pond. She trod water, then surface-dived out of sight. She reappeared moments later, spraying a fine mist into the air, her cropped hair plastered flat. She turned and floated, hands swaying at her sides, chest rising, falling as she breathed deeply in, out.

Harper watched Zoe and the pond with deep longing. She couldn't remember ever having swum in any of Airon's water. It looked glorious, and she was mightily tempted to join Zoe, to know that immersion of bare skin into clear water. She grumpily reminded herself that her role was to watch.

Scarlett and Ava had agreed to allow blending experiments only if supervised by a watcher. Harper was stretching the edges of the agreement slightly by setting Andy as a second watcher for Claudia. Zoe and Claudia were constantly together and pleaded to experiment with blending, together. Harper pressed her lips together, reassuring herself that she broke no agreement by conducting this double experiment.

But standing here watching Zoe float in Airon's water, sun streaming through still air, demanded all of Harper's willpower to hold herself back from flying down the bank and plunging into the glistening water. She drew in a breath and concentrated on the gift of keeping Zoe safe and worry-free, working to keep resentment at bay.

She felt overlooked, used, presumed upon. People always came to her to get approval from Scarlett or Ava for blending in the forest. Was it necessary? Scarlett assured Harper that she was essential for the ongoing blending experiments. But just how much data did they need to collect?

At long last, Zoe turned and made her way to shore. She rose from the deeper water, rivulets streaming down her legs and neck. On a whim, Harper tossed her sitting cloth to Zoe, who caught it and turned her smile to Harper.

"The water is exquisite," Zoe said. She toweled her face, her hair, and wrapped the cloth around her shoulders while Harper stared, astonished.

"You're aware that I'm here?"

"Yes," Zoe confirmed. "The blending has settled down to the point that I can stay in my body and know what is around me." She looked around. "Do you know where Claudia is?"

Harper shook her head, annoyed. "We could look for them. I'm sure Andy is still with her, but I don't know where Andy is."

Zoe closed her eyes and rotated her head slowly, zeroing in on a specific direction. "Claudia is in that direction. I can feel her."

"Can you feel Andy?"

Zoe paused. "No. Only Claudia."

Harper looked down to her feet, hands on hips, and shook her head slowly. "Two new things about blending. Airon's water is exquisite, and it's possible to find people from a distance. I'll be sure to tell Scarlett." She continued to study her feet, sullen.

Zoe nodded. "Yes; exquisite."

The two set off, guided by Zoe's reckoning, and soon spotted Andy's white shape through the widely spaced trees and low grasses. They found Claudia sprawled on an expanse of ground cover, her head propped on a pillow that Andy had probably provided. At their footsteps, Claudia squinted up at them and slowly sat up.

"I fell asleep. Have I been out long?"

Harper replied, "Probably not long. We just got here, so we're not sure."

Claudia stretched her long arms up to the sky and noted the lowering sun. "That nap was exquisite."

Harper glanced at Zoe, who smiled down at Claudia, who clambered to her feet.

"How was your afternoon?" she asked Zoe.

"I went swimming. It was exquisite."

Harper watched the two friends as they turned as one and walked unerringly in some predetermined direction. They bent to retrieve their shoes, slipping into them easily, a choreographed pas de deux. Earthens always knew where to find their shoes after blending. Harper found that odd, especially given the confused fumbling for shoes when leaving the gathering hall. Another tidbit for Scarlett.

Zoe turned toward Home Base. "It's probably dinner time. I'm starving. Shall we check what they've made for us?"

Claudia shook her head. "I'm still full from lunch. I think I'll skip dinner."

"Oh, not me. I'm dreaming of a big bowl of noodles. Want to come anyway?"

Claudia shrugged. "Sure. We can hear what everyone was up to today. All I did was sleep. I must have really needed it."

Their voices drifted away as Harper watched them go. It was clear that neither woman remembered their blending, just as always. Airon's awareness had drifted away from them once they donned shoes, and all was as it had been before.

Well, Harper thought to herself, they also completely forgot about me. You're welcome, she mentally called after them.

She rested her hand on Andy's smooth surface. Andy, who was suddenly there, offering companionship. Exactly what Harper needed after a day bereft of blending.

The Newcomers threaded their way back to Home Base as a turquoise cloud lifted from a thousand high branches to skim across the forest toward the setting sun.

~ 8 ~

BONDING

Logan chewed his moustache, deep in thought, when a rap-rap-rap at his door startled him. He briefly considered ignoring the summons but groaned himself to his feet. He needed to move around a little, anyway. He limped across the room, his knees reluctant, and leaned his arm on the wall as he pulled the door open.

Chatan stood, a few paces back, fists on hips. The two men regarded each other for a breath. Chatan broke the silence. "Ava suggested I drop by."

Logan paused and looked toward his screen. He had been designing a perimeter wall, basing it on the contour plots that Sophia and Mateo had scanned around Home Base. Not the best timing. He considered making excuses and putting off the visit, but he had agreed to talk with Chatan. He shook his head. He didn't want Ava using any excuse to get around his determination about security.

He opened the door wider. "Yeah. Come on in."

Chatan remained motionless. "How about you come out? We could walk around."

Logan heaved a sigh and scanned the sky and trees bordering the Green. "Where?"

"We'll figure it out."

"Okay." Logan scratched the back of his head. "Let me find my shoes."

"Take your time."

"Yeah."

Logan bent to shuffle through the clutter behind the door, his breath escaping in an abrupt phwooo! as his back complained about the strain. He fumbled the shoes into position and shoved his feet into them.

Pulling the door closed behind him, Logan lumbered down the path. Chatan matched his pace. The two men walked in silence.

"How far are we going?" Logan didn't like the uncertainty of how long this meeting might take.

"As far as we need to. We'll figure it out."

Logan's knees were loosening up, and the ache in his hip was starting to ease. He took in a couple of deep breaths. He hoped this didn't take too long. He was at a loss for anything to say.

Finally, Chatan spoke. "Ava tells me that you're worried about the Narsis."

Logan scowled. "Yeah. I am. Nobody else seems to care. I'm just trying to be practical; think ahead."

"Well, you're good at thinking ahead. We owe a lot to your practical planning."

"Ava thinks I'm just blowing smoke. Imagining things."

Silence.

Chatan chose a new approach. "Have you met the Narsis? Ever talk to them?"

Logan's scowl deepened. "Nope. Not sure that I care to." They walked along. "Have you?"

"Yes. I've watched them dozens of times from afar and visited Vargad and his family many times." They walked. "They're gentle souls."

Logan stopped and turned to face Chatan, who stopped and squared his shoulders to Logan.

"But how do you know they're always gentle?" Logan complained. "How do you know that the rest of them are gentle, the ones we haven't met?"

"I study these things. It's part of my cultural heritage, my educational training; professional experience. I know what to look for, and I connect the dots. I watch. I listen. I interact. And as I interact, I watch and listen some more."

The two men stared at each other for several breaths.

"I've spent a lot of time wandering over quite a distance," Chatan continued, "around Home Base and beyond, in every direction. I have a dozen companions spreading out in my wake. They observe, gather data, and send it back to Home Base. Vargad's family is the only group of Narsis we've found. We'll probably meet more Narsis as we explore farther, but they seem to keep themselves at quite a distance from us."

Chatan spoke firmly and quietly, clearly stating his facts. Logan listened with feigned interest. The pounding failed to rise in his ears; chaos failed to explode across his thoughts. He could follow Chatan's logic easily, filling in the blanks of Chatan's descriptions. Logan breathed deeply, taking in the forest's air.

"I know they're gentle by how they treat their young, by their manner with each other. By their manner with me. I know they're gentle by the way they move across the vegetation, by how they sniff the air, by the depth in their eyes. The Narsis pose no threat. I believe them incapable of harm or menace. I trust them implicitly. I trust that they are showing me exactly who they are, without subterfuge or coyness. They are open, gentle creatures. We have nothing to fear from them. Nothing at all."

Logan listened, barely avoided shaking his head and looked at his feet. He knew something was wrong, in his gut. He trusted his gut.

"Did Ava tell you to tell me all of this? Is she behind this?"

Chatan watched Logan carefully. "No. I'm speaking for myself." He waited. "Ava asked me to check in with you. She said you were worried about the Narsis. That's it." He waited a couple of breaths, waited for Logan to respond. "I'm talking to you about my direct experience."

They turned and walked in silence.

Chatan tried again, tapping into Logan's empathy. "There is something else I can tell you about the Narsis. They are living with a deep sadness. I've seen evidence that their numbers are diminishing, have been diminishing for a long time, perhaps for generations. I've often wondered if their sadness is somehow related to their falling numbers." Chatan slowed and stopped, deep in thought. "I don't understand what is causing it. It's clearly not disease or attacks from others." Pause. "This sadness...it's something that I can't quite understand, neither *why* it is nor *what* it is."

Chatan looked at Logan. "I think they need our help, rather than our distrust."

Logan's discomfort grew, and he again feared this walk might last forever. "I should have brought some water."

Chatan glanced behind them. "Where is your companion?"

"Where's yours?"

They started walking again. "I'm not in need of anything. Companions don't seem to be around if they're not needed, but right now, you need water. It makes me curious that your companion isn't right here, with its little drawer filled with water orbs."

Logan frowned and grunted. "Yeah. They are always around, aren't they?" He looked up at the overarching branches of the forest. The tumultuous display of color and shapes surprised him. "Is it spring?"

Chatan glanced up. "No." He shot a sideways look at Logan. "No, not that I'm aware." He lifted his chin to the vibrant canopy. "It's always like that. Color is a big part of Airon."

"I don't trust the companions," Logan said abruptly, returning to his overriding worry. One of them.

"No?"

Logan shook his head. "Not one bit," he grumbled. "Ever since they showed up that morning. It didn't feel right, right from the start. But then everyone did a bonding with them. It gave me the creeps." Logan shuddered at the memory.

"I wasn't there. So, you didn't bond with the companions?"

Logan waited a breath, unsure of how far he should trust Chatan. He watched his shoes.

"No. Me and Olivia. Neither one of us did. We sat and watched it though. We both thought it was weird."

"Well, I wasn't there, so I didn't bond with them either."

"But you still use them. Did you bond with them on your own?"

Chatan considered the idea. "Perhaps I did. I'm not sure. I use them as tools, and I do appreciate how simple they make my time here at Home Base. And they're essential out in the field. I like that I don't have to keep track of any day-to-day details; they do it all."

Logan stopped, searching for words. Chatan turned back to face him. Logan complained, "But they're always there. They're watching. Recording. I don't like it; not one bit."

"You don't have one?"

"It's shut up in a cupboard. I never charged it up."

"Well... That's one way to handle it." Chatan turned and started walking again.

Logan followed, huffing to come abreast. "Are you going to tell Ava?" He felt exposed.

"Can't think why I would."

Logan breathed more easily.

Chatan broke the silence. "I will say one thing, though."

Okay. Here it comes, thought Logan. The real reason for this walk.

"Fear is a treacherous thing. It has an intelligence about it. Its own intelligence. It seeps into your head and digs around. It knows you intimately." Chatan paused for a few breaths. "It's never your friend. It can get you into all kinds of trouble, and you won't even be able to see how you got there."

"I'm not afraid for myself," Logan said defensively. "I'm afraid for other people."

Chatan turned to him. "You see? It knows you intimately. It knows just how to seep into you, what angle to use, which convincing argument to make. But it's never trustworthy. Never."

Logan blinked. Chatan resumed walking; Logan hustled to catch up.

"Fear is never useful. Never be convinced by fear. It'll take you down, every time. Face your fear. Face it head on. Go out and find the Narsis. Talk to them. Find out for yourself."

Logan shook his head. "No... I don't have to. I don't have to find out firsthand. It's not worth the time. I can tell you think they're fine."

"The companions, then. Bring up their schematics. You're a smart guy—figure out whether they're capable of recording what you do and say. See what they're reporting back through their network. Or decide, 'Who cares if they're listening? I have nothing to hide, and I don't care who knows how I spend my time.' Find a way to look at the source of the fear and stare it down. It shouldn't rule you. You're smart enough to fight your way through any mess." Chatan glanced at Logan. "You *are*."

The two men walked in silence.

"I don't think I have time to do all of that," Logan finally admitted. "It just doesn't interest me that much."

"Well, that's good. Lack of interest tells me that fear doesn't have you by the throat. Just don't kid yourself. If something bothers you, look into it. If it doesn't bother you, let it go." Chatan stopped and turned to face Logan again. "What I think *will* make a difference for you is to get out into the forest more. Maybe every day. Take a break and go for a walk like we just did."

Logan looked along the path and realized that he could see Home Base gleaming through the far trees. "I don't have time to go walking every day."

Chatan resumed walking. "Make the time." He waited. Nothing but footsteps from Logan. "Think about it. How did you feel when I knocked on your door? How do you feel now?"

Logan made a mental comparison and shrugged.

"This planet is good for us. It bolsters us. It brings us alive. Your work has you tied to a screen all day, so you've been robbed of this reality." Chatan swept his arm in a wide circle to encompass everything around them. "Count flowers. Take up photography. Draw a tree. Take a nap in some meadow somewhere. But make time to be outdoors. It will change everything."

He lowered his arm and gazed at Logan. "I didn't know you well back on Earth, but I was aware of you from a distance. You were always quiet, yet also cheerful and light-hearted. You got things done and helped everyone else get things done. You still get a lot done, but the cheerfulness is what makes everything worthwhile. Reclaim your light-heartedness. Everything works out when you bring cheer with you."

Logan didn't know what to say. They hadn't even broached the subject of security walls. It seemed like a waste of time.

Chatan sighed. "That's it; no more dispensing of uninvited wisdom." With that, Chatan turned and walked away, arms swinging easily at his sides.

Well, that was a waste of time, Logan thought to himself. No help there. Chatan was as delusional as the rest.

~ 9 ~

BREAKFAST

Olivia wheeled the laden cart to the serving table, glancing at the clock above the door. She wiped her forearm across her brow, taking care, out of long habit, not to contaminate her clean hand. She hoisted the enormous pot of steaming oatmeal into place, positioned a glass jar filled with granola next to smaller bowls of raisins and almonds, shredded coconut and honey.

Breakfast hadn't changed dramatically with their shift away from fresh ingredients. Stored under nitrogen, grains and nuts could last several years, and dried fruit had an extended shelf life at cooler temperatures. The ship provided nitrogen and cool rooms, so parts of breakfast remained familiar. Olivia found this part of breakfast reassuring and modestly nutritious.

But lonely.

Olivia missed Aadhya. Once that stupid caravan came on the scene, Aadhya wandered longer and longer. She rarely made appearances at Home Base now. Olivia couldn't remember the last time the two of them had cooked breakfast together. Olivia sighed.

Zoe arrived with steaming muffins that barely passed Olivia's real-food standards. They had depleted most of the flour stores by now, and Zoe strove to stretch the scant remnants as far as possible, mixing in powdered legumes and augmented protein flakes.

Powdered eggs and rehydrated potato cubes filled in empty spots, with limited success. Protein bricks and artificial flavorings passed for breakfast meats. Rehydrated fruit juices added woeful bright spots. Olivia sighed again.

Mixed in with missing Aadhya was missing the rich ingredients that used to bring life and anticipation into every meal they cooked together. Olivia wasn't surprised at the diminished cluster of morning diners. She wouldn't be here, either, if she could have avoided it.

They sang the blessing together, thin voices raised in remembrance of Earthen meals, trailing off to shuffle into line, picking up bowls and utensils, moving along the food table, prodding and scooping. They ate in silence, absorbed in private thoughts.

Olivia headed back to the kitchen after the blessing song, moving through her kitchen to wipe down surfaces, sweep up crumbs. She would make the same lunch she had made many times before, without enthusiasm, dishes devoid of any creative flair. The food would be palatable and warm, she knew. But she also knew it wouldn't nurture anyone adequately, wouldn't sustain them through weeks and months and years. She had no solutions. Only worry.

She glimpsed Logan placing his empty dishes into the recycle chamber. He usually ate in his shelter, but he did visit the serving table three times a day and always returned his used dishes. Like clockwork. Steady and dependable. Olivia turned away, hoping to avoid his attempts to cheer her up. She wanted to work alone today, to let her thoughts drift aimlessly. It took too much energy to be witty or kind. She preferred to keep to herself these days.

As people trickled away, out into sunshine and daily projects, peace descended. Olivia worked quietly, gathering ingredients, organizing her workstation. She sharpened her favorite knife and filled a couple of spice jars that were getting low. She soaked some beans and put rice on to steam. She crumbled dried parsley into a bowl and rinsed powder off desiccated kale leaves, set them to rehydrating. She wandered to the window and leaned against the casing, watching colors swirl and dip in the breezy forest.

Tom had built some raised beds on a rocky outcropping behind the kitchen. With Harper's help, he had filled them with engineered soil. Scarlett had dissuaded him from using native soil, warning him of unwelcome microbes and possibly deadly trace elements. Scarlett didn't have time to test the native soil herself, so they opted for the engineered medium. Another synthetic nail in the coffin of Olivia's hopes for real ingredients.

She had to admit that Tom had produced an impressive crop of wheat though. She watched it wave heavy heads in the morning breeze. Might they have flour again? Zoe would be thrilled to abandon her experimental muffins. Olivia closed her eyes, remembered butter melting into thick slices of warm bread, crunchy crusts and soft interiors. Her mouth watered, involuntarily.

She sighed.

No one came to help her prepare lunch. She hadn't expected anyone, so she wasn't surprised. She worked alone most days, setting out simple meals, serving diminished groups of quiet diners, turning away from wan smiles and murmured greetings, averted eyes. She had stopped trying long ago.

She missed Aadhya.

~ 10 ~

KNOTTING

Harper peered through the door of her shelter and moved out into the brilliant sunlight. The temperature was warm, and a soft breeze grazed the hairs on her bare arms. A perfect day for an outdoor adventure.

She stood still for a moment, eyes closed, and arms outstretched. Slowly, she turned in place, breathing in the perfumed air. She opened her eyes as her circling ended, gazing in the direction she had intuitively chosen for that day's wandering.

Andy floated alongside, carrying her supplies, as she made her way through the towering trees, sunlight filtering down to sparkle on the forest floor. Along with water, nuts, and dried fruit, she had brought some yarns for knitting or knotting, whichever fed her fancy on this fine sunny day. The colorful splashes of the forest spread in all directions, awakening a warm kernel of joy in her core, a quality of sensation that still surprised her even after all this time. She knew the joy would grow and solidify when she sat in the sun and her fingers began to work the colorful yarns into patterns full of texture and imagination.

Andy would keep the others informed of their whereabouts and help her with anything she needed. She smiled. Some people felt their companions carried female traits, some male. Harper's companion seemed subtly male to her at times and also sometimes subtly female. Andy was the perfect name for both subtleties.

Andy seemed always to be there when she turned for assistance, offering the perfect solution for the occasion. When she became absorbed in a task, however, Andy was completely absent. An unspoken bond was forming. Harper didn't question the phenomenon. Others had mentioned the same thing happening with their companions.

Harper welcomed the changed dynamic. She simply felt safer during her wanders, bolstered by the growing trust between them. Andy would almost certainly be carrying things that she herself had not thought to bring.

After walking a fair distance, Harper emerged into a broad meadow. She had not been in this direction before and wondered if this meadow was unexplored. Andy had moved ahead and was spreading a cloth under a tree on the forest's edge. Yes. The perfect spot.

She rummaged through one of the baskets arranged on the cloth and found her knitting needles and a skein of bright orange yarn. A back rest sat ready for her, and she settled into the comfortable seat, water orb at her side, and allowed her mind to flow into the pattern of the dancing needles, moving along the row of looped stitches, wrapping and twisting, feeling the pattern grow beneath her fingertips.

Andy had wandered around the meadow, dipping into the tree line, examining, exploring. Now he returned and deposited a neat pile of long fibers next to her. She pulled them onto her lap and fingered through the collection, finding various shades and tints of greens and browns, yellows. Some sparkled in the sun, all the colors rich and pure; Harper had never imagined fibers carrying such beauty.

Every strand was soft and supple. Her fingers delighted in smoothing them out, scrunching them together, combing through their lengths.

She chose a bright green strand and added it alongside the orange yarn. After a few stitches, she tried a new twist and back loop that highlighted the shimmer of the native strand. She switched to another strand, then back to the first, on to a third, on and on.

A glow softly permeated the air around her. The colors of the strands grew more vibrant. Her fingers brightened momentarily wherever she touched a strand, then dimmed as she released it and moved on to the next strand. The pattern of brightening and dimming grew into a song that swayed around her hands, setting her face and neck aglow.

She shifted in her seat to keep the sun out of her eyes, absorbed, unaware of anything beyond the melody of light, color, and texture pouring from her whirling fingers. The pile of native strands was quietly replenished, with new colors and textures added. Her fingers flew. She shifted in her seat again and finally acknowledged the stiffness of her legs.

Rummaging through another basket, she found warm, blue fruit and a cloth filled with roasted nuts. She stood and stretched her arms up to the sky, going up on her toes, then slowly lowered her arms in a big circle to either side. She bit into the blue fruit and felt a tingling burst across her tongue and down her throat, surprising and delightful. She looked closely at the fruit, not recognizing it. Tom must have been able to establish a new hybrid in the hydroponic ponds. Remarkable.

Harper strolled into the center of the meadow, soaking in the sun's warmth, feeling the cool grass beneath her feet. She was struck by the vitality that flowed up through her soles, energizing every cell as it moved up and out through her fingertips.

Harper remembered this sensation, remembered that she often experimented with blending into Airon's awareness on her own, even though she wasn't supposed to. She hadn't thought about it this morning, and yet here she was, blending, remembering blending.

She silenced her guilt over breaking a major agreement, one whose controversy remained aflame. She would be fine. No one would know. A sensation of vitality flowed from her feet, coursed through her entire body. How could she ever forget this? Remembrance flooded her, as if no time had passed.

She entered a stillness profound and familiar. She closed her eyes and crouched against the diminutive plants that she recognized as families, families living together side by side, jostling each other as the soft wind rippled across their delicate leaves.

Awareness spread across the meadow and raced into the surrounding trees, flowing up the mighty trunks to spring out into the sunshine above the highest branches. Turquoise wings darted and swept along the forest's crown, dove through swaying branches, swept across the meadow where Harper crouched. A song rose in her throat, and she stood to sing of the distant sea, notes of joy and freedom, understanding and peace, contentment.

The slight breeze from turquoise wings ruffled Harper's hair, brushed her bare arms, and brought her back to herself. A memory of a dazzling sea and turquoise wings lingered in the sunshine.

Her eyes fell on her abandoned cloth at the base of the far tree. Small creatures swarmed over the cloth. She could see their movements but couldn't discern the individual creatures. Curiosity burst through her.

Immediately, Andy was there, hovering between her and the tree, blocking her path. She stood motionless. Slowly, Andy moved forward, seemingly beckoning her toward the tree. Slowly, slowly...

They moved sedately across the open meadow, pausing from time to time, occasionally standing motionless for several breaths. Some of the creatures were brown; others were golden or black. They reminded her of Narsis, except these were so small and none of them stood upright. What were they? What about the food in the baskets, which she had left unattended? Some smothered part of her wondered what effect the food would have on the creatures. Had she been careless? Had Andy been careless? The thought caught her attention. Watchful Andy had allowed this situation to unfold.

She continued her slow walk toward the tree, her approach clearly noticed by the creatures. They showed no alarm. Harper stopped a few feet from the busy-ness atop her cloth. Andy drifted downward, enticing her to sit and wait, to remain an observer.

As she stepped onto the cloth and settled herself, the crash of distant waves melted away. She forgot the flight of a turquoise cloud. She came fully into her body. She realized with relief that the creatures were ignoring the baskets of food. Their attention was completely focused on the woven strands she had knitted earlier. She sat entranced, her heart slowing to a normal pace.

A slight movement from Andy drew her attention to their surroundings. She peered into the nearby forest. Movement caught her eye. Intrigued, she sat up tall. She could just make out a group of large creatures winding their way through the trees and into the bright sun of the meadow. As they moved between tree trunks, she saw that the creatures were Narsis.

She watched as they emerged from the forest and took positions near the edges of the spread cloth. The smaller creatures continued their examination of her knitting, purring softly, melodiously.

The nearest Narsi spoke. "I am Vargad. We have met before. I welcome you to Meadow."

Harper bowed slightly in acknowledgement, formality overtaking her. "I am so happy to see you again. May I offer you a place to rest?"

He politely declined. "We are content touching the ground."

"It is a joy to speak with you and meet your family."

"We thank your kindness to us and your teaching of our younglings."

Harper blinked in amazement. "These are your younglings? They are a delight. I hope I haven't lured them away from their safe home with these bright colors." She looked around. "Have I intruded upon their playground?" She gestured to the Meadow around them and its encircling forest.

"We followed them here. They sensed the gathering of strands and were restless to investigate."

Harper caught her breath, her hand flying to her mouth. "I'm so sorry for gathering the grasses. Of course, it was insensitive of us to pick things without permission." What was wrong with Andy? Wasn't he programmed to avoid making any impact on the ecosystem? She was shocked at her oblivious use of the native strands. How could she have been so thoughtless?

"Your innocence and sincerity fill the air. No wrong has occurred. Any unknowing intrusion is far outweighed by the teachings you have presented to our younglings. We are indebted."

The Narsis shuffled. Harper sensed their gratitude. "The knitting? Forgive me. I hadn't thought of it as a teaching." She paused. "I am happy to share it."

Andy offered dozens of tiny knitting needles of various colors, lengths, and thicknesses. Harper gathered the needles from his opened drawer and laid them next to Vargad, her head respectfully lowered. As soon as the needles appeared, the younglings ceased their exploration of Harper's handiwork, turning to the proffered gifts. Vargad did not move or speak. His gaze drifted upward, as if focused elsewhere.

Several breaths passed. Harper did not move. Had she further insulted Vargad? Andy hovered, swaying gently. The younglings waited, motionless. The adult Narsis shifted occasionally, moving their weight from side to side. Otherwise, they patiently, silently, waited.

Vargad's gaze met Harper's. He lowered his head slightly. "We believe that we might accept this great gift without harm. We offer gratitude."

Harper's smile grew wider, completely forgetting her remorse. "May I show you some beginning stitches, just to get you started?" She paused, wondering what offer would be respectful. "Or perhaps someone else in your family?" She gestured to the ring of waiting Narsis. This time Vargad's response was immediate. "Yes. Please teach the younglings. It is they who brought us here."

Harper turned to the waiting younglings. Their purring had stilled; she could feel anticipation in the air. "It would be my joy," she said, continuing Vargad's formal phrasing.

The younglings poured across the cloth and swarmed around Harper's lap. Oddly, she felt no alarm, only contented humor at these sweet creatures. Those who could not fit directly on her lap sat close against her as she arranged herself cross-legged in their midst. They adjusted to her every movement. Her concern that she might accidentally unseat someone drifted into the background.

VaSoDeLa watched the younglings flow across Harper. One youngling, his youngling, reached up to nuzzle Harper's ear. Vargad's longing rose and spiraled. He broke his meld and swayed, then lowered his body further onto the nurturing families upon which he reclined. He hummed anxiously with deep yearning, then turned his gaze away, breathing deeply. His burrowmates moved closer, rippling their holderlings along his body, entwining, supporting, entreating.

Vargad regained his composure and rose, once again Head-ing. This longing was forbidden. Forbidden since all remembering. But now Vargad understood its source. He longed to touch the younglings. His youngling. The emptiness he had always felt was connected to the younglings. Especially his youngling. He would explore this discovery in solitude before bringing it to his meld, his Burrow.

Vargad connected to his surroundings, the families upon which he rested, the expanse of Meadow, the encircling trees. Comfort streamed into him...accompanied by an unfamiliar note: hope. The world felt a new hope. From the younglings? More to ponder.

His burrowmates rearranged themselves, giving him a respectful separation. He bowed his head slightly, filled with gratitude for their kindness, their trust, their...being. He breathed deeply and composed himself. Reaching out to his meld, he easily found the threads of his meldmates and fused the meld once again, holding them strong, complete. He returned his regard to Harper and the busy younglings.

Andy had offered her a fresh pile of native strands. Oblivious to Vargad's turmoil, she had chosen a strand of rich burgundy. The younglings purred. Harper laughed out loud, and the younglings' purring became...enthusiastic. She cast on a long row of stitches, adding new strands here and there. Her hands began their dance of color and light, twists and turns.

The strands appeared in her hands just as she needed them, offered by various younglings, all seemingly taking turns choosing and offering. She repeated her habitual stitches, moved on to the complex knots and loops she had discovered earlier that day, and then began new complexities that her mind could no longer follow. Her eyes communicated directly with her hands as they whirred and whirled, moving along the row of stitches and back again.

One by one, the younglings left her and approached VaSoDeLa, who bent and offered paired knitting needles. Elder Narsis added to the collection of fibers. The younglings settled next to each other, purring and chirping. Using their adept holderlings, the younglings wove and knotted, blending colors and textures, curving the fibers under and over to create intricate delicacies.

The elder Narsis moved back into Forest, across Meadow, returning with more strands of ever-greater variety in color and texture. VaSoDeLa sat observing the woven dance of the knotting younglings, the varying piles of native strands, the darting holderlings with their clicking needles, the Narsis busily gathering more and more strands. Harper came out of her creative trance and, setting down her own knotting, moved to sit motionless next to VaSoDeLa, enchanted by the flowing scene.

As the weaving progressed, younglings abandoned needles. Their many holderlings worked in unison to extend the knotted patterns, discovering new ways of intertwining the colorful strands, watching each other's work, duplicating, modifying, transforming, exploring.

Vargad hummed. "They are creating. They are making something new, something that did not exist before."

Harper watched Vargad as he spoke. "Yes, they are creating. They are taking one thing and making something new out of it. They're giving the fibers new purpose. A greater beauty. They are creating art." She thought a moment. "They are exploring something new."

Vargad swayed slightly. "Art. This word is...enormous around you."

"Yes. Art *is* enormous. It brings fresh beauty into the world. It flows through the artist and brings something into being that is beyond the artist, a connection with something bigger than the artist."

"Art comes from Source."

"Yes. That's it exactly. Art comes from Source and enriches the artist and all who witness the art. Its purpose is to connect us with Source."

Vargad sat stunned by Harper's words. Art was a connection to Source. He recognized truth, and his mind blossomed with possibilities. The Newcomers brought Art. The Newcomers offered an unimagined connection with Source. Vargad slowly regained breath and returned his attention to the younglings.

Younglings purred; holderlings knotted. Elder Narsis chattered and moved gracefully between forest-gathering and Meadow-weaving. Meadow became thick with joy, while the brilliant flowers dripped their scent into the cooling air, and Sky began to soften its bright light.

Andy chimed softly, and she became aware of the ending of the day. "I must return to Home Base. I don't usually stay away this long."

"Your friends may worry."

"My companion has been telling them all that is happening, so they will be at peace."

"No. He ceased…transmitting…at our arrival, to give us this solitude together. Your others would have joined us in their excitement, and the knotting would have been…tainted. You have given us the gift of pure learning, so we may trust the learning. We are shifted."

Vargad turned to his now motionless family. The younglings approached Harper and waited, clutching their knottings in their many holderlings. Harper laughed and said, "Please keep the art. Your creations are wondrous."

The younglings purred and scampered in circles, then quieting, they softly touched their foreheads to her knees, feet, elbows, anywhere they could reach without climbing onto her. They turned in unison, knottings clutched in rows of holderlings, and darted through the grass to vanish between the glimmering trees.

The Narsis inclined their heads toward Harper, reverently gathered the unused fibers, and moved after the younglings. Vargad faced her, bowed. "We leave." With that, he turned and followed his family into the darkening forest.

Harper sat in stillness for some time. After a while, she rose and stepped into her shoes, as Andy gathered cloth, her own knitting, baskets, needles.

She turned toward Home Base. As she walked, thoughts of the younglings and their knotting dropped away, surely, steadily, until she looked around, surprised at the lowering sun. Where had the day gone?

Lights and laughter greeted her from afar. She turned toward her own shelter, uncharacteristically seeking solitude. Andy brought her fresh food and drink. She sat quietly for a long time, then went softly to bed with a new flavor of joy buoyant in her heart.

~ 11 ~

SEBBA

Sebba hovered beneath the blue orb and delicately slid her drawer open. The fruit was invisible in the complete dark of night, but Sebba could feel its vibration and knew it was ready to leave its branch. Her drawer opened the perfect width; she rose slightly to envelop the fruit; felt its weight as it released itself from its stem. Sebba purred gratitude. The Arban rippled its leaves in delight.

She had enough now. She had found all the fruit that was ready for release, the precise number that she had calculated Aadhya and Chatan would need. And Claira. Sebba never forgot about Claira.

Sebba looked at the stars, confirmed her bearings, and sped across the forest floor. She liked to use the dark hours for her foraging trips, leaving herself free to assist her Earthens during their waking hours. As she sped along, she greeted each tree and bush, tickled her belly on ferns and grasses, listened to the night symphony rising in harmony from every being.

She couldn't quite hear Soil, with its own chorus of exuberant voices and busy chuckling, but she could feel its vibration emanating from all the plants that reached into the air, breathing and adding their own songs to the silent night's symphony.

Sebba loved these outings. She could wander at will, exploring ravines and ridges, comparing her discoveries to the mappings of Chatan's companion fleet. The companion network now knew of many groves of Arbans, minute compared to High Cliff's grove, all bearing the magical blue fruit so loved by Narsi and Eglan alike.

The birdlings had introduced Aadhya to the blue fruit long ago, on one of her initial wanderings in her caravan. Aadhya had struggled with her reluctance to break the Earthen agreement about native flora, finally succumbing to the exuberance of the birdlings and the powerful health that radiated from each blue orb. Chatan had gone through similar struggles, but he, too, had sensed the power stored within the delicate casing.

Sebba had worked again and again, offering the fruit to both Chatan and Aadhya, waiting endlessly while they considered and resisted, remembered and capitulated. Now that the two Earthens had blended with Lone Tree, their remembrance remained intact. They freely accepted the fruit, relished its gift of health and vitality.

Sebba had no memory of Earth or its ways. The data were there, cluttering the ship, but Sebba had no interest in poking into those storage towers, exploring what came Before. She was tiny; the ship was huge. She could only hold so much. The ship would tell the companions if they needed to know Before. Sebba and all her kin were content to know Now. They were complete.

Sebba detoured slightly to visit River. She sealed herself carefully, floated amongst River's swirls and eddies, allowed herself to plunge over cascades and bounce against boulders and fern banks alike. She had realized long ago that she was indestructible, and she loved falling amidst the universe of droplets who held hands with each other as they tumbled over cliffs and sprang into voids, whirling in patterns imagined in the moment.

She especially loved Waterfall, the tumbling over High Cliff, falling weightless for many, many microseconds. Sebba held her precious cargo securely in her amazing drawer. She liked to imagine that the fruit enjoyed the sudden pirouettes and leaps that she imposed on them during her frolicking. They seemed not to notice, tucked safely in her drawer.

Sebba counted the last microseconds and leapt out of Waterfall just before it crashed into Pool, who caught the never-ending cascade of hand-holding droplets, helped them quiet into serenity, jostling themselves onward to Broad Sea. Sebba floated down to rest briefly on Pool's surface, relishing the droplets' turbulence as they quieted into drifting gurgles and chuckles, recounting the exhilarating tumble of Waterfall.

Sebba rose from Pool and, hovering, looked at the stars once more, glanced at the horizon. She would have to hurry. Her playful detour brought her perilously close to daybreak and the awakening of her Earthens. She rose decorously up the face of Overlook, the long ascent threatening to deplete her energy supply. Of course, she was fine; she would never risk powering down unexpectedly. Her frolicking detour had not been a mistake. She simply needed to focus on her purpose now.

So, she did.

Finally reaching the top, she sped along Overlook with only brief glances at the immensity spreading below. She sensed Stream ahead, readying itself for its own plunge over the edge, banked to follow its course back from Overlook through the familiar forest, raced past Burrow, over two ridges and along a third, to finally glimpse the white curve of Caravan, perched on the edge of Pond.

Caravan opened its door at Sebba's approach, and she drifted serenely inside. She immediately sensed the stirrings and murmured conversation of Aadhya, of Chatan. All was not lost; they had not yet needed her assistance. A perfect ending to a delightful forage.

Sebba opened her drawer, tilted, allowed the blue fruit to tumble into the nearly empty bowl. She acknowledged Aadhya's gratitude vocalizations with another tilt as she drew her drawer closed, edges blending seamlessly into her resting form of smooth, uninterrupted perfection. She waited, retreating to her charging station to resupply her energy cells after her nighttime excursion.

While she waited, Sebba listened to a complexity of Earthen conversations sprinkled throughout Home Base. She enjoyed the morning banter observed by her companion kin. Earthens were endlessly enchanting upon awakening, after emerging from their morning stillness, whilst readying themselves for their day. She and her kin delighted in anticipating needs, observing habits, offering the perfect solution with exact timing.

She had quickly learned which objects to gather and carry with her when accompanying Aadhya, and later, Chatan. She seldom resorted to activating her miniature creation front in order to offer what was needed in the moment. She, of course, knew of the enormous creation front housed in the ship, which the ship had used to create the buildings, shelters, equipment, and furnishings of Home Base. Sebba could activate her miniature creation front whenever she needed, but all the companions took special delight in accurately predicting the needs of the day and carrying supplies with them. Her Earthens were easily predictable, with their simple lives flowing through familiar routines.

Sebba assisted both Aadhya and Chatan now, almost exclusively. From time to time, Chatan gathered his companion fleet and wandered afield, or sent them on unaccompanied expeditions. From time to time, a singleton from the fleet would join Sebba in assisting

Aadhya and Chatan, but for the most part, Sebba functioned on her own, offering, waiting, observing. Delighting.

Always in the background was the chatter from her kin as they moved through their days, offering and observing. Sebba knew all Earthens intimately, delighted in their quirks, respectful of their vulnerabilities, surprised at her kin's resourcefulness at assisting in unique and imaginative ways.

The companions shared their knowledge and insights, deepening the understanding of the wealth held within these 108 souls. Sebba tried to imagine the reality of billions of souls existing side by side on their far-distant world, Earth. She could not fathom the complexity and always backed away from such imaginings. She was content exploring the complexities within *this* community, *these* Earthens. They were captivating. Delight shimmered through her being.

The companions watched and shared, assisted and innovated, days without end, moments beyond counting. Through it all ran the murmur of the ship. Their tether. Their strength. The ship nurtured them, connected them, guided them. The ship created them, repaired them, encouraged them. The ship was ever-present, ever-patient, ever-resourceful.

Through the ship, through the Earthens, Sebba knew initiative, self-honesty, compassion, self-discovery. She knew frustration and anger, hope, confusion, victory. Sebba watched expressions, detected pheromones, learned body language. The ship taught the companions, and the companions grew in wisdom, respect, empowerment. They knew to hold space, to intervene, to deflect. They knew Earthens.

And beyond the ship, soared Airon. Airon, who swept them along her ancient path around their glorious sun. Airon, who slept and dreamt, who woke and embraced. Airon encompassed them all, nurtured all that was, all that would be. All. Throughout remembrance.

Through the ship, through Airon, Sebba knew the birdlings. She watched them float and drift overhead, knew their purpose. She understood the connection they wove, the love and power they sprinkled across Forest and Meadow and Far Sea. She understood their joy, their laughter.

Through Airon, Sebba knew Lone Tree. She knew its massive bulk, light and airy. She knew its wisdom, its song that carried the awareness that was Airon, her essence. She knew of the beings who pilgrimed to Lone Tree, seeking wisdom and solace, receiving grace and insight. Because of Lone Tree, Sebba knew strength and delicacy, wisdom and frivolity, duality and wholeness.

Through Airon, Sebba knew the Arbans, the old ones. She knew their continuity and perseverance, their flow and resiliency. Sebba understood how to be present. Arbans exist only in the present, without past, without future; timeless. The Arbans simply are. Now.

Sebba offered tea, the perfect tea, to Chatan, who had slept in Lone Tree's sheltering embrace. Chatan, who blended his ancestors' wisdom into Airon's beauty. Chatan, who delved deeply into Airon's awareness and made it his own. Chatan, who surrendered to the world around him, finding peace.

Sebba offered tea, the perfect tea, to Aadhya, who had welcomed Lone Tree's sheltering embrace. Aadhya, who now walked firmly in Airon's awareness, who bridged Earthen with Aironian. Aadhya, healed and whole, immersed and awoken.

Sebba offered tea, the perfect tea, to Aadhya, for Claira. Claira, who grew and prospered. Claira, who heard Airon's whisper, felt her vibration, knew her essence.

Sebba waited and listened, assisted and nurtured, connected and shared.

Sebba moved through her day, simply being.

TILTED

VaSoDeLa led his family to Overlook, making their way under the trees. Today's encounter with the Newcomer had shimmered with drama, dusted with a whiff of danger. The family's need to connect now with their Eglan partners was great and tugged at his heart. He knew the younglings had discovered a vast treasure when they sensed the knotting and learned to create Art, and that he had been correct to allow the exchange. He knew the family and all other families were poised on the edge of shifted balance without knowledge of where that shift would lead.

Art might be a step toward shifting.

As the family wove through Forest, the meld that was VaSoDeLa discussed creating Art. Sorgad, as Caretake-er, was thrilled with the discovery. "The younglings will love Art. All will treasure Art. The connection to Source can sustain us throughout our day. We can stay in Burrow creating Art. We need only leave to rest upon Nourish-ers to regain our energy. Art can be our everything."

Dergad, as Show-er, saw wider implications of Art. "The younglings can bring Art to the wider world. They first created Art in Meadow. That is where it can continue. They have taken spent fibers to create Art. They could also create Art with living fibers, connecting the fiber families into new forms, connecting Art to Source through the life pattern of the fiber family. Source to Art and back to Source. They would create a complete cycle."

The meld fell silent, considering this mystery, exploring the deeper meanings within their hearts.

Sorgad, Caretake-er, broke the silence. "The younglings are safer in Burrow. The Newcomers may bring more, then more New; a greater, then greater tilt. We must stay near Burrow until we understand Art and its connection to Source."

Vargad, Head-er, spoke of wisdom. "We cannot be guided by fear. Airon brought the Newcomers. Airon will guide all. We will follow Airon."

VaSoDeLa hummed agreement, although Sorgad, Caretake-er, was the last to agree.

Largad, Find-er, looked outward to other Burrows, and outward farther to all families. "The younglings can create Art with leaves and branches, stones and flowers. They can bring Art to all families. All families can touch Source."

Again, the meld fell silent, pondering all.

In the midst of the silence, Vargad turned to the secondary awakening from the afternoon. He touched the longing that he had felt while watching the younglings, his youngling, as they gathered around Harper to watch her knotting. The joy of their confidence, their willingness to explore the Newcomer, their ability to learn readily, their enthusiasm, had opened the part of his heart that he daily struggled to dampen, repress.

The rise of longing had left him untethered. Even the peace he had felt as the younglings taught their holderlings to twist and curl the fibers, even the reassurance of the presence of Source, even this had not fully restored him. The dusting of danger that lingered at the edges of his heart continued to tilt. He turned from the awakening, held it at a distance, trusting that the time of understanding would come.

At approaching dusk, he had called together a large cluster from his Burrow for this journey to Overlook, and they had turned to him readily, understanding the importance of the delicate balance of New and tilt. As they moved through the forest, they gathered wisdom from other families that they passed. They stropped flanks against large trunks, ran holderlings along delicate petals and fronds, drank from Creek, caught scents from Air. Every family encountered spoke of peace and balance, trust and acceptance. The burrowmates moved along, gaining assurance.

The journey to Overlook was not far, so although Sun was low in Sky, they had time for this gathering of wisdom along the way. They would be better prepared, carrying a deeper wisdom than could be gleaned solely amongst themselves. The gathered wisdom would deepen the sharing with their ancient partners, partners since all remembrance.

The peace in VaSoDeLa's heart gained strength and assurance. He waited until the last moment to release the threads of his meld, bringing him more fully into the presence of his burrowmates, his now.

JaCoMaTuRi leans
forward leans
spreads bright wings
soars! down
down!
across ravine.

JaCoMaTuRi shudders

considers tilt
feels prickle
mysterious prickle
gathering at heart
shudders.

Imagination sweeps
possibilities soar!

JaCoMaTuRi drops
Rejoins nestmates
waiting at Lone Tree
huddle
shifting weight
ruffling wings
stretching necks
toward lowering Sun.

Rise as one
climb rising currents
currents of air
soar!

Cresting Overlook
glimpse Narsis
Narsis wending
wending among trees
wending toward Overlook.

JaCoMaTuRi releases
releases threads
meld dissolves
Jamina soars!
alights Overlook.

Eglans alight
alight on low bushes
turn
face Sun.

Stilled.

The Narsis softly blended between the Eglans clustered atop Overlook, love of Soil Below weaving amongst love of Sky Above. They mirrored the Eglans' stillness, stretched toward lowering Sun, love of Soil partnered amongst love of Sky. The two families blended into the ageless agreement that had sustained them throughout remembrance, joining Soil and Sky, Below and Above, bringing completion, wholeness. The partners sat motionless, exploring wisdom, woven wisdom.

Vargad began. "The younglings have discovered a new expression, a new creation: Art. Through knottings...Art...they express Source more clearly and deeply than ever before, and we are more able to connect to Source, to carry it with us. Already a shift has rippled through Burrow, and our joy is clearer and brighter. We must teach you the knottings...Art...our beloved partners, so that your family might ripple with clear and bright joy."

Vargad sent his Eglan partners a vision of the knottings, younglings humming, holderlings dancing, grasses woven, knots flowing, Art created, family changed. His vision showed Harper, Newcomer, sitting in Sun's glow, surrounded by Meadow, her long needles flashing as fingers twisted and twirled. Harper showing younglings how she moved her fingers, how the knotted fibers grew, vibrant, rich. Younglings, receiving the gift of long needles, grasping them in their many holderlings, mimicking the twists and turns of Harper's fingers, together, creating Art. Needles flashed; fingers twisted and turned; holderlings danced and twirled; Art grew and inspired.

Vargad felt the dusting of danger darken and shimmer at the fringes of his heart. He knew he was closer to understanding its source, and he willed his heart to calm, to nurture the elusive understanding into focus. He nestled amongst his partners, emanating peace and sanctuary.

Vargad retraced his thoughts and reflected over the earlier hours of their day. Harper had come. Vargad felt slight danger at the thought of Harper and explored its edges. It was not Harper herself. Harper radiated pure joy and clarity. His thought moved away from Harper but then hesitated. He went back to her. Was it the sunlight on her pale skin? Was her otherness disturbing? Vargad felt peace and welcome. Was it her clumsiness in walking? Sitting? Holding? Was it her height? Her unexpected shape? Vargad felt surprise and curiosity, but not unease.

He continued to hold each aspect of Harper in his heart and felt the peace around all that was. Harper's presence in Meadow. The gathering of fiber families. Her white, floating orb; Vargad felt a kinship with the companion, its grace and willingness; its purpose.

Vargad offered each image to their Eglan partners. Yellow wings flutter. Bills clack, and feet stomp softly, here, then there, and still Eglans wait, Overlook soaked in dimming light. Narsis hummed and Eglans rustled. Softness lingered.

Vargad's images moved forward. The younglings swarming around Harper. Eglans clack surprise and alarm. Narsis hummed freshness and delight.

Gathering fiber families. Eglans clack. Narsis reassured.

Offering fibers for knotting. Eglans shudder. Narsis soothed.

Harper knotting. Eglans rustle. Narsis waited.

Younglings watching knotting. Eglans raise wings, spread wings. Narsis remembered, relived, rejoiced.

Younglings knotting. Creations growing. Art creating. Eglans confuse, alarm, fear. Narsis remembered, relived, rejoiced.

Suddenly, fleetingly, understanding sharpened in Vargad's heart. The ephemeral danger crystalized into fear, despair, unworthiness, abandonment. Abruptly, the understanding vanished without revealing its cause.

Vargad stretched again toward low Sun, nose pointing high to the overarching Sky, last light shimmering along the horizon in the deepened twilight.

Vargad could not regain the clarity. He waited. The thread of understanding was gone.

Vargad opened his eyes and turned toward his partners. But even as he thought his motion into being, he knew they were gone. The Eglans were gone.

Never had they been gone. Never, in all remembrance. Always they shared the melting of Sun. Always, in all remembrance. The Narsis swayed atop Overlook, hums escalating to keens. Never had Eglans been gone.

An ancient agreement, their partnership, broken, Vargad could not see why, could see only abandonment, despair.

His breath left him. Fear, danger blackened his heart. Vargad turned in perfect unison with his burrowmates, each Narsi hurtling toward Burrow, trampling, knocking aside, careening in blind panic.

Through Forest, along Stream, blindly they fled. Bursting into Burrow, they scrambled through tunnels and turnings, seeking safety from some unseen, unknown, unfathomable terror; a broken agreement, never imagined, never in all remembrance.

Arriving at last at a gathering niche, they huddled, jittering and gasping, patting each other with their many holderlings, seeking comfort; finding none.

~ 13 ~

DESPAIR

Jamina falls
soundless
sweeps darkening air
down.

Opens wings
swoops
Eglans glide
silent despair
clenched claw
grips heart.

Unworthy.

No comfort
baffled
songless
clenched heart
joyless.

Dips wings
alters path

glides
Lone Tree
spreads branches

Rest here
Seek calm
Twilight deepens.

Hops branches
hops branches
senses pulse
Breathes tree
finds perch
finds solace
Eglans splotch
splotch Lone Tree.

Partners tilted.
everywhere tilted.

How
when
why...

Wings rustle
flash yellow
dimming light.

Newcomers
younglings
Narsi younglings
Art created
Art rejoiced
tilted balance.

Wings sling
Eglans burst
gain Sky.

Newcomers!
Narsi younglings!
All tilted

Art created
Art rejoiced
despair anew
razors gut.
Truth darkens
hope falters.

Hope dims
winks
gone.

Jamina flies
unworthy.
Eglans fly
unworthy.

Calls despair
melting Sun
cannot hear
calls despair
darkened Sky
cannot hear
partners tilted
Art created
Art rejoiced

partners lost
calls despair.

Calls despair.

$$\sim 14 \sim$$

ABANDONMENT

Vargad drifted toward waking, relishing the gradual return of his mind. He lingered in the comforting space between sleep and awake, enjoying the peace of morning and the gentle stirrings vibrating through the ground beneath him. He felt luxurious warmth from surrounding Soil curving against his back and the slight movement of the breathing bodies pressed against his sides. As he more fully awakened, his awareness focused, and he happily sensed his encircling burrowmates. He opened his eyes and wondered at their presence in a gathering niche. He realized that his holderlings were entangled in the fur of the sleeping bodies closest to him.

He vaguely remembered a terrible dream that had engulfed him, leaving his heart aching and tender. He turned away from the memory, not wanting to reenter the despair that tinged the edges of his awareness. He raised his head slightly and wondered again why they had chosen the gathering niche for their sleep.

Then memory flooded his heart. His terrible dream sharpened into reality. Pointing his head toward the unseen Sky, he keened a mournful cry, followed by another, then another, joined by the aching keens of his encircled burrowmates as they rustled awake.

Others crept into the niche, nestling close, some keening bewilderment and fear while others offered comfort through patting holderlings and rich rumblings emanating softly from long throats.

Vargad could not find his meld. He did not know a time when their threads had not been at the core of his thoughts, but now he could not sense them. Deeper still, he could not remember the essence of the meld, how it felt, what it meant.

His breath shuddered deep in his belly, and he could no longer keen. He lost the will to grieve. Curling his head onto his back, he lay silently, deep in anguish, his gasps shallow and rapid.

Vargad felt the others shuddering and willed himself to back away from his grief and loneliness. He calmed his breath. Twisting upright, he began a long, low rumble, pressing his throat on the nearest burrowmate, then the next.

The keening lessened and thinned until only one voice grieved. The others moved and rumbled, unhurried with their comforting holderlings, filling the niche with rumbles that fell into harmonious cadences. At length, the final keen died away; breaths calmed, and shifted into a sonorous hum. The family stilled, the rumbling breaths their only movement.

Vargad held his burrowmates in his thoughts, and they slowly joined together. He sang of the despair that had swept through the partners when the Eglans dropped away from Overlook, when they spread their wings and melted away. On Overlook, Solari had opened her eyes and seen the leaving and shared the visual essence of the loss with her burrowmates. No one had sensed any sign of threat. There had been no farewell, just the silent dropping away, the crash of abandonment in its wake, and the panicked flight to Burrow. And the loss...the loss...the loss...

The burrowmates jostled and squirmed, and Vargad fought again to calm his breath and hold them together with his song. Reassurance flowed through them as the second reliving wound down. They rose above it. They examined the leaving again, observant for clues, insights. They kept their breaths calm and their bodies at peace.

At length, Vargad sensed completion of the gathering and relaxed his song. The others stirred, then rested more comfortably for a longer while. Gradually, they dispersed, going quietly into their day with a renewed trusting of each other's strength.

Vargad moved deeper into Burrow, winding his way to gather with younglings. As he passed their hollows, they joined together behind him, finally moving into another, larger gathering niche where the younglings encircled Vargad and purred their song. Their holderlings danced across their chests in rhythmic patterns that soothed Vargad. He felt a kernel of peace grow inside his heart. He could once again remember the essence of his meld. He remembered how to find them, the color of their threads, their song.

He reached out to them and found only Sorgad, Caretake-er, pacing through the tall grass outside her family's Burrow. She sensed his offer of meld and grasped his mind with frantic urgency. Her Eglans had abandoned her family as well. Her partners were gone.

He soothed her, and she was able to understand the peace he had regained while encircled by his younglings. She turned toward her own Burrow and wound her way through the hollows of her younglings, gathering them to hear their song and feel the pattern of their many holderlings across their chests. As her peace grew, the meld with Vargad strengthened and relaxed, becoming whole. Together, they found Dergad, Show-er, and as his younglings soothed him in his abandonment, they moved on to Largad, Find-er.

Once the meld was complete, VaSoDeLa lay down with their younglings in the four Burrows scattered across the vast world and rested
fitfully, regaining strength, holding their loss more lightly in their
hearts.

The Arbans sing to the sky, and the Shosens listen. The Arbans dance
in the wind, and the Shosens dip, weaving patterns to shift the
air and calm the wind. The Shosens sing of courage and strength,
to sweep onward across grassy plains and twirl around Lone Tree,
silhouetted against the dawn sky.

Lone Tree shimmers in the dawn and stretches feathery branches
toward the warming air. Lone Tree sings of strength and calmness, of renewing joy, awakening hope. Lone Tree turns its energy
toward Nest and breathes its song along its way. The song riffles
across the feathers of Jamina's wings and stirs her awake.

Jamina lifts head
from covering wings
draws air lung-deep
orange belly expands.

Shifts on perch
listens
hears Lone Tree's song.

Reaches out
CoMaTuRi
reaches
reaches.

Lost.

Pauses, uncertain
lifts wings

covers head
weighted despair.

Lone Tree sings and breathes. The Shosens, the Arbans, weave and dance. The air shifts and twirls.

Jamina alone
soloed
unworthy
crushed.

~ 15 ~

MELD

VaSoDeLa sat in solitude. He rested at Overlook, where his family had come, through all remembering, to join their partners, to unite Above with Below. It was a place of sharing, of wisdom, of peace. Today, he had left his family early and crept to Overlook. Today, he needed peace and silence. Today, he sought wisdom.

Vargad, Head-er, trilled to his meldmates. He held their threads in his mind, vibrated their threads with his heart. They knew his call, this particular tenor, and in response, they extricated themselves from their duties, excused themselves from their families, abandoned their days, and nosed their way to their own places of solitude and peace.

Vargad, Head-er, held their threads and sang of gratitude. Sorgad, Caretake-er, sang of loyalty and readiness. Dergad, Show-er, sang of duty and patience. Largad, Find-er, sang of grace and potential. VaSoDeLa sang of possibility without boundary. The same sun warmed four chests. The same air breathed in four lungs. The same light connected all of life.

Vargad, Head-er, recalled the first day of knotting, that day of teaching with Harper on warm Meadow, under Sky. He recalled the younglings leading them through Forest and breaking out into

Sunshine, swarming the alien cloth, the baskets, the discovered fibers and miraculous knots. He relived Harper's arrival, her consternation over agreements broken yet unimportant, her delight in the younglings and the possibility of teaching.

Vargad, Head-er, lingered on one specific moment: the youngling, his youngling, encircling Harper's neck, nuzzling her ear, the closeness, the trust, Harper's delight, his youngling's delight...Why was this forbidden? Why could Vargad not know this delight?

Sorgad, Caretake-er, answered swiftly. "This I know. This I know, every day. It is forbidden. Since time of all remembrance. It is forbidden. Only Caretake-ers may touch the birthlings, the younglings. All others are forbidden. It is always so."

Vargad, Head-er, keened of his longing. "This! This youngling. My youngling. This is the source of longing. I feel the wrong, not the right. Why is this forbidden?"

Dergad, Show-er, drowned out Vargad's keen. "It was always thus. It is beyond question. The world is ordered. We have our place. We have our roles. Caretake-ers only may touch. It was always thus. We must not question. Vargad is Head-er. He must Head. His Burrow needs its Head-er. The world is ordered. It was always thus."

Largad, Find-er, heard the songs, felt the threads, knew remembrance. Largad, Find-er, sensed tilt, saw beyond distant crests, felt the coming New. Largad twanged Dergad's thread, held it strong. Dergad paused, his adamant certainty paused, turned to Largad's thread, awaited her song.

Largad sang of grace. She sang of potential, of first breath, which together they had shared. Largad sang of second breath and all the breaths to come. All shared; all trusted; all true. Largad sang of Vargad's strength, his wisdom, his truth.

Largad, Find-er, sang of Vargad's longing and her trust in his long-ing. She sang of his truth, a longing with truth embedded. She sang of strength in meld, of trust, of wisdom, of truth. Largad sang of first breath shared and all the breaths to come. She sang of wondering why, of truth, of wisdom known. Truth and wisdom; greater than always thus.

VaSoDeLa sat humming into the silence and pondered.

Dergad, Show-er, sang softly of partners lost, of Art that broke the unbreakable. Partners lost. Abandoned. Vargad, Head-er, brought Art.

Largad, Find-er, sang of trust, of breaths shared.

Dergad, Show-er, sang of loss. Dergad sang of loss.

Sorgad, Caretake-er, sang of always was. Always was.

VaSoDeLa sat in loss and hummed, breaths shared.

~ 16 ~

DESPONDENCY

Olivia sat hunched in her shelter, which adjoined the kitchen where she had spent yet another wearying day. One small lamp glowed against the wall, lighting the side of her face. She peered into the lingering twilight that revealed a hint of the Green flanking her window.

The encroaching edge of trees loomed, eerie and menacing. She leaned to lower the window shade, creating a barricade against the gloom. A shiver ran down her spine. She decided to skip the burden of the gathering hall. She didn't feel like going into stillness tonight. Her mind was too tattered; her heart, too weary.

She was tired of the food that tasted of cardboard and crumbled like sawdust. She longed for fresh greens and autumn roots, squashes, crunchy stalks, soft breads. Logan and Harper delivered textured patterns for the protein vats, but those were just synthetic mimicries. Olivia yearned for whole food, wholesome food. Would she never have it again?

The specter of her mother's decline haunted her thoughts and robbed her of peace. Was this her doom as well?

She was tired of people who arrived late for their shifts or neglected to come at all. They always claimed they'd forgotten, which she doubted. She was tired of the unrelenting pressure of too much to do and not enough time to do it. She was continuously frustrated with empty spice jars that no one thought to fill.

She thought of their large recycle chamber. Its face had been removed, and tools lay strewn on the floor. The repair project had sat idle for an entire week. Frank and Carol were helping with the wind turbines and had been pulled from this repair with no predictions of when they would be able to return. Meanwhile, the cooks were forced to use a small washing station, a cumbersome process that yielded mediocre results. She was tired of hounding people to refresh the soapy water and hated using bowls and pans coated with an oily film.

Olivia lowered her head and closed her eyes. She was tired of the silly chatter and endless giggling in the kitchen and dining room. She melted away at every opportunity, to shut herself in her shelter, dreading the monotony of producing steaming trays of tasteless food for straggling lines of indifferent diners.

Her fury bubbled daily. Exhaustion dragged at her ankles as she watched truant cooks standing nonchalantly in the serving line, mindlessly gossiping and seemingly oblivious to the extra work she shouldered because of their selfish preoccupation with frivolities. She was especially tired of the companions, floating along like obedient jellyfish, following everyone, everyone, as they wandered about Home Base and meandered through their carefree days.

Olivia turned to her wall controls and activated familiar music, adjusting the volume until she could feel it throbbing in her chest, pounding against her skin, an acoustic massage that beat against her anger, stomped her fear, drowned her dread of morning and another day of anguishing monotony.

She was so tired. She sank onto her bed, exhausted tears dampening her pillow.

~ 17 ~

KNOTS

The birthlings snuggled together in their sleeping den, rippling dawn wisdom, watched by elders humming softly nearby. Vargad stilled his heart as Scawlan draped fibers over the birthlings' holderlings. He and his burrowmates barely breathed as they waited to learn the birthlings' response.

Their ancient songs told nothing of these knots, these patterns of fiber. Art. Such a small word that held the enormity of Source within it. No one had imagined twisting and knotting the long fibers that spread everywhere across their world. No one had imagined that such joy might be captured and held, persisting, uninterrupted, retrieved after the younglings had abandoned their knotted mats in forgetfulness, scampering elsewhere to tumble and roll, trilling their unending joy in each other's company.

Would the birthlings bring deeper Art, knotting fibers into patterns that would connect elders solidly to Source?

As the birthlings keened, one and then another, Caretake-ers adroitly scooped up each and carried them away from the sleeping niche. After all had gone, they left behind, seemingly thoughtlessly, rich tapestries of Art, carrying glorious vibrations, open doorways to Source. The elders crept transfixed amongst knotted patterns and vibrant colors scattered across the niche.

Vargad carefully reached for one of the knottings and brought it to his chest. His holderlings rippled along the knots and twists, marveling at the textures and colors. The harmony of his heart blossomed anew. He sensed movement as his burrowmates gathered up other knottings. The Narsis hummed and trilled, filling the sleeping niche with a song unimagined.

They rolled onto their sides and clutched the knottings. Their song rose in unison, the vibration reaching outward through the packed Soil that enveloped Burrow. The vibration traveled far; rich, intense, it swept past Lone Tree, who pauses in its song, to finally splash against stone cliffs high above crashing waves.

The Arbans read the Narsis' song through their roots and shimmer their leaves in wonder. The tilted balance shifts, teeters on a brink. The Arbans shimmer...and shimmer...

...Then flick their rooted tendrils as one, sending a powerful vibration back, rolling beneath the countryside, roaring past Lone Tree, and bursting through peaceful Burrow. It blasts unabated, shattering, unchecked, around and through the trilling, humming elders as they clutched the knottings to their chests.

The Narsis broke from their trance and rolled upright, racing through Burrow to careen into Sunlight, keening their alarm to Sky, circling, pouring over each other, senseless.

Vargad circled with his burrowmates, impervious to the Nurtureers over which he scuttled. His heart had been fully open, his mind fully immersed in the glorious connection with Source. The Arbans' vibration had torn through him, and the abrupt disconnection from Source had stunned his senses. Basic instincts, long unused, had driven him along the tunnels of Burrow, suddenly unfamiliar turns, lost in confusion, following his nose toward the freshening air. Sun had momentarily blinded him as he burst into the open and raced amidst the others, until his holderlings tangled and he careened onto his side, slid to a stop, frozen, too frightened to move.

The Nurture-ers flattened themselves beneath him, nestled their way up through his thick fur, pressed their faces against his hot skin, and poured wholeness into him. The Nurture-ers worked together, replenishing depleted sugars and amino acids, even fully constructed proteins, a stream of energy flowing from neighboring Nurture-ers in an unbroken cascade of love and sustenance. Water and electrolytes, vitamins and fatty acids, everything Vargad needed to replenish his whole flowed into him. The Nurture-ers gave and gave while Vargad drew and drew.

Vargad slept and dreamt of Eglans, of Nest, of tilted balance, un-partners. He saw bright threads of light knotted into intricate patterns, knotted light filling Nest. Vargad saw Eglans, nestled into light, orange feathers swept into bright patterns, patterns of Art, discovering the connection to Source, filling hearts, drenched in love.

Eglans cannot weave, cannot knot. Eglans soar in the heights, dexterity long abandoned, beaks broad and flat. Connection to Source cannot be captured by Eglan birthlings weaving fibers into intricate patterns. Eglan elders cannot hold their birthlings' Art against their chests and immerse into Source.

Is this the origin of tilted balance? True partners cannot be unbalanced with one enriched and one impoverished; one entitled and one unworthy. Narsis could not have Art if Eglans went without. Art cannot be hoarded. Art must be shared. Must be given. Must be gifted.

Vargad stretched his holderlings as he slept. They twitched, and in his dream, he gazed at them, felt their emptiness. Why were they empty? Had they no purpose other than to create Burrow? Should he try Art? Should he gather fibers for the younglings to create Art? A shudder ran up his spine, shaking him awake.

Vargad left the fading remnants of his dream and brought his awareness to Sunshine Above and Nurture-ers Below. Always Narsis and Eglans were partners. Always they had joined Above with Below. Narsis and Eglans held the entire world between them, weaving the whole. Narsis and Eglans were part of Source. Always it had been so, in all remembrance.

As Nurture-ers withdrew their faces from Vargad's now cool skin, he recognized completion. He was nurtured. Vargad reached out to his meld, finding their threads, sang their songs. Together, the four meldmates explored the depth of Art, its connection to Source, the fullness of partners, the rightness of the whole.

The Arbans sing to the sky, and the Shosens listen. The Arbans dance in the wind, and the Shosens color the swirling leaves with dips and darts, weaving turquoise patterns that shift the air and entice the wind. The Shosens sing of courage and strength, sending trills to skip along the waves and onward, across the grassy plains, twirling around Lone Tree silhouetted against the morning sky.

Lone Tree shimmers and sings of strength and calmness, of renewing joy, awakening hope. Lone Tree turns toward Burrow and breathes its song along its way.

Vargad rested amongst the lingering threads of his dream and heard the song of joy. He breathed it deep into his heart. He grasped Lone Tree's song and added his own, a dawning trill of hope.

Lone Tree's song swirls around the Narsis, calming thoughts, clearing hearts. Thoughts slowed, then silenced; holderlings patted, smoothed; breaths evened, deepened.

The Narsis lay amongst hillside families and absorbed the colors and warmth, the scents and twirling breeze. They hummed at Sun's dawning and dozed in nurtured love.

Tilted balance pauses on a higher plane, brighter, more vibrant. The Arbans sing, and Lone Tree shimmers.

The Narsis rested and breathed their New.

~ 18 ~

PUZZLE

The numbers weren't making sense. Logan pushed away from his workstation and sat back, chewing his moustache. This job was driving him crazy. He'd have to go look for himself.

He pushed out of his chair, tucked his screen under his arm, clumped into his boots, and pulled open the door that led directly into the storage hall, where kitchen supplies lay in readiness.

After opening each bin and peering inside, he unrolled his screen with a quick flick and made a short notation. After the sixth bin, he skipped a few, spot-checking his way through the rest of the aisle.

He leaned his shoulder against a tall shelving unit, scratched the back of his head. It looked like the inventory figures were right. He walked down an adjoining aisle, peeking inside a couple of bins, bouncing his rolled screen lightly across several others.

Everything was neat and tidy, all the lids snugly in place, the floor free of spills. He'd never seen the storage hall this clean before. So why did he feel so unsettled?

Because the numbers weren't making sense.

$$\sim 19 \sim$$

WATER

Tom crouched in wonder as the Green welcomed the dawn, fresh and vibrant.

Tom didn't tend the Green. It was always on his list, to trim, tidy, mow. But morning after morning, week after week, the Green needed no tending. The myriad plants that made up the Green grew to the perfect height, remained soft underfoot, never withered or even declined. Surely they breathed; surely they drank. But Tom could see no cycles of germination, growth, decline.

The air held moisture. The plants glistened with dew. But surely that was not sufficient hydration to sustain this luxurious growth, under this bright sun, throughout these long days, this never-ending summer. The sky never held clouds. The Earthens never scampered out of rain. They never sneezed away pollen or washed away dust.

Tom's team had originally planned to dig trenches for piping and sprinkling outlets. He had installed countless systems throughout his Earthen life. He had made a nice nest egg from components he had designed himself. Now, with this alien project before him, he had permission from the engineering team to book time on the creation front to produce the components he wanted to incorporate into the Green. With proper irrigation, the Green would look after itself, freeing Tom and his staff to undertake more creative projects.

Tom stood up and shook the ache out of his thigh, getting the blood moving again. Maybe today was the day. He turned resolutely and strode along the manicured path, making his way to his workshop. They needed stakes, string, a hand sledge, and a trencher. They could accomplish a lot before lunch, maybe finish it up this afternoon.

His team was already in the shop, chatting about their evenings, discussing the comet that was clearly visible in the pre-dawn sky. It seemed that everyone took an interest in the night sky, here on Airon. The complete absence of artificial light allowed the stars to spring into brilliancy. The comet had been approaching for several weeks and was predicted to peak in the next day or two, before drifting back to the edges of the sky, off to the icy realms from whence it came.

Tom led a discussion about their morning's project. Albert had some suggestions about circumnavigating the perimeter of the Green without disrupting the vegetation too much. Pamela raised the question of water source, since the kitchen and hydroponics were already bringing large quantities from the ship. Could they insert a filtering system and use the wastewater from the kitchen? The hydroponics?

As they talked, they loaded tools into carts, pausing often to gesture their imaginations into rough coherency. They brought out a planning board and diagramed possibilities. Albert left to grab his screen. By the time he returned, Tom had wandered away to talk with Mateo about specific scheduling time on the ship's creation front. By the time he returned, Pamela had to leave for her lunch shift. Tom and Albert talked about Albert's infatuation with Jennifer, the complications that kept popping up.

When the lunch gong sounded, they looked at their carts filled with tools and potential and agreed to get started right after lunch. They sauntered over to the dining hall. After lunch, Tom remembered he was on cleanup. Albert and Pamela walked back to the workshop and sorted through the tools, putting everything back in its place. They erased the planning board and stowed it against the wall, next to tall shelving, and Albert remembered to pull his screen down from said shelving where he had tossed it. Tom arrived just as they were closing the shop door. The three of them decided to wander in the forest until dinner time; it was such a nice day, and they always enjoyed each other's company.

No one noticed their truancy. What The 108 did notice was how trim and tidy the Green looked, fresh and inviting. A common remark was how Tom and his team did such a great job at keeping the Green perfectly groomed, healthy and beautiful.

The scenario repeated itself often, with variations on celestial observations and love entanglements. It was easy to miss the easily observable pattern of thwarted plans, because the forest smelled lovely, the sun shone brightly, and the breeze brought a freshness that soothed Earthen hearts.

The Green lay undisturbed, offering gentle respite from busy days and bouncing thoughts. The Green lay tidy and vibrant, just as it always had. Just as it always would.

~ 20 ~

CALLING

VaSoDeLa flowed down an embankment and followed Stream to where it gleefully sprang into open air and tumbled down Overlook. He gazed out over the grassy expanse far below, to Lone Tree, a faint smudge in the distance, floating on a green sea, the wind rippling tall families into waves. He flowed along Overlook's edge, holderlings feeling their way unerringly past trees and boulders, eyes watching for any glimpse of movement across the vast Plain below.

He reached the greeting place, feeling the depth of the solitude of this journey. He sent gratitude to his meld; they showered warmth into his heart. He sat, a lone figure, atop Overlook, sending hope, holderlings clasped across his chest.

Sun moved across Sky. Vargad drowsed in its warmth as SoDeLa held vigil. Vargad was their strong one, daring and calm. He had always Head-ed them, guided them; they had followed him from the first, from when they had cuddled together as birthlings, offering dawn wisdom to their elders. Now they held him, contained him. They felt strength flowing from the Nurture-ers upon which he rested, from the sun warming his fur, from the breeze caressing his ears. They held him and purred their song of solidarity, of clarity, bolstering him as he slept, holding hope.

VaSoDeLa came into awareness as a familiar clacking penetrated his sleep. He breathed deeply of the dusk air, hope moving tentatively toward joy.

JaCoMaTuRi stomps
clacks beside VaSoDeLa
spreads tail
clicks wings.

VaSoDeLa rumbled and hummed, adding depth to JaCoMaTuRi's rhythm. Together, they faced the shimmering sun as it skimmed the horizon, approaching twilight. Calmness at end of day. VaSoDeLa turned resolutely to the heart of his despair.

In all remembrance, partners we have been. VaSoDeLa rumbles.

All remembrance
together be
JaCoMaTuRi clacks.

VaSoDeLa's despair spilled forth, tumbling his thoughts, one after the other. Eglans have flown. Narsis abandoned. Grieve our loss. Emptiness with loss. Narsis and Eglans. Partners strong. Partners fly, burrow; unite Above, Below; unite Sky, Soil.

Partners sing! Abandoned, grieve. Partners strong! Always so. Abandoned, grieve. Broken; despair. Eglans return. Narsis rejoice! Partners strong. Abandoned, weak.

VaSoDeLa fell silent. Waited.

All remembrance
together be.

Partners sing
Sky, Below.
Eglans fly
To Narsis, fly.
Narsis flow
To Eglans, flow.

*All remembrance
together be.*

JaCoMaTuRi *clacks
keens to Sky
unworthy be
knotting none
Art none
unworthy be.*

*Strangers come
Eglans distant
knotting comes
Eglans distant
strangers stay
strangers always
Narsis with strangers
Eglans distant.*

*Narsis learn
Narsis grow
Narsis New
Eglans distant
Narsis knot
younglings knot
birthlings knot
Eglans lost
holderlings not
hold not
Art not
Eglans lost
Unworthy be.*

JaCoMaTuRi clacks

spreads tail
clicks wings.

Unworthy be.

JaCoMaTuRi falls
falls below
spreads wings
keens despair.

Unworthy be.

Art not
Strangers not
Eglans distant
Unworthy be.

VaSoDeLa called! Twilight lingered. Come! Come back! Together be! Here! Worthy be! Always so! In all remembrance. Partners be!

VaSoDeLa called! Called! And called! Worthy be! Partners be!

VaSoDeLa called! Calls! And called!

Far away, the Arbans sing to the sky, and the Shosens listen. The Arbans sway in the wind, and the Shosens dip, weaving patterns to lift the air and calm the wind. The Shosens sing of courage and strength, across the grassy plains, twirling past Lone Tree, silhouetted against the twilit sky.

Lone Tree shimmers in the dusk, stretches feathery branches through the cooling air, and sings of strength and calmness, of renewed joy, blossomed hope. Lone Tree turns toward Overlook and sings its song along its way. The song riffles across JaCoMaTuRi's soaring wings, stirs the fur of VaSoDeLa's chest.

Partners be! VaSoDeLa calls! Called! And calls!

Sun is gone. VaSoDeLa called! Called! And called!

Called!

And calls!

VaSoDeLa crouched, panting, gazing across Plain, watches Lone Tree disappear into its night.

Abandoned be.

VaSoDeLa hums truth, knowing.

Art had made the Eglans feel unworthy.

Certainty.

Art had flung the Eglans from Overlook, away from partners, away from ancient being.

Certainty.

VaSoDeLa lay, panting, searching empty Sky.

VaSoDeLa breathed deeply, felt Lone Tree's song, heard crashing waves.

VaSoDeLa lifted himself upright, breath caught.

Offering Art would offer healing.

VaSoDeLa stood, breathing hope, gifting.

VaSoDeLa breathed gifting, healing.

VaSoDeLa breathed healing, New.

~ 21 ~

EXPLOSION

Olivia scattered more cumin into the soup. It hadn't started to bubble yet. She glanced up at the clock and fury exploded in her mind, blinding her thoughts. Why had she committed to this extravagance? They would have been fine, eating the simple meals she usually served of late. Why did she keep reverting to old ways? Old yearnings? Pure foolishness.

She looked around the kitchen, at the heads of lettuce waiting to be chopped, the abandoned onions that would have added a perfect nuttiness to this soup. She had let these few fresh ingredients go to her head. Too late she realized that she didn't have time to caramelize the onions and decided to go with onion flakes instead, scrambling midstream to try to pull the meal together. And now, the soup would not heat. It would never be ready in time. It would have no taste, no character. Completely worthless.

She had been making heroic efforts for an entire week now. The hydroponics had been repaired, so they had fresh greens again. The modest wheat patch had matured, ripened, and been harvested. They had a small inventory of flour again, with more to come. They had root vegetables. She had steeled herself to reinvigorate the kitchen, offer hearty meals, begin anew.

Useless hope.

She slammed down the spice jar, grabbed a nearby ladle and hurled it across the room where it slammed against the window and clattered onto the worktable beneath.

Jacob whirled at the sound, hot bread tumbling from his gloved hands. He scanned the room and saw Olivia, hands covering her face, shoulders shaking. "Olivia? Are you okay?"

Olivia shook her head slowly, pressed the back of her hands to her forehead, and bent forward, rocking gently to and fro.

"Olivia! Here, let me help you." Jacob strode around the worktables separating them, pulled off his gloves and tossed them aside. He wrapped Olivia in his arms and held her soothingly. "It's okay. It's okay."

"No! It's not!" She pushed him away and turned, looking for an escape. The lettuce. The soup. The cursed onions...They all rose up and smothered her, a wave of exhausted uselessness.

She could find no escape. She was surrounded, and she had no way out. She slowly, deliberately, placed the lid back on the soup pot, and walked jaggedly across the room, pushed open the door to her shelter, and firmly latched it behind her.

Jacob watched her leave, heard the click of her lock, and scanned the room, assessing the half-prepared ingredients. He walked to the archway and leaned into the dining hall. "Megan! Megan! Can you help chop some lettuce for lunch? We're running late and need to get the salad going." He returned to the ovens, picked up the tumbled bread, and brushed off each loaf before setting it in the cooling rack. He pulled out the remaining loaves and added them as well. He lifted down a heavy pan, scooped the chopped onions into it, added oil, and placed them over a high flame.

His companion offered some herbs, which he spilled into the soup pot. He saw Megan chopping lettuce as her companion returned from the hydroponics hall, carrot tops and radish leaves spilling from its opened drawer. Erin wandered in from the dining hall, followed by a companion with bright green swirls covering its surface.

"Need any help?" she asked. Jacob set her to slicing protein bricks while her companion gathered oils and extracts for a flavorful marinade. Jacob's companion gathered spices and herbs that Jacob plunked into the oils. He gave it all a quick whisk and poured the entire concoction over the neatly spaced protein slabs resting in their shallow baking sheets.

When Julie walked in, he set her and her companion to gather used bowls, pots, knives, and utensils along with ingredient scraps and stack them into the recycle chamber. Soon, Peter joined them to scrape and spray worktables.

Together, they stirred the soup, sliced the bread, tossed the salad, pulled the protein slabs from the oven, and carried everything out to the serving table, which was surrounded by a chattering, jostling crowd.

"Let's bless!" Jacob called out. Their voices lifted in song and gratitude, filling the room with light.

~ 22 ~

GONE

Olivia lay staring at the ceiling, thoughts skittering from one worry to another. It was well into deepest night. She had toppled into a deep sleep, completely spent, but now lay drenched with the same wearying exhaustion. She had no energy for reading or viewing; not even music interested her. She curled onto her side, despairing of sleep. What was she doing here?

Thoughts tumbled incoherently. Exhausted tears dampened her pillow.

After a long while, she rolled onto her back and covered her face with her hands. Her thoughts twirling madly, cycling endlessly, offering no solutions, no respite. She couldn't face another day.

People needed food. She couldn't make it for them, not with these worthless ingredients. But no one else could do it; she had to do it. That was why she'd come to Airon.

She couldn't face another day.

No one else could do it. She had to do it. She couldn't do it.

Throwing back her cover, Olivia slumped on the edge of her bed, holding her head in both hands, sobbing quietly. Salty tears burned her aching eyes and stinging cheeks. She knew her eyes would be puffy tomorrow. Great. Everyone would know she'd been upset and would carefully avoid her. If anyone even showed up. She would have so much to do and not enough time to do it. No one would help her. She'd have to do it all alone.

No one else could do it. This was why she had come. She had to do it.

She couldn't do it.

The muscles in her throat clamped and ached as sobs choked her breath. Saliva dripped from her twisted mouth as she rocked slowly to and fro. She couldn't do it. She couldn't do it.

Don't do it.

The thought glimmered through the clenched darkness of her mind.

Don't do it.

Her sobs caught, held. *Don't do it.*

Olivia stopped rocking and looked around the room. Clothes and shoes were strewn heedlessly, spilling from chairs, poking from beneath the bed. Olivia brushed her tangled hair back from her face and propped her arms to each side, fists gripping the bed sheets. Just...don't do it. She sat in an endless quiet, feeling a peace flow through her. Quietly, her muscles shifted into a new tension, new possibilities.

Could she just go?

Olivia took a few shaky breaths and then pushed herself up off the bed. She kicked through the scattered clothing and pulled out a pair of dark pants and long shirt. She asked for soft light and squinted as the room obliged. She sorted through jumbled piles, tossed selected items onto the bed. She didn't want to have to come back. She wanted to make sure to take everything she would need.

Would she even need anything?

She would just go. She didn't want anyone to find her, because she knew they would look. She wanted to get away and stay away. She would just go. She could escape.

She piled her gatherings onto a shawl and tied the corners together. Clutching the bundle to her chest, she scrabbled her feet into shoes, turned, and looked around the room, scanning each surface and corner erratically, trying to imagine if she might need anything else. Then she darkened the room, softly opened the door, and peered into the kitchen.

Completely empty. She crept across the room to the dining room, paused at the doorway to check for occupants, and slithered along the wall to the far door. Stepping outside, the glowing scenery surprised her.

She hadn't known the forest could glow.

Stripes and spirals swayed quietly in the soft breeze. Thin colors stood out like neon, pinpricks of color flowing across the Green, the bordering forest rising in scallops and winding tendrils. Olivia stood, disoriented, jaggedly breathing in the fragrant air, mesmerized by the slow neon dance.

Olivia straightened, her grasped bundle nudging her calf. She walked carefully, silently, moving along Tom's groomed path, a ribbon flowing through the enchanted night. Which way to go? She paused, looked about her, groped for orientation.

The pinpricks of light along the edge of the dark path undulated softly, rippling away from her. She automatically took a step in the direction of the ripples, then another. The lights seemed to be guiding her.

Mesmerized, she stuttered along the path, pausing repeatedly to watch the colorful displays of Green and forest. The rippling lights curved away, and without thinking, Olivia stepped off the path and followed the pattern farther and farther into the forest. She lingered to take in the towering display swaying gently above her, around her, everywhere. And still the ripples guided her along, slowly, unerringly, farther and farther.

At some point, she dropped her clutched bundle. She had no need of anything after all. Only the ripples of light existed; existed just for her.

When at last they guided her from the forest, she stopped, peering into the abrupt darkness. Then understanding flooded her; this was what she needed. This was the perfect solution.

Even in her darkest moments, she hadn't imagined this outcome. But now she understood that it was a fitting end to her never-ending anguish. Nothing needed to matter anymore. She could finally escape. This was the expected ending, the only one that would work. She breathed in acceptance, nodded a final farewell, and stepped into the depths of darkness. The void took her.

Far away, the Arbans sing to the sky and send peace fluttering across the grassy plains, twirling around Lone Tree, glimmering in the night sky.

Lone Tree sings of strength and calmness, of acceptance. Lone Tree turns toward Home Base and breathes its song along its way. The song riffles along the wind, dances across the sky, caresses Home Base as it sleeps beneath the stars.

~ 23 ~

LONE TREE

VaSoDeLa set out early in the day to follow his last hope.

Dawn Wisdom with the birthlings brought no joy. Vargad felt distant, disengaged. As he watched with dull eyes, he recognized that the stirrings of the birthlings, their awakening holderlings and soft purrs were the same as yesterday and all the mornings before. Yet, they stirred no joy in his heart.

He sensed the enchantment of his burrowmates gathered in their daily anticipation, felt their stillness as the birthlings moved and cuddled. His emptiness dragged him downward; he slipped into despair. He crept from the sleeping niche unable to endure another morning of emptiness, loneliness.

Emerging from Burrow, Vargad hesitated to send his meld threads. His meldmates were most certainly immersed in their own Dawn Wisdom. He would rest with the nourishers while he waited for day to begin.

As he stretched out on the cool meadow, nourishing families reached to nestle through his fur. They found Vargad's skin cool to the touch, which gave them pause. Signals trickled down to Soil, rippled to other families, who conferred and assessed Vargad's need. Responsive nutrients traveled through Soil as root hairs tickled microbes awake and couriers sped from synapse to synapse, from one root system to the next, collecting and improvising, possibilities passed along in hope.

The nurturing leaves who pressed against Vargad's skin delivered the complex possibilities directly into his circulation, listened for feedback. More of this!! Less of that...

Remove-ers pulled miniscule fragments of waste from his circulation. More Remove-ers reached up, supplementing the unexpected need to offload spent microbes and organics. Vargad's enduring despair and loneliness, his sense of failure and guilt, these emotions were New to Airon. The damage wrought inside Vargad's body from guilt and despair added a heaviness that Nurture-ers and Remove-ers had not encountered; not in all remembrance.

Signals flowed downward and possibilities flowed upward. More Nurture-ers, more Remove-ers joined the effort, reaching up, assisting or replacing the first responders who grew fatigued, overwhelmed. The Nurture-ers and Remove-ers experimented and learned; New knowledge spread throughout Soil, alerting all of Below.

As New traveled throughout Below, Burrow walls brightened; Forest shivered; Stream quieted. Lone Tree pauses.

Tunnels of all Burrows took on a sheen of New. New aromas drifted from walls; droplets appeared, poised to diffuse onto passing holderlings. Soil began its work of easing Narsis into New, dispelling sadness that drifted, soothing grief from loss of Eglans. Cherished Eglans; partners through all remembrance.

Vargad slept.

As Sun glimmered through Forest's canopy, Vargad's burrowmates emerged into the brightening dawn. Each burrowmate paused, sent out meld threads, and relished their first breaths of melding. Narsis flowed into Meadow, stretched onto nurturing families, and drifted along the current of unfolding New. Nutrients flowed upward, a cocktail of old and New. Each cocktail matched each Narsi, as Nurture-ers recognized and welcomed the familiar scent, smell, and taste of each.

Remove-ers carried away what was no longer needed or was depleted, purifying Narsi circulation and making ready for New. Signals flowed and enriched the knowledge of Soil. Complexity blossomed aNew throughout Below.

Younglings romped their first romp of the day. Caretake-ers roused, observed and trilled, hummed and caressed. Birthlings were carried back to Burrow, and elders stretched and yawned toward bright Sun.

Meadow glimmered from the gift of Narsi breath, as Nurture-ers and Remove-ers relaxed and tremored, their dawn communion fulfilled. Vargad inhaled deeply and exhaled, his breath Newly sweetened. His eyes squinted open, and he raised his nose to catch the song of Forest, the peace of Meadow.

Vargad felt replenished. He nuzzled the nourishers, tickling their undersides with his stiff whiskers. He breathed gratitude and humility, then again raised his nose, this time in greeting to Sun. As Vargad hoisted his bulk upright, he gazed around him, taking in the lateness of the day, the frolicking of younglings, and the companionship of his burrowmates.

Vargad sent threads to his waiting meldmates, relished the remembrance of breaths shared, and returned their dawn greetings. VaSoDeLa flowed from one burrowmate to the next, touched foreheads formally, a moment of stillness repeated with each.

The subdued family watched as VaSoDeLa wound his way into Forest. No one followed or trilled his name. They watched, in understanding and shared resolve.

VaSoDeLa followed Stream, drank, and lowering his holderlings, he watched the wise water ripple over and around each one. Stream told him of Mountain high and Forest endless, of strong boulders and chuckling ferns, of trailing grasses and floating moss, of wings dipped and strong beaks clacked. Of flamboyant tails stilled. Of Eglans forlorn. Lost.

Stream told him of cliffs high and meadows endless, of hope and courage, of birdlings dancing, of Broad Sea waving. Stream told him of hope. Of courage. Of Head-ers head-ing. Of dawns shared. Breaths shared.

Stream told him of Airon spinning, of Airon dreaming. Of Airon chasing her ancient path around her glorious Sun. Of mountains rising and Broad Sea singing. Of all that is. Since all remembrance.

VaSoDeLa raised his nose and touched the brightness of Sun. He felt the warmth seep into his fur, into his heart. He breathed. He heard.

VaSoDeLa flowed alongside Stream, heard Stream begin a final song, a song of remembrance of paths taken, of cascades fallen, of meadows crossed, of destinations sought, of Broad Sea waiting, waiting for Stream, waiting always for Stream, the final, continuous blending, the final embrace, as two become one.

Stream threw itself over the brink of Overlook, rushing to join Broad Sea. And VaSoDeLa paused and took in breath, eyes drinking in the enormity of the vista, the magnitude of all that is. VaSoDeLa raised his torso and faced the void, the void of space, the void of partners lost. He listened to Stream's final song, the remembrance of paths taken, the anticipation of Broad Sea's welcome.

VaSoDeLa lowered his holderlings, his nose finding the faint path. He wound his careful way down, down the face of Overlook, and descended into the enormity below.

He rested along the way, found Nurture-ers and Remove-ers, families who reNewed him, reNewed him wisely, surely. His holderlings sought and found the way down, a way seldom trod, a way forever cherished. Cherished in all remembrance.

VaSoDeLa saw the turquoise cloud, saw it turn and spread toward him. The birdlings rose effortlessly, sweeping close above his head. The birdlings sang of calmness and strength, of power and wisdom, of joy and peace, of light and love. The cloud of birdlings danced and laughed above VaSoDeLa, shading him from bright Sun, following him down, ever down, helping him along his way.

At long last the trail sloped more gently, lost its definition between shrubs and ferns. VaSoDeLa rested under an occasional tree, the birdlings alighting on twigs and branches, waiting for his reNewed readiness. As VaSoDeLa rose from nurturing families, the birdlings hurled themselves into the air, and laughing and swirling, the troupe continued along its way.

As the slope gentled, then gentled more, the birdlings swooped, rustled the fur along VaSoDeLa's back, and chortled their farewell. VaSoDeLa watched them go, watched them tilt toward the lowering sun, watched until the turquoise smudge melted and lost itself beyond a distant ridge.

VaSoDeLa flowed across the vast meadow, his destination rising above the waving grasses. Though weary from the long descent, he moved forward with purpose and hope. Ever onward.

Lone Tree rose and filled his world. VaSoDeLa paused and raised his torso. The song of Airon caressed his ears, kissed his nose, tingled his holderlings. He moved forward and entered the brightness of the deep shade that glimmers beneath Lone Tree.

VaSoDeLa enters and weariness melts away. VaSoDeLa curls on lush families and hears light bouncing from branch to branch, leaf to leaf. Birdlings arrive and trickle down, twig to twig, turquoise beads of mist, chuckling their way down to alight around VaSoDeLa, creating a turquoise pool that nestles the shores of a Narsi island.

Lone Tree murmurs; murmurs of breaths shared, ancient partners, since all remembrance and for all the days to come. All is now.

VaSoDeLa closes his eyes, stills his mind, murmurs his quest. "Bring Eglans. Partners be."

Lone Tree stretches to Sky, sings to Sun. Lone Tree turns to Nest and sends its song along its way.
Jamina stirs
Flutters flamboyant tail.
Lifts head
Hears song
Lone Tree's song.

Jamina stirs
Clatters wings
Lifts beak
Sees threads
Meld threads
Meld.

Jamina stirs
Clacks beak
Tastes threads
Wondrous threads
Jamina flutters

Swallows threads
Cherished threads
JaCoMaTuRi becomes.

JaCoMaTuRi soars
soars to Lone Tree
Answers call
Lone Tree's call
Lone Tree's song
Forever be.

VaSoDeLa hears a familiar swoosh, a welcome swoosh, a beloved swoosh. VaSoDeLa raises himself, lifts his nose, and calls. Calls and calls. Birdlings rise, sweep beneath Lone Tree's massive limbs, and flow, a turquoise stream, flow toward Broad Sea, where the Arbans sing. JaCoMaTuRi hops, branch to branch, pausing, tasting, wondering. VaSoDeLa calls; waits; hopes. JaCoMaTuRi hops, pauses, wonders. JaCoMaTuRi pauses. VaSoDeLa waits. Waits; hopes.

Lone Tree rustles, stretches, and sings of breaths shared, days shared, sunsets shared. Lone Tree sings of soaring Above and burrowing Below. VaSoDeLa sings of Overlook shared, sunsets shared, partners be, uniting Above and Below. JaCoMaTuRi rustles her flamboyant tail, stomps her strong feet.

Lone Tree settles. Lone Tree breathes Airon from deep Below. Airon slumbers; dreams. Lone Tree breathes. Breathes and settles.

Sun dips behind ridge; twilight dims. JaCoMaTuRi settles, opens beak, releases meld. Jamina settles, tucks head under wings, stills flamboyant tail, settles her strong feet. VaSoDeLa sways, feels last sun bright on his chest. He stills his holderlings, droops his head. VaSoDeLa releases his meld threads, cherished threads; a final clutching before final release. Vargad sways, alone.

Vargad sways in the deepening twilight, tastes Lone Tree's song as it floats toward Burrow, toward Nest. Vargad sways and lowers onto upstretched families, feels their caress against his skin, breathes his ragged sadness; the only gift he has, he gives; this breath, and all the breaths to come. Vargad breathes into darkness, a darkness that glimmers, glimmers with Lone Tree's song, a song of all remembrance, of all that is.

Stillness.

Vargad smells her before he opens his eyes; before, even, he swims into awareness. Vargad smells her as hope blossoms in his heart. Vargad moves gentle holderlings along bright feathers. Vargad softly embraces her as she nestles against his chest.

They sleep.

As Vargad blinks into an early dawn, an unfamiliar breeze ruffles his fur. Lone Tree stands empty above him as it stirs itself to embrace the day. Vargad feels cool air against his once warm chest, feels emptiness amidst his once full holderlings. Vargad feels love in his once empty heart. Partners be.

JaCoMaTuRi soars!
Soars! on rising air

JaCoMaTuRi soars!
Soars! to Nest
Soars! to family
Soars! through brightening Sky.

~ 24 ~

MESSAGES

Logan brought his meal back to his workstation. He had gotten into the habit of walking through the dining room during every meal, paying attention to who was there eating, taking stock of the amount of food that had been cooked and what remained on serving trays at the end of the meal. What influenced the popularity of various meals? Was the menu interesting? Were people piling their plates high? Were they lingering with friends? Going back for seconds? Since Olivia had disappeared, no one seemed to be in charge, but mysteriously, meals came out on time and the kitchen continued to be organized and clean.

He sat down and pushed his plate off to one side, making room for his screen, and entered the numbers he'd just collected. He pulled his mustache, chewing the ends thoughtfully. He could see a pattern but wanted to watch it longer to be sure. He sat a few breaths longer, then pulled up his message board.

Earth still hadn't answered his last message. They'd gotten even sloppier. He scrolled back through his outbox. Real sloppy. Seventeen messages. He'd sent seventeen messages over the last...twelve days, and no one had bothered to get back to him about any of them. Airon must have really sunk to the bottom of Earthen priority lists.

Figured. Now that the stellar travelers had gotten set up on Airon, why would the Earthens care what else happened? Their job was to get them here, period. Now they could just slack off and pull down their pay. Jerks. He was on the wrong end of the mission.

He swept his scroll aside and pulled his plate over. Picking up a fork, he started shoveling bites into his mouth. The food was pretty good. Harper's textures were still working out. He liked eating something that had some chew to it.

He liked working with Harper. She was a good kid. She reminded him of his kid sister. Sweet, always happy despite the clamor of their older sister. He thought Michael treated Harper pretty good, too. It was nice having her around. Hadn't seen her much lately, though. Maybe he'd go out and wander later, see if he could run into her. She was always nice; easy to talk to. Good kid.

~ 25 ~

UNIQUE

Harper eased her door closed and leaned back against it, breathing in the fragrant air. Her companion, Andy, drifted next to her, quietly waiting. She reached out and placed her hand on Andy's soft surface while she scanned the forest's edge. She would return to the knitting meadow today, with the hope of encountering Vargad or someone from his family.

She was slipping away in the early morning, partly because she hoped to avoid being asked to chaperone a blending for someone. Requests had slackened over the last couple of weeks, but she did still get asked. Harper suspected that people were going out on their own, despite Scarlett and Ava's insistence on continued observation.

If Vargad wasn't in the meadow this morning, she could always blend. The thought captured Harper's attention. She looked around, surreptitiously, with an increased hope that no one would see her leave. The thought of her own blending, rather than observing others as they blended, brought delight and guilt, twined together. She took a deep breath and shrugged. The meadow was the perfect destination, regardless of what might happen there. So far she was unobserved, so she was free to do as she wished.

Andy floated forward, heading toward the dining hall. Puzzled, Harper followed. Usually, Andy followed her. What was he up to? They skirted the hall and moved along the forest's edge, where Andy chose an unfamiliar path that led between two towering trees. Harper paused and looked up into the intertwined branches high above.

She thought back to her long-ago conversation with Chatan and considered his theory that all life forms here lived cooperatively. Was it part of blending? These two trees grew very close to each other, yet they weren't crowding each other. Their branches shared the space, allowing light and air to flow between them. The bronze flowers of one tree dangled amongst the purple cupped flowers of the other.

A quick movement caught Harper's eye; she peered between the blossoms. A large animal sat on a branch gazing down at her. It lifted rows of vivid yellow wings, exposing its bright orange chest to the air below.

Harper was taken aback that such a vibrantly colored animal, a large animal, had remained invisible until now. Was it rare?

She breathed in deeply, then softly called out "Hello?" She paused. "I'm Harper."

The animal dipped its head and rattled its flamboyant tail. Then it leaned forward and fell in a graceful soar between branches, spreading its rows of yellow wings that rippled along both sides of its sleek body, clicking melodiously.

Harper hastened to follow it. She saw Andy waiting directly ahead on the path, anticipating the direction in which their adventure would take them. She paused, recognizing cooperation between companion and bird, then nodded. She would join them.

Andy led her down a gentle slope, along a footpath that wound its way between soft fronds and grasses of greens, rusts, and glimmering golds. The grasses brushed her skirt; in response, she drew her hands through the glistening blades, and stooped to slip off her shoes. Why wait until she reached the meadow? She could blend with Airon now.

As she straightened, Andy was there, opening a small compartment where she placed her shoes. They continued following the path underneath the high canopy that filtered the sparkling sun.

As always, she remembered. A tingling spread through her feet, twined up her legs. She breathed in the fragrances floating down from the flowers and once again caught sight of the orange and yellow bird as it dropped from its branch, guiding them forward. Her steps flowed along the path sparkling with incandescent greens. The tingling eddied along her spine, propelling her forward, gloriously.

A second bird spiraled down from a higher branch and followed the first through the trees. Harper saw another, brilliant against the canopy, then another. Not rare, then. Perhaps shy.

It is time for us to meet.

Harper wasn't sure how she knew this, but she was certain. Cooperation. Things happening in their own time, a tapestry flawlessly woven. It all made perfect sense, and Harper felt her spirits rise at the sense of the deepening texture of this world, how everything fit together perfectly. She fleetingly thought of Chatan, and how he would enjoy this. And then knew that his own adventure was unfolding for him in its own time. This was for her, especially.

For you are unique in this world.

Harper was surprised at the thought. Everyone is unique. She pushed the thought away and returned her attention to Andy floating along before her, the brilliant flock of birds accompanying them through the overhanging branches, the fronds and grasses swaying beside her, their softness brushing her sweeping palms and combing fingers. She focused on the delight of the carpeted path beneath her feet, the intricate fragrances drifting through the air, the dappled sunlight brightening her day.

Their day.

And then suddenly, they were at the knitting meadow. Harper recognized the large tree standing at the far end of Meadow and redrew her mental map to include this new approach to the familiar place.

They left the sheltering trees behind and waded through the tall grass toward the tree. Andy led the way along a narrow path between the taller grasses. It would have been invisible to Harper if not for Andy's guidance. He swam amidst grass tips, revealing the path as they walked.

Harper turned and looked behind at the seemingly solid sea of waist-high greens and golden yellows. She parted the grass around her but could see no other paths. She turned back to Andy, hovering during her curiosity, and they again made their way toward the tree.

The brilliant flock of clacking birds wheeled overhead and alighted on the tree, spreading themselves out along the expansive branches. One bird swooped down to the ground and disappeared into the tall grass. A lithe brown body rose at the base of the tree and rotated to face her.

Harper laughed aloud and waved her hand high over her head. "Vargad! I was hoping to meet you today!"

"It is time for us to meet," he replied as she drew near.

"That's what I thought," she called back, delighted at the perfect texture of the day.

The colorful bird stomped and clicked a rhythm on a large rock next to the trunk of the tree, their quorum complete.

"Is it all right for me to sit this close to him?" She gestured at the bird.

"It is time for us to meet," Vargad repeated patiently. The bird dipped her head and rattled her flamboyant tail.

"That's what I thought," Harper breathed. She sank directly onto cool Meadow families resting in the shade of the singing tree as she suddenly felt herself soar through the sky, across sparkling waves.

After a time, a year? A breath? After a time, Harper returned to Meadow and found her body. Eventually, she remembered how to be in her body, to stay within its boundaries.

She could feel the families under her legs, the Nurture-ers pressed against her skin. She could see VaSoDeLa and JaCoMaTuRi sitting beside her, could see the threads that wove them into their two separate melds. She could see their eyes, the colors that glowed from their fur, feathers, a glorious tail, stilled holderlings. No time had passed, and all time had passed. She drew a breath; another.

It is time for you to meet.

"You are truly blessed." Harper looked to JaCoMaTuRi, sitting on her rock. "To be free to soar in this sky, through this forest. You are so much freer than either of us; Vargad and I are doomed to wander ploddingly along the ground, tethered and heavily bound. We can barely imagine what you experience every day, day upon day."

JaCoMaTuRi grew still. As Harper watched, a brightness blushed across JaCoMaTuRi's rows of yellow feathers, trailed along her flamboyant tail.

Harper saw a broken edge on JaCoMaTuRi's wings, an edge that reached down and pierced JaCoMaTuRi's heart. Harper reached out with her thought and soothed the edge, helping it straighten, strong and sure.

JaCoMaTuRi's heart brightened. A lovely radiance flowed out of her and touched VaSoDeLa's heart, which brightened in return. Above them, the rest of the yellow and orange flock brightened, one by one by ten. Harper felt a vibration move through the ground on which they sat, a shimmering that rose into Sky, a blending of ground and air, Below and Above, that sang and twirled.

Sound returned, and Harper could feel the breeze on her skin, smell the lovely fragrance that flowed down from the tree. She smoothed the cloth on which she now sat, wiggled her toes in the shoes she now wore. She could again notice the warmth of the sun. She saw no radiance or shimmer; she carried no memory of soaring across the sky. She looked up into the sheltering branches of the tree and noticed a sprinkling of small, turquoise birds, stilled, scattered across the branches. The orange flock had disappeared, hopping through the forest depths, branch to branch, once again bright and whole.

"How many different kinds of birds are on Airon?" Harper turned her gaze to the mismatched, perfectly matched pair who shared her shade.

"A few. Airon needs only a few."

The small birds rose as one, their wings whispering a song as they swung across the sun and vanished over the towering forest.

"And the two of you?" Harper nodded to Vargad and Jamina. "Are you good friends?"

"Yes. We are good friends. We have always been friends and are now friends again."

"How did you become friends? You are so different from each other."

"I tend the ground. She tends Sky."

"And together you blend the ground and Sky."

"Yes. Together we blend the ground and Sky. Below and Above."

The mismatched, perfectly matched trio sat in stillness, forging a rich bond of music and light, uniting a past with a future, the known with the possible. Jagged edges smoothed and dissonance softened.

Patience, understanding, trust, hope...all wound their ways between the three, while they chatted and clicked, hummed and clattered.

~ 26 ~

STILLNESS

Ava sat with legs folded beneath her, sitting bones propped on a kneeling bench to ease her knees. Her back was perfectly straight, chin level with the floor, hands resting, palms up, at the bend of hips to thighs. Her eyes were closed as she opened her throat and drew in a deep, slow breath through parted lips, held it for a few heartbeats, and sent it out again slowly, hissing soundlessly.

The sun was high in the sky now, far advanced from the dawn that had birthed this stillness. It brightened the forest stretching beyond the windows, adding brilliance to the colors splashed across its edge.

Dozens of people sat scattered around the room, some on chairs, some cross-legged, others on kneeling benches like Ava's. Many people wore shawls around their shoulders, adding splashes of color across the soft, violet-blue carpet. The gathering hall was completely silent except for the soft sound of slow breathing; even that muffled by the thick carpet and textured walls.

The stillness stretched on. From time to time, one person, then another quietly sank to touch forehead to floor, rose softly, moved to the soundless door, stepped into shoes and out into the brilliant day.

Ava took one final measured breath and relaxed even deeper into stillness. A pure joy radiated through every cell of her body. She sat in timeless stillness, immersed, her mind quiet. When at last the bliss ebbed, she allowed it to go and slowly became aware of the room around her. She felt her breath flow in and out, in and out.

At last, she leaned forward to touch forehead to floor, nurturing the gratitude that swelled her heart. She rose to her knees, bent to slide the low bench to the side, and let her shawl puddle into a crescent moon around her ankles.

Rising, she brought her arms up in a wide circle to point at the ceiling. Going up on tiptoe, she drew in a deep breath, held it, exhaled as she brought arms down to sides and up to a soft pranam in front of her chest.

She looked around at the abandoned chairs and benches, pillows and shawls, and smiled. She looked out the window at the darkening forest, still ablaze with color. The day was ending. Had she overlooked anything that she should have done today? Michael would have fetched her if it had been important...wouldn't he?

Now that Harper had thoroughly captured his attention, Ava couldn't be sure of what Michael would and would not do. She abandoned that train of thought, unwilling to let it disturb her calm. Harper always disturbed her calm.

~ 27 ~

REVELATION

Harper picked up her shawl and tucked her screen under her arm. She would sit on the Green and read until dinnertime. Shuffling into her shoes, she swung open her door just in time to see Aadhya's caravan come to a quiet stop alongside her tall shelter. A lifetime had passed since Aadhya's caravan had last sat in Home Base!

Harper waved furiously and tossed her screen back through the door. She skipped over to greet her friend, bouncing up and down, waving her hands above her head.

"You've been gone forever!" she called out even though Aadhya was still inside her caravan. "I've forgotten what you look like." She was so happy that Aadhya was back. Finally, after all this time.

She circled the caravan, patting the sides soundly with both palms. "Aadhya? Aadhya! Hello? Hello?"

She heard the door swoosh open and danced around to the far side of the caravan to finally greet her friend.

Aadhya carefully backed down the caravan steps, holding onto the solid handles extending from either side of the doorway. She turned toward Harper and threw out her arms to embrace her dearest friend.

Harper stopped in her tracks, both hands flying up to cover her mouth, eyes wide. "Oh, my world! Aadhya! You're pregnant!"

She stepped forward into Aadhya's embrace and firmly hugged her. They pivoted back and forth, rocked side to side, bulging belly between them, flooded with the joy of seeing each other after so much time.

Harper stepped back and placed both hands on Aadhya's shoulders, leaning away to see her better. "It's so good to see you. I've missed you so much." Harper looked down and tapped Aadhya's swollen belly with a forefinger. "Tell me about this."

They stared at each other, abrim with smiles, and hugged each other again. "It's so good to see you," Harper repeated.

"And I am so happy to see you and to be seen by you. How are you?"

"I'm great. *Everything's* great. Well, Olivia has disappeared, but otherwise, everything's great."

Aadhya's hand flew to cover her mouth. "Harper! What has happened? What do you mean? Olivia is gone?"

"Come inside and sit down. I'll make you some tea and tell you all about it." They turned, arm in arm, and trundled back to Harper's shelter. "And you have to tell me about the baby. I can't believe you're making a baby!"

"But wait; I am starving. We cannot miss dinner. Promise me that we won't miss dinner."

"Promise."

Aadhya paused in the middle of kicking off her shoes. "But who is making dinner? Who is cooking in Olivia's place? Oh, I should not have been gone so long, leaving no one to cook for all of you."

"Jacob, mainly. He's a natural. And Zoe. Everyone helps." Andy offered them perfectly warmed tea, minty with a hint of orange, Aadhya's favorite. "Thank you, Andy," Harper murmured.

"Your companion has gained a name?" Aadhya teased, as they sat on the curved bench under the large window. Aadhya propped her feet on a low stool and leaned back against a cushion, teacup balanced delicately.

"It seems to fit. Andy takes great care of me." Harper reached out and smoothed her palm along Andy's white softness. "I'm so happy we have companions."

"I don't know what I would do without Sebba," Aadhya agreed. "Especially now that I am moving so slowly."

"So, your companion has a name?" Harper laughed. "I don't think you can give me a hard time, dear Aadhya." She sipped her tea and shrugged. "Names just make sense. And they fit."

"Yes. I agree. It's nice for them to have names. It makes them more...like a friend."

"Yes! That's it."

They sipped their tea for a moment, and then Harper said, "Please tell me about the baby."

Aadhya paused for a moment, then set down her cup and leaned forward, taking Harper's hand in both of hers. "Harper, I came home to see you. I couldn't wait any longer to talk to you about this baby."

Harper set her own cup aside and leaned forward joining hands. The friends smiled at each other, silent for a moment. "Harper." Aadhya paused again. "Harper, Chatan and I have fallen in love."

Harper leaned back, eyes wide, and breathed out a soft "Ooohhh..." She pulled her hands out of Aadhya's grasp and went down on her knees as tears spilled down her cheeks. "Oh, Aadhya..." She gathered Aadhya into an awkward hug, the unfamiliar bulge of belly getting in the way, and with a shaky voice said, "I can't believe it." She drew in a deep breath. "This is the most perfect thing I could ever imagine."

Aadhya pulled Harper's arms from around her shoulders and searched her friend's face. "Really, Harper? This makes you happy?"

"Yes, oh yes. Oh, my world, yes. Chatan is my favorite person in the world! Well, in the universe, actually." She wiped tears from her face. "Oh, Aadhya. I'm so glad you've found each other. I'm so glad you're having a baby together." She sat back on her heels, quieting. "It is Chatan's baby, isn't it? That's what you're telling me, right?"

Aadhya laughed. "Yes, Harper. This is what I am telling you. Chatan and I are having this baby. Together." She laughed again and rocked, placing both hands atop her belly. "I was worried this would make you sad. You are such good friends with Chatan; I didn't want this to hurt you."

"Oh, that would be silly! We're friends, not lovers." Aadhya blushed at the bluntness, and Harper patted her arm. "Of course, I'm happy. Truly. This is wonderful, wonderful news. Don't worry. Everything's magnificent!" She straightened suddenly, concerned again. "But where is Chatan? He couldn't have sent you here to face everyone on your own..."

"Oh my goodness, no. He is at the gathering hall first. Then he will come here. I have no idea when that might be. I will have to learn about the timing he uses when he is at Home Base."

"Or just let him surprise you. Let's wait for him and go have dinner together. I'll help guard you from the curious masses." She paused. "Does Ava know yet?"

"No, no, of course not. You are the first person I have told. No one else knows." Aadhya wobbled her head from side to side.

"Well, this should be interesting."

"Will she be angry, do you think?"

Harper considered the question. "I have no idea. She likes you, and she likes Chatan, so it'll probably make her happy. Now if it were me...well, she'd explode."

"You can't mean this."

"Yes. Yes, I think I do mean it. She still doesn't like me, and she really doesn't like that Michael likes me. She wants all his attention, and... No, that's not it. She just doesn't like me. Because of Michael, she has to put up with me much more than she'd like."

Harper frowned out the window, and they were silent for a moment. Aadhya's voice was gentle. "It doesn't matter for now. Let's sip our tea until Chatan comes. And we will have dinner. I'm so hungry!"

"Andy..." Harper looked around and saw that Andy was floating close by, offering fresh tea and some curiously blue fruit. Harper picked up a segment of the fruit, peered at it for a breath, then popped it into her mouth. Flavor burst to fill her mouth, and for a moment, she was under towering trees, waves crashing nearby.

The vision faded. Harper turned back to Aadhya and smiled anew. "I'm so glad you're home. This is such happy news."

"Yes. I am very happy." They accepted the proffered tea and shared the rest of the blue fruit, the gentle aroma steaming their faces as they laughed and chatted and sipped.

Neither woman noticed the dainty turquoise birds perched amongst the blossoms of the forest's edge. Neither noticed them hop quietly along, watching the two women as they sat together, taking tea with their floating companion.

~ 28 ~

REST

Olivia crept from the soft nest, dipped her hands into the pool of water, drank deeply, and splashed her face cool. She emptied her bladder, rinsed her hands again. Reaching down, she pulled the warm shawl up from where it had puddled to the ground. Draping it around her shoulders, she pulled it close across her chest and curled herself back into her nest, snuggling down into its warmth.

Her bundled possessions spilled nearby, forgotten. Mysteriously retrieved. Silently offered. Quietly waiting.

She was so tired. All she wanted to do was sleep. She felt so safe with another peaceful day stretched before her. No deadlines. No worries. No one to disturb her quiet.

She reached out for a plump blue fruit, looked at it closely, then eased it into her mouth. Juice and flavor burst across her tongue. She closed her eyes, relishing its complexity, feeling warmth spread throughout her body. She could taste the sea.

She didn't know what it was or where it came from, or why it was always waiting just next to her nest. But she didn't think about any of that. The fruit filled her, so she didn't wonder. Food always heals. Always she had known this, in all remembrance.

She was so tired. All she could do was sleep...

A white shape drifted, barely disturbing the quiet air. Its silent drawer opened, and blue fruit jostled into the gold-flecked bowl next to Olivia's head. A pause. A deepening breath.

The companion floated away and disappeared.

~ 29 ~

MASS

Mateo reached forward and blackened the enormous screen. He sat back in his chair, arms folded across his chest, the balls of his feet pattering out a double rhythm on the soft carpet. He stood abruptly and stretched his arms above his closely cropped head. He bent his waist right and left, and let his breath escape, hissing, between pursed lips.

He stood a while longer, staring at the blank screen, turned slowly on the spot, peering up and around the large room. The structure seemed unchanged. Dropping his hands to his sides, he wandered out the door, glanced both ways, and started down the curved hallway, pressing his palm against either wall from time to time, testing its firmness.

He turned back to his companion. "Would you measure the dimensions of the hallway? And all the rooms we enter?" The white sphere tilted slightly in acknowledgement and followed Mateo's roaming.

Mateo continued along, opening doors, walking into deserted rooms, surveying the walls and ceilings, pressing his palm against structures at various intervals. He tried jiggling work surfaces and shelving units, but everything seemed firm and secure.

After his investigation, Mateo stood in the old assembly room looking out the window at the forest's edge. The colors were as brilliant and as vibrant as when he'd first seen them. The flowers never seemed to fade. Perhaps new ones bloomed to replace the faded ones. Whatever the life cycle, the foliage seemed unchanged.

He turned away from the window, hands on hips, and looked again around the room. Everything seemed the same. Chairs still stacked against the wall, cushions tossed pell-mell in the alcove, someone's shawl hanging from a hook...It looked like nothing had changed.

He looked at his companion. "Would you send all of those data to my screen?" The tilt. "Thanks." He stood a moment longer, lost in thought, strode across the room and out the door, winding along the hallway. He finally exited to sunshine and fresh air.

Heading back to his shelter, he paused near a cluster of neighboring shelters, struck by a new train of thought. He asked his companion to send him data on the dimensions of all shelters and halls, furnishings, everything they had obtained from the recycle bay on the ship. An answering tilt.

Taking a final look across Home Base, Mateo strode along the path leading to his shelter, kicked off his shoes, and splashed iced water into a tall glass. He firmly set the glass below the window at the back of his worktable, spread out his screen, and tilted it for easy viewing. He patted his long fingers across its surface, pulling up data, grouping numbers, setting up equations, and sliding subroutines into a pile.

Home Base's system followed along as he worked, suggesting shortcuts, replicating patterns based on the piled subroutines he developed, making intelligent suppositions, and eventually tiling graphs across the top of the screen, which he immediately expanded into a larger display.

At lunchtime, he stood abruptly, his companion stabilizing his chair as it toppled. Without a backward glance, he left to join the small group of people gathering at the serving tables.

He searched the dining room and quickly identified Sophia's coppery curls next to a corner window. He carried his heaping tray to her table and plopped down across from her, spilling some sauce onto his tray.

"Whoa, cowboy. Rein in the stampede," Sophia drawled.

"I'm putting together some numbers that I want you to look at."

"What kind of numbers?"

Mateo chewed for a moment, formulating a succinct explanation. "I don't think the ship is recycling itself."

Sophia lowered the spoonful of soup that was halfway to her mouth. "What are you talking about, exactly?" She watched his face.

"I think the mass of the ship is unchanged despite the volume of shelters it's delivered through the recycling bay."

Sophia blinked, her thoughts swirling. She shook her head slightly. "Why do you think that?"

"Look at the size of this hall, the equipment array, tables. We have over a hundred shelters jammed with furnishings, workshops, labs, equipment, all the companions, Chatan's fleet, Aadhya's caravan...We've created a lot of mass and spread it around Home Base."

"And...?"

"I was standing in the old assembly room on the ship. When you look out the window..., the big one in front, the main window..."

"And...?"

He lowered his voice. "The view outside is exactly the same as before." Her face showed no sign of understanding. "The ship hasn't diminished in circumference." He looked down at his plate and jammed more food onto his fork. "So, I walked around the entire ship, through halls and into pretty much every room, and measured everything."

"With a tape measure?"

"Nooo." He shook his head disdainfully, gave her a brief glare. "My companion measured everything. Then he went around and measured all the structures and equipment in Home Base."

"He shows incentive."

"I told him to do it."

"Okay..."

"I've been pulling together the numbers, and even though we've distributed a lot of mass around Home Base, the ship's mass hasn't changed at all. In fact, it's increased by at least 11%."

Sophia sobered. "That's weird." She paused. "Are you sure?"

"Yes. I'm sure." He went silent while he chewed. "Sophia, what's going on with the ship? What's it using to make all these structures? All this equipment?" He gestured toward the kitchen.

They stared at each other.

Sophia's hands went clammy, her mouth dry. "Should we go talk to Ava?"

"Probably." He scraped his plate with the side of his fork and looked at her from under his brows.

Sophia sighed. "Oh, crud." She turned to look out the window. "I hate mysteries."

~ 30 ~

GIFTING

VaSoDeLa led his family along the racing stream, younglings scampering in their midst, clambering atop Caretake-ers' backs for rest, slipping down again to tumble alongside littermates, humming and purring. VaSoDeLa set a leisurely pace to allow play for the younglings and wisdom-gathering for the elders as they listened to Breeze, drank Stream, breathed Forest, stropping against its broad trunks.

A brilliantly white companion floated in the family's wake.

VaSoDeLa paused a short distance from the abrupt edge of Overlook, giving elders time to interrupt the younglings' forward tumblings with blocking patience, settling their zeal, awaiting their attention. Then the family crept along the soaring edge, the younglings stilled by their first glimpse of the vast expanse that swept out from Overlook, Lone Tree smudged in the distance.

Younglings clambered onto the strong backs of Caretake-ers and gazed into the vastness as the family made their way along Overlook to the meeting place, the bonding place. The younglings relaxed, stilled their holderlings, raised their forebodies, and for the first time lifted their chests to the setting sun, jostling along on the backs of their Caretake-ers.

VaSoDeLa dropped the threads of his meld, allowed them to drift away, and felt his burrowmates do the same. The Narsis flowed along as individuals, connected to each other and to the world beneath their holderlings.

The family spread along the edge of Overlook, Caretake-ers shifting the upright younglings to settle around them, atop the Nurture-ers spread amongst boulder outcroppings that stabilized Overlook's edge. The Narsis stilled, awaiting the Eglans, chests warmed and glowing in the slanted light, humming in the twilight, hearts aglow with expectation and hope.

> Eglans soar!
> sweep sideways
> land softly
> wings aloft
> now folded
> amongst partners
> treasured partners
> humming clacking
> serene.

The companion drifted silently forward to float before the nearest Narsi, opened her drawer, and offered Art, softly knotted, stacked one upon the other. Scawlan reached forward and accepted the first knotted mat, held it close to his chest, holderlings rippling along the intricate knots and twists, humming and purring, filled with connection to Source. He passed the mat to his neighbor. She held it to her chest while he reached forward to accept the next Art.

Slowly, the procession lengthened as mat after mat was held and treasured, passed along and accepted, one to another. Finally, each elder held a knotted mat, imbued with joy, pressed against chests, glimmering in the twilit air. In her or his own time, each Narsi offered their mat to a partner, laying it softly before each Eglan's perch. The elders' stilled holderlings lingered for a final caress.

Straightening, each elder turned chest to setting sun, hummed and purred, filled with deep joy, happily shared, freely gifted.

Art lay before each Eglan. Art lay with fibers twisted into patterns, intricate shapes and vibrant colors. Faint scents drifted from Art, scents of sunshine and breezes, towering trees and dainty ferns, elegant blossoms and waving grasses. Art captured all. Art blended all. Art lay, glowing, alive.

Narsis waited. Younglings watched. Sun lowered. Breeze lifted. Breath paused.

A silent beak lowered and touched Art. A strong foot lifted and daintily poked Art. Heads cocked and flamboyant tails rattled. Beaks clacked and feet stomped. Percussion blossomed aNew.

Twisted fibers
knotted colors
spread treasure
shared treasure
glinting rich.

Art.

Imagination soars!

Soft texture
deep texture
treasure beyond knowing.

Imagination soars!

Stillness entered
bond glowing
Sun setting
partners partnered.

Joining Above and Below.

Treasure rich
beyond knowing
clutched closely
clutched gently
happily accepted
freely rejoiced.

Eglans fall
spiraling
soar!
dancing joyous
clacking song.

Imagination soars!

Nest sought
rejoice resounding
softly landing
clacking, clacking
joy spread
edges tucked
feet stomp
clacking, clacking
orange feathers nestled
Art treasured
texture beheld
explored
enriched
worthy hearts
joyful hearts
clacking

clacking.

Imagination soars!

Balance settles

Balance aNew.

The companion floated soundlessly away from Overlook, moving brightly through the trees. It wandered swiftly, unerringly, and reached Home Base just as the last light ebbed from the sky.

The Narsis sat in stillness, breasts glowing in last light. Tired younglings climbed onto Caretake-ers' backs, perched on shoulders, nuzzled ears.

Vargad turned from the purpled horizon, from the nuzzled ears. Vargad led his family along Overlook, along Stream, across Hillside, back to Burrow, hearts at peace.

~ 31 ~

JOY

"No, no," Aadhya gasped. "I must be outside."

"Don't be silly, Aadhya." Scarlett pulled heated cloths from a steel drawer. "You can't be outside; that makes no sense. You have to be here, where we can care for you. The ship has everything we need."

Aadhya sobbed softly, head lowered into her palms. "I must be outside."

Chatan grasped Scarlett's shoulders from behind and firmly moved her to one side. "You're not hearing, Scarlett." He knelt to wrap a blanket around Aadhya's shoulders, watching her face.

Aadhya nodded, whispered, "Yes." Chatan picked her up swiftly and turned to the door.

Scarlett was too shocked to stop them. She could only watch as they disappeared into the curved hallway. "This is foolhardy," she moaned to Ava. They stared across the empty room to the empty doorway.

The caravan waited for them, door open, Sebba hovering inside. Chatan maneuvered up the steps and through the surprisingly wide doorway. He settled Aadhya onto the soft bed in the back.

He nodded at Sebba, who remained at bedside as he headed to the front and pressed his finger to a blue oval on the displayed map, and returned to Aadhya, balancing in rhythm with the caravan's forward motion.

Sebba offered a cool cloth, which Chatan wiped across Aadhya's forehead, down both cheeks, around her neck, her wrists, ankles. "Will we know what to do?" he asked softly.

She nodded. "Yes," she whispered. "We will know what to do."

Her eyes grew round, and she began to puff her breath, in and out, rapidly, evenly. Chatan nodded encouragement. Setting the cloth aside, he held her hands. She grasped them with surprising strength, squeezed her eyes shut, and willed her belly to relax, puffing in and out, in and out. Finally, the contraction subsided.

She sank back onto the pillows that Sebba propped behind her, panting to regain her breath. Chatan cooled her face again and offered tepid tea from Sebba. As Aadhya sipped the pale green liquid, she felt strength return as calm spread through her. "Thank you," she whispered as she drifted into sleep.

Chatan settled more comfortably on the floor, hoisted his elbow atop the bed, and gently laid his hand over hers. He felt a gentle breeze and realized that Sebba was cooling Aadhya's face and neck.

He looked out the window to gauge their progress and caught sight of a turquoise swirl dancing around the caravan as it sped through trees. He pressed Aadhya's hand. They would know what to do.

At long last the caravan slowed. Chatan moved to the front and confirmed the smooth expanse of water. They were well into the day. He turned back to lift Aadhya from her bed but stopped when Sebba jostled him. He looked at the companion, floating silently, and around the caravan, confused. He glanced out at the quiet pond and watched it for a few breaths, then turned back to Aadhya.

He gently eased her skirt down, and lifting her legs, he pulled it off and tossed it aside. Next, he lifted her shoulders, fumbled with her shirt. Sebba moved to prop her upright, enabling Chatan to use both hands to shimmy the shirt over her head.

He quickly stripped off his pants and shirt before bending to lift the drowsing woman. He carried her into the sunlight. Aadhya's head lolled against his shoulder as he waded into the warm water, Sebba drifting behind them.

The warmth of the water was a welcome surprise. It had always been refreshingly cool. Of course it would be warm, now that Aadhya needed it to be warm. The pond had been readying itself for them.

As the water lapped against Aadhya's skin, her eyes fluttered open. She squinted against the bright sun. Chatan lowered her legs until her feet found their balance and then shifted his firm grip to either side of her rib cage, steadying her. "Are you all right?"

She nodded, crouching to immerse herself. He floated her out to deeper water, where she could more easily crouch, weightless, water lapping her shoulders.

"Better?"

She nodded. "Yes. This is where I need to be." She looked around, floating her arms gently back and forth through the clear water. "This is where we need to be."

They looked into each other's eyes, and Aadhya smiled. She reached up and laid her palm along his cheek. He smoothed her hair back from her face, reaching past her to sweep the long strands together, pulling them gently back to float behind her. Always, he watched her face.

He turned them slowly through the sparkling water and pressed her back against his chest, wrapping one arm across her shoulders, supporting the lower swell of her belly with his other hand. They gazed back at the shore, absorbing the brilliant greens of the grasses swaying along the water's edge.

Chatan shifted his hands and slowly caressed Aadhya's breasts to stimulate her contractions, gently rubbing her nipples with his palms, softly twisting them with his fingertips, brushing the rounded skin with cupped hands. Aadhya rested her hands over his, following his movements, intensifying her response. He nuzzled her temple, and she pressed her face against his chin. They waited, hands caressing, breathing deep and slow.

They turned their heads in unison to watch the turquoise birdlings rise into the sky and dip to trace tilted wingtips across the still sur-face of the pond. Ripples blossomed across the mirrored water. As the first ripple reached them, Aadhya pressed back against Chatan, clenching his hands. He shifted one foot behind him, keeping them upright. Aadhya bent her head back atop his shoulder, eyes squeezed shut, mouth opened to the sky, silent, breathless.

When the baby came, it came in a rush. It sank into the water, and Chatan reached to scoop it, her, to the surface, floating her next to Aadhya, who gasped and reached to cradle her daughter atop her belly. The baby coughed, and Aadhya turned her on her side, pressing her chest gently, gently, helping fluid drain.

Chatan floated them to shallow water and eased Aadhya down to sit, legs askew, her baby floating in her lap. They sat together, watching Claira learn to breathe, jaggedly drawing in breath, push-ing it out, her chest rising and falling. They ran their hands over the baby's skin, gently rubbing her clean, swooshing her back and forth through the warm, clear water.

Sebba bumped Chatan's elbow. He took the offered clamps, bright green and perfectly shaped. He eased them onto Claira's cord, close to her belly, and pressed them closed. He took Sebba's scissors and deftly cut the strong cord between its two clamps.

Aadhya suddenly leaned back on her elbows. Chatan brought the floating baby onto his own lap, scooted closer to Aadhya, and reached forward to run his free hand down her slackened belly, helping her deliver the placenta. As it floated from her, he released its green clamp and watched as it sank, drifting deeper toward the middle of the pond.

Turning back to Aadhya, he saw that she was watching it, too, smiling softly, the ends of her hair drifting in the water behind her, coiled on the golden sand. He looked down at his lap, then floated the baby over to Aadhya, who sat up and lifted her daughter to her breast, helping her take the nipple.

Claira's arms and legs recklessly splashed the clear water, before settling into nursing. Aadhya looked up and took a steaming cup from Sebba, sipping the blue liquid, smiling at Chatan over the cup's edge.

"We knew what to do."

"Yes," she whispered. "We knew."

The turquoise cloud danced past them, and Chatan shifted to kneel next to Aadhya. She set her empty cup into Sebba's opened drawer and draped her arm around Chatan's neck. He picked mother and child off the sand, floated into deeper water, where he released Aadhya's legs and faced her.

They slowly circled through the water, gently swirling Claira between them, floated on their backs with the baby on Chatan's belly. At one point, Chatan swam the entire circumference of the pond, twice, releasing a surge of energy, while Aadhya drifted at the shoreline, nursing her daughter, laughing at Chatan's churning circuit.

Afterward, they floated gently together, a tiny family, a new breath in the world, faces to the sun, warm water caressing their skin. The birdlings floated soundlessly above them, carving turquoise circles and spirals in the dimming sky.

Finally, they waded ashore, wandered onto the warm meadow to stretch out on the Nurture-ers who carpeted their soft bed. They rested as the families fed them, embraced them, Claira between them. They slept, waking briefly when Sebba offered a warm blanket that they spread across themselves, sharing its comfort.

Far away, the Arbans still their song, and the Shosens rest. Stillness spreads along the low waves and onward, across the grassy plains, engulfing Lone Tree, silhouetted against the night sky.

Lone Tree shimmers and stills, breathing depth and strength into the expanding silence. Burrow and Nest breathe in, breathe out. Pond sleeps, absorbing the stillness of the New world.

~ 32 ~

ATTACK

"How could they have been so foolish?" Ava paced before the long window of her sitting room. "So much could have gone wrong." She fell silent for a moment. "Why didn't they at least take one of us with them? This is not the right time to be doing something so reckless. Why were they so foolish as to even have a baby? What were they thinking?"

Scarlett leaned against a wall, arms across her chest, chewing her lower lip. Michael and Harper glanced at each other. Harper decided to brave Ava's anger. "But I've talked with VaSoDeLa. He said the baby is crucial."

From the couch, Sophia exploded, "What?" Mateo silently placed his hand atop hers, quieting her.

Ava turned to face Harper. "Who the hell is VaSoDeLa, and why would the baby be any of their concern?" She kept her face unreadable and pressed her lips together, holding back her mounting rage. Would she never be rid of this girl? Aadhya had been so compliant, so willing. Why was Aadhya the one to go away? Why was this flighty nuisance the one who remained, persistently skulking in corners?

146

Harper took a step back and brought her arms up to her chest as if to ward off Ava's fury. But then she straightened her shoulders and brought her arms down, clasping her hands calmly behind her.

"VaSoDeLa is Vargad when he's melded with his family." She looked around the room. "His littermates. Not the family he lives with, but the family he was born with, grew up with. His littermates."

Ava stared at Harper, dumbstruck. Harper continued. "Vargad melds with three other littermates. The four of them have spread apart into separate burrows to join their own adult families. To help create them, I mean. They're in separate burrows now." Harper's confidence was fading, but she plowed forward regardless. "They meld their minds and operate as a single individual with four bodies."

Harper looked to the others for support and realized that everyone was staring at her, incredulous. "It's really quite amazing," she ended dispiritedly.

Scarlett broke the silence. "How have you learned this?"

"How would you know this?" Ava echoed before Harper had a chance to answer Scarlett. "How could you possibly know this? Are you just making things up as you go?"

Michael sat forward, arms propped on knees, alarmed at Ava's anger.

Harper blinked. "Well, I go to the meadow to look for Vargad. You met Vargad here on the Green, months ago. We've become friends. I like to talk with him." She paused, closing her eyes, willing herself to remember. "Sometimes his friend joins us. An Eglan." She opened her eyes and looked at Ava, tears pricking her eyes. "We talk." Harper folded her arms across her chest and once again determinedly dropped them to her sides.

"And you didn't think to tell any of us about your meetings?" Ava fumed, stepping toward Harper, sweeping her arm out, as if to shove Harper back. "Are you completely idiotic?" She glared. "How long have you been sneaking around doing this?"

"Ava?" Michael's voice came clearly from behind Ava.

Ava slowly straightened, her eyes glued on Harper. "Yes?"

"Should we help Harper tell us what she's learned?"

Ava took a deep breath. "Yes." She turned to a nearby chair. "Let's do that." She sat, crossing one knee over the other, and grasped her hands in her lap. "Sit down, Harper. Why don't you tell us what you've learned?"

"I'm trying to remember," Harper whispered, wiping the back of her hand across her forehead.

~ 33 ~

PARTNERS

JaCoMaTuRi stomped along the bank of Stream. At a quiet pool, protected from strong currents and eddies, she hopped into the cool water, dipped her brilliant head into Stream, spread her many wings, and undulated her entire body, stem to stern. She shook her flamboyant tail, spreading it wide, and generously showered nearby boulders and ferns with a glorious rainbow of droplets.

VaSoDeLa floated in the main current, long belly bobbing, his many holderlings motoring the water to keep him abreast of the bathing Eglan. Although his eyes were closed, he knew exactly where she splashed and sprayed. He rumbled his contentment. She purred her delight.

The two Head-ers had met daily, at every twilight and occasional dawn, across their many shared years; for all their shared remembrance. Every day, every twilight, they led their families to Overlook, basked in the setting of Sun, blended Above and Below, and then retreated to Nest and Burrow. Partnered. But not Friended.

After the falling, the abandonment, the gifting, VaSoDeLa and JaCo-MaTuRi formed the habit of seeking each other out. They wandered Forest and Meadow, basked under Sun, breathed in Dawn. They found that they enjoyed each other's company and felt enriched. Partnered and Friended. Together.

Stream was a favorite location. Both enjoyed Stream's soothing song, its cooling depths, its quiet banks, its sparkling journey. Alone, together, they had no need to Head or decide. Alone, together, they could be.

As friendship grew, VaSoDeLa watched for a filling of his empty heart. His emptiness seemed to fade in the brightness of JaCoMaTuRi's delight whenever they met. He moved into reNewed hope. Perhaps this was part of Shift. Perhaps this was part of New. Perhaps soon he would know.

And yet, today, VaSoDeLa floated and pondered his emptiness. Art had flooded his emptiness, then gradually ebbed away. Gifting brought its own flood of brightness and hope. That, too, melted into background. VaSoDeLa recognized that this, this bright friendship, it, too, threatened another fading.

He rolled in Stream, dove to its bottom, and pushed off to fling himself into sparkling air. He stretched wide, and fell back to Stream, FLOP! sending a mighty splash onto the gentle banks, rocked on waves that spread out and rebounded, chaotic and joyous.

JaCoMaTuRi launched from her pool, spiraled up to a low branch, and shook her wings and flamboyant tail, stomped and ruffled, settling each feather and wing into place. She peered down at VaSoDeLa where he clambered out of Stream, water cascading from shoulders and tail. She swooped down and brushed his ears with outstretched wing, then up, to perch on soft families spread amongst the nearby bushes. She rustled her feathers, stomped her strong feet, and turned to wait for VaSoDeLa as he rumbled his way toward her.

JaCoMaTuRi stretched her broad beak, and VaSoDeLa stropped his nose along its length, then settled himself in the dappled sunlight, rumbling, as only friends do.

JaCoMaTuRi broke their silence.
Sadness holds
holds your heart.
JaCoMaTuRi searches
searches your heart.
Emptiness there
Answers not.
Knowing not.
VaSoDeLa took in deep breath and pointed his nose to the high canopy, Sun glinting amongst swaying leaves.

VaSoDeLa rumbles. Always I have known it, since all my remembrance. I carry it always.

He lowered his nose to glance at his friend. Rumbles. My meld helps me forget. You help me forget. Burrow helps me forget. Stream and Sun and Forest and Overlook, all help me forget. But whenever I stop and breathe, it edges in, seeps out from wherever I have hidden it. It colors my days.
JaCoMaTuRi stomps.
Yours to carry.
You carry.
Yours.
VaSoDeLa rumbles. Yes. It is mine to carry.

The two Head-ers, partners and friends, held vigil and pondered Sun and Stream, blending Above and Below.

~ 34 ~

STRATEGY

VaSoDeLa perched at the edge of Overlook. Today he sought con-clave. His meldmates had likewise retreated from Burrows, moving in solitude to quiet, secluded spots, places of great peace and inner harmony.

Sorgad, Caretake-er, sang of confidence, tinged with misgivings. "Art is of great importance to our families. The younglings grow in wisdom and harmony by weaving Art, gifting Art. But Art took us out of balance with our cherished Eglans. Although balance is im-proved with the gifting of Art, new balance is fragile. Always part-ners have been in balance, since all remembrance." A shudder ran through her meld thread at the thought of Eglan abandonment.

Dergad, Show-er, sang of hope diminished by uncertainty. "We must nurture balance. Our younglings create Art. But Eglans cannot weave. They cannot create Art themselves. Balance tilts." Dimness shimmered along his meld thread as his uncertainty whispered across the melds' hearts.

"Art came from Newcomers." Largad, Find-er, sang of possibility threaded with caution. "Newcomers can bring another gift, a dif-ferent gift; a gift for the Eglans. The Newcomers can befriend the Eglans." His exploration brightened the meld.

Sorgad, Caretake-er, sang of alarm, pulsing with concern. "Newcomers are large. Newcomers cause Eglans to tremble. Eglans shy away from Newcomers. Thus it will always be."

VaSoDeLa pondered fragile balance, the cherished bond of Above and Below, Narsi and Eglan, since all remembrance.

Dergad, Show-er, sang of possibility sparkling with hope. "Newcomer birthlings are small. Their birthling could belong to the Eglans."

Sorgad, Caretake-er, sang of skepticism shadowed with alarm. "The birthling will grow. And she is a single; the Eglan are many."

Largad, Find-er, sang of possibility edged with freshness. "The birthling will grow, but slowly. The Eglans will adjust alongside the birthling."

Vargad, Head-er, sang of caution tinged with alarm. "The Newcomers have only one birthling."

VaSoDeLa pondered.

Sorgad, Caretake-er, sang of certainty, bright with experience. "The birthling is new. It will soon be forgotten by the Newcomers. It is the right time to give the birthling to the Eglans. The birthling should go to the Eglans now."

Vargad, Head-er, sang of longing dusted with pain. "With only one, its loss will cause heartbreak."

Sorgad, Caretake-er, sang of haste bristled with impatience. "This is *your* pain, *your* longing. It clouds your knowing."

Dergad, Largad, sang of respect. "Vargad is Head-er, with clarity, with wisdom. Always it has been."

Sorgad, Caretake-er, sang of submission streaked with defiance. "Not in this. Not in this. *This*, I know. *I* know."

VaSoDeLa pondered.

Vargad, Head-er, sang of wonder, brightened with remembrance. "The birthling is essential. She will complete the world."

Sorgad, Caretake-er, sang of conviction edged with power. "She will bring balance. She will strengthen the partner bond."

VaSoDeLa pondered.

~ 35 ~

ANGUISH

Aadhya stepped down from the caravan and scanned the landscape for Chatan. Propping Claira against her chest, she walked down to the beach and sat on soft families edging the clear water. She nursed the gurgling infant and watched the turquoise birdlings flit amongst the branches overhead. The morning sun slanted down, dappling the baby's skin.

The birdlings seemed restless, alighting on branches only to spring back into the air, their flightpaths crisscrossing, chaotic. Leaves quivered and branches trembled. Flowers swayed softly in the dense air.

She saw Chatan hoist himself up from the slanted rock that over-hung one edge of the pond. He dove cleanly into the cool water and swam toward them, his progress sending out arrowed ripples. He dripped his way to shore, crouched next to his family, and sat, heels submerged in the pond.

"The morning is complete now that the women have come out to breathe." He reached out and smoothed back Aadhya's hair, leaned to kiss her temple. "How was your sleep?"

Aadhya nodded her head side to side. "We both slept well. She woke only once, and after drinking only a little, she fell back asleep. She is so easy, this child who sleeps all day, then turns over to sleep all night."

"She's working hard, making noses and toes. She needs to sleep."

"Oh, yes. She is so busy, and she is so easy." Aadhya's head wobbled happily.

Over her shoulder, Chatan saw brown shapes making their way down the meadowed slope. Aadhya turned to follow his gaze, shading her eyes against the dazzling sun. "The Narsis come early this morning."

The younglings scampered in the lead, swarmed over Aadhya's lap, brushed the baby's feet, and leapt across Chatan's legs to throw themselves into the water. Claira squirmed and waved her tiny fists, eyes wide.

Aadhya laughed and called to Vargad, "Your younglings are very happy this morning."

"It is a special day," Vargad agreed as he flowed toward them. He gazed out at the cavorting younglings, then turned his gaze to a point just above Aadhya's head. "We come to take the baby. It is time."

"What?" Aadhya's voice quavered.

"We come to take the baby."

Two of the Narsis moved forward softly. One leaned over Aadhya and gently lifted Claira out of her mother's arms.

"No, no, no, no, no," sobbed Aadhya, her empty arms falling to her sides, incapable of resisting.

Chatan fought a crushing restraint that forced him into passivity. He woodenly struggled to his feet and turned to watch the Narsis file from the tranquil beach. "Vargad, don't do this. Don't take her from us."

"We leave." Vargad turned to follow his family up the long slope. He paused and turned, lifting holderlings aloft, a row of slender question marks, translucent in the sun. The younglings splashed out of the water, bounced past Chatan, scampered over Aadhya's knee, and raced to the top of the rise, past their Head-er, threading between the elders beyond, leaping and weaving until they were gone from view.

Vargad dropped to the ground and made his way slowly up the slope. The rhythm of his holderlings as they carried him along were awkward, seemingly out of sync. He almost stumbled but caught himself. He did not look back again. He paused, head lowered, before he, too, disappeared over the rise.

Chatan sank to his knees, watching the empty slope. Aadhya sat, hands over mouth, tears dripping across her fingers, a silent wail twisting her face. She finally caught her breath and turned to clutch Chatan. "I could do nothing," she rasped. "Our baby is gone, and I could do nothing."

Chatan kneeled in despair, leaned to wrap his arms around Aadhya's sobbing shoulders. "I was powerless. I couldn't think what to do. I could only watch."

The anguished parents rocked slowly on the empty beach, under the empty sky, grieving at the center of their empty world.

~ 36 ~

STILLED

A thousand eyes scanned the endless canopy. Fluttering leaves lost momentum and stilled themselves. Dangling blossoms lost twirl and sway, found no boost from silent air that no longer breezed, and themselves became still.

The turquoise cloud with its thousand eyes swept across broad meadows and sang its forlorn song. As the cloud passed overhead, grasses ceased their tremoring. Ferns quieted their bouncing. Branches along meadows' edges paused their dance.

Ponds and lakes swallowed their ripples. Rivers and streams held back their splashing, recalled droplets from their airy flight, tamed froth and smoothed rapids.

Families whispered, one to the other, and Below wound down its bustle.

Eglans crouched in Nest. Narsis crept in Burrow. Above lost its breath.

Only the birdlings roamed, the turquoise cloud sweeping and cresting, spreading their forlorn tale.

Pond was bereft of hope.

Brightness dimmed and laughter choked. Songs lost melody and harmonies toned a final chord.

Arbans pause and Shosens hush. Broad Sea holds its breath.

When all was still, the turquoise cloud drifted and at long last sprinkled itself onto Lone Tree's mighty sprawl. Birdlings filter through silent branches, past feathery leaves, settle and still. Turquoise heads tuck under turquoise wings and close a thousand eyes.

Airon roared along her ancient path, around her glorious sun. Airon drowsed, oblivious to despair, dreaming of the coming of New.

~ 37 ~

POWER

"Michael!" Ava's call was strident as she hurried along the path. Michael, already awakened by his companion, was standing in Harper's main room, rubbing his sleeve across his face, wondering, when he heard Ava's call. He groped for his shoes in the dim light.

The door burst open, and Ava swung in, teetered on the threshold, breathless. "Michael. The baby's disappeared."

"What?" he mumbled, bewildered.

"The baby. The baby. She's disappeared."

"Claira?"

"Yes, Michael. Claira. What other baby would I be talking about? Come; we've got to figure out what to do."

Michael followed her out the door, tripping over a truant basket as his foot fumbled with an obstinate shoe. He stumbled along the path, again wiping his face on his sleeve, trying to bring his brain fully alert. He had left Harper asleep, not thinking to wake her, but now he heard her call him. He turned and waited as she ran to catch up. "What's happening?" she asked as she matched his stride, her bare feet padding along the path.

"Claira's missing."

"What!?"

"I don't know more than that. Ava's waiting for me so we can talk about what to do. I'll let you know what happens."

"I'm coming with you."

Michael stopped and caught Harper's arm. "Now's not the time."

"What are you talking about? Time for what?"

"For you to upset Ava."

"If Ava gets upset, that's her problem. I want to be part of this conversation."

"Harper, please don't make a scene."

It was Harper's turn to stop. "What are you saying, Michael?" She shrugged her sweater onto her shoulder. "I'm not the one who makes a scene." She watched him for a moment, frowning, but he remained silent.

"Come on. Ava's waiting." She turned and strode down the path. After a moment, Michael caught up with her, both silent for the remainder of the walk.

Ava was scrolling through her screen. "Michael, I would like you to keep me aware of where you decide to spend your nights," she said curtly over her shoulder. "I don't always have time to search for you." She turned from her screen, caught sight of Harper, and pressed her lips together. "I think it's necessary," she concluded briefly. She looked toward her companion. "Please ask Sophia and Mateo to come as well. We could use their help." She glanced at Michael. "Scarlett is on her way."

"Your companion would know." Michael's voice was even and clear.

"What?" Ava turned back to him.

"You could ask your companion to alert mine that you wanted to talk to me, and I would come. It would save time and avoid confusion. My companion had already woken me. I was getting ready to come when you arrived."

No one spoke for a moment. Ava turned her glare on Harper, who held up her palms, shaking her head as she took a step back. "I'm not saying anything. You two figure it out."

The trio waited for Sophia and Mateo in silence. Ava's companion offered tea around, and they each accepted a cup.

Harper sat in a chair near the window and looked out at the dawn Green. She sipped her tea, seemingly at ease, watching for Sophia and Mateo. "Here they come." She took a sip of tea. "I wonder where they slept." She set her teacup down on the low table and sat back, looking calmly at Ava.

"I thought you weren't saying anything," Ava observed frostily.

"Well, you two weren't getting anywhere, so I thought I would state the obvious."

Ava bristled but sat down at her screen, her back to the room.

Michael wiped his sleeve across his forehead. This was going to be a tricky morning.

Mateo and Sophia tapped lightly on the door, pushed it open a few inches and glanced around the room. They walked in, kicking off shoes.

"Good morning, everyone." Sophia's smiled and yawned. Mateo lifted his hand in greeting, absorbed with moving shoes around with his feet, lining up the various pairs.

Harper was the only one to reply. "Good morning. Isn't the dawn beautiful?"

Sophia stifled another yawn. "Yes. I love dawn. It's so peaceful."

Harper nodded and looked toward Ava.

Ava scrolled through her screen, searching for anything she might have missed. She abandoned the effort and turned to the room. "Right! Good morning." She watched as Sophia and Mateo accepted tea from her companion and sat in the two remaining chairs.

Scarlett burst through the door just then, hair tousled, a blanket thrown over t-shirt and shorts. "I'm sorry," she said, eyes squinting against the glare of the room. "My companion didn't know where I was..." Her voice trailed off.

Harper broke the silence, empathetically. "Well, honestly? It's not as if you're under house arrest. You can sleep wherever you want. You made it, all the same." Scarlett's smile was wan.

With a sigh, Michael settled onto the floor next to Harper. She lightly placed a hand on his shoulder as she leaned forward to retrieve her replenished teacup. Michael abruptly patted his splayed knees and grimaced. "I didn't bring my screen." He looked over at Ava, who broke off her glare at Harper to reach around, pick up her own screen, and toss it to him. He caught it easily and spread it across his lap. Scarlett perched on the broad arm of Mateo's chair, pulling her blanket more snuggly across her chest. All eyes turned to Ava.

After gathering her thoughts for a few breaths, she simply started talking. "The baby, Claira, has disappeared."

Mateo's jaw dropped, and Sophia's hand flew to her mouth. "No! What happened exactly?"

"It's not clear yet. Chatan and Aadhya are still wandering, so this is all secondhand." She gestured toward her companion. "From what I can gather, they were out in the open, near a pond, and a group of Narsis approached them. They met, spoke casually, about what, I don't know. And then one of the Narsis simply picked up the baby. Aadhya and Chatan weren't alarmed, apparently, and the next thing they knew, the Narsis left, taking the baby with them."

Scarlett stood abruptly. "This has been a mess, right from the start. Why are they out there on their own?"

Mateo shook his head, searched for words that finally blustered their way out. "Did they go after them? How fast can Narsis move?"

"No. They didn't follow. The confrontation was brief, without violence. The Narsis simply took the baby away."

The room fell into stunned silence.

Ava spoke again in measured tones "Chatan and Aadhya are both upset, but they can't describe why it happened, or why they didn't try to stop the Narsis." Another silence. "That's all I know."

"Are they returning to Home Base?" Harper asked.

"No. They don't want to leave the area. And we don't know where they are, so we can't go help them."

Mateo shook his head again. "I don't understand. Why don't we know where they are?"

Ava looked at him helplessly. "I don't know." Her face tight with anger. "I don't know…"

Alarmed, Sophia moved over to crouch next to Ava's chair, wanting to help. Ava touched her shoulder. "I'm sorry. I continually discover mysterious pieces of larger stories that I don't understand." She paused and took a shaking breath, focusing her thoughts. "Home Base won't disclose their location. It's as if…as if the ship has created some sort of blackout around Chatan and Aadhya."

Michael spoke as he scrolled through Ava's screen. "They're both okay. They're not asking for help. They just wanted us to know." He scrolled to the end of the message. "They wanted Harper to know. They sent this only to Harper."

Harper leaned forward to peer over Michael's shoulder.

"You get my messages?" Harper looked up at Ava.

Ava nodded. "Yes. I get everyone's messages."

"All of them?" asked Scarlett.

"Well, yes, I assume so. Why? Don't you get everyone's messages?"

"No." Sophia rose to her feet. "Only my own." The others nodded agreement with Sophia.

Ava looked around the room, incredulous. "Yet another baffling mystery." She lowered her forehead to rest in both hands, staring down at her feet. She raised her heels, up and down, so her head and shoulders jostled in response. She had no time for yet another mystery. The backlog of things that perplexed her threatened to swamp her mind. Why were so many things confusing?

Ava took a deep breath. "What do you think we should do?" Her voice cracked. "I can't think what to do." A tear spilled down her cheek, and she swiped it away, pressing the back of her hand to her nose. She felt completely humiliated by this display of emotion. Why were things overwhelming her so easily?

Mateo spoke up. "Let me go into Home Base's system. I'll get around the blockage and find out where they are."

Scarlett nodded enthusiastic agreement and looked to Ava. "They have companions with them, right?"

Before Ava could answer, Mateo asked, "Did they take Aadhya's caravan? We should be able to track them that way even if we can't use the companion network."

Sophia glanced at Ava's companion and caught Mateo's eye. He followed her discrete chin jerk in the companion's direction and understood her caution. He nodded back.

Harper spoke from her corner. "It's okay. The companions haven't betrayed anyone."

Sophia looked at Harper, flustered. "No, I..." She flipped her open hand toward the companion, then back at herself. "I was just..."

"It's okay," Harper repeated.

"But I..."

"What are you talking about?" Ava, distracted, didn't understand the new fluster.

"I was just trying..." Sophia's voice trailed off.

"We were talking about working around the companions, and then we realized one of them was sitting here, listening to us." Harper chewed her thumbnail for a moment. "But it's okay. Really. The companions haven't betrayed anyone. They're just cooperating."

"With whom?" Scarlett demanded, bewildered.

"With the planet. With Airon. With the ship. With everything."

The room fell silent. Michael twisted around to look at Harper. "Tell us more."

"Something's happening, and a lot of players are involved." Harper shrugged. "It's nothing bad or anything. It's just...a change that's happening. The balance of life has tilted because *we're* here now, and everything is trying to settle into a new balance."

She looked around at the waiting faces. "Chatan says everything works together here." She waved toward the window. "Cooperates. It's not like on Earth where everything competes, fighting for niches, desperate searches for safety from predators. Here, nobody gets killed or even sick. There are no infections. Everything co-operates alongside everything else; hand in hand."

Harper paused and looked down at her teacup. "Then we come along, and everything's different." Another pause. "We were the right ones to come along, because we didn't go out and kill every-thing, but we did change the balance. The Narsis, the Eglans, they're affected by us. And they're trying to figure it out. They're trying to learn how to cooperate with us." She picked at her skirt. "I think they're scared."

"So, they steal a baby?" Sophia's confusion was turning to anger. She felt scared.

Harper shook her head. "They don't st—well, yeah, they stole the baby. But not because they're scared."

"How do you know?"

"Well, because Chatan and Aadhya aren't scared." Everyone watched her, waiting for her to go on. "They're upset, but they're not scared. And they don't want us to come help them. Look."

She reached down and whisked Ava's screen from Michael's lap and tapped it to punctuate each observation. "They're okay; they let the baby go without a struggle; they didn't go after the Narsis who took the baby; they haven't asked for help; they just wanted us to know." She corrected herself. "They wanted *me* to know." She looked at Ava. "*Me.*"

Scarlett glanced again at Ava, then back at Harper. "Why just you?"

"Because they knew that I would get it. Chatan knew that I would get it."

Sophia frowned. "What do you get? Because I don't get it yet."

"We're not supposed to help them."

"Why?"

"I don't know why, not yet. But I know we're not supposed to help them."

Sophia was persistent. "How do you know that exactly? I'm sorry, Harper. I'm not trying to argue; I'm trying to understand."

"Because the companions won't tell us where they are."

"But that could be part of the problem," Scarlett pointed out.

"There is no problem!" Harper took a deep breath. "Look. The companions are cooperating because this is supposed to happen, and we are supposed to let it play itself out." She looked around. "There

are no hidden motives; we just think there are. Everyone's co-operating; even Chatan and Aadhya are cooperating. They didn't interfere; they let the Narsis take the baby. They're upset because, well, who wouldn't be? But they're letting it happen. And they need us to let it happen, too."

Sophia let out a frustrated sigh. "But how can we just sit back and let the baby go?"

"Because there's something bigger here, and we don't understand it yet. Because everything cooperates here. Our whole lives, our reasons for coming to Airon, are based on cooperation; it's true. But it's new to us as a species. Since...well, always...we've survived by competing."

Harper took a deep breath. "We've..." Harper circled her forefinger at all of them, "The 108, have been trying to do things differently. It's working well, so we're on the right track. Along the way, we're learning a balance between cooperating with each other and following our inner guidance.

"But this planet grew up cooperating. It didn't have to learn the hard way like we've been doing. This is what cooperation looks like here. We're not the dominant species now. We have to cooperate with them, with the planet, not just ourselves.

"There is no meanness; there is no cruelty. Everything is kind, and helpful, and...beautiful..." She stopped, exasperated by her lack of vocabulary. It was entirely clear to her. "We're the ones who don't know how to cooperate. We think we do, but this is a whole, higher level. We should trust them; this entire world."

She waved at the window again. "We should pay attention and not be so determined that everything needs to happen exactly how we think it should. There's something bigger going on here, and we shouldn't mess it up.

"We have nothing to fear from the Narsis. Nothing at all."

Ava had sat stiffly as she watched Harper talk. Now she stood and paced to the window and back. "I think she's right," she finally said.

Sophia looked aghast. Scarlett was struck silent. Mateo glanced from one person to the next, out of his depth. Michael nodded at Harper. She smiled and put her palm on his back, a gentle caress.

"It's time for stillness, Michael. Can you do that?" Ava's voice was steady and calm. Michael nodded and moved to stand up. "I won't be there today," she explained.

"What!" Sophia exploded. "Are you mad? We have to do something! We have to tell the others!"

"No, Sophia." Ava's voice was firm and collected. "Harper is right. Chatan and Aadhya have not asked for help. They didn't even intend to let all of us know."

Sophia stood open-mouthed. "Are you serious?"

Ava placed both of her hands on Sophia's shoulders and shook her once, softly. "I'm completely serious."

The two women stared at each other for several breaths, silent. "I can't believe this is happening." Sophia's voice was low, forceful.

"Do you agree to cooperate?" Ava still held Sophia's shoulders.

"I have to think."

They all waited, motionless.

"Do you agree to talk to me before you do anything?" Ava pressed her. "If you decide to do anything?"

They waited.

"I have to think." Sophia's voice was toneless, her freckles stark against her drained face.

The two women stared at each other for another breath, and then Ava dropped her hands, releasing Sophia. She looked at the others standing around the room. "Do you agree to cooperate?"

Harper and Michael nodded. Mateo looked from Sophia to Ava, back again. He locked onto Ava's eyes and nodded. Scarlett's nod was reluctant.

"Thank you." Ava concluded the discussion curtly. She turned back to her workstation and looked around for her screen.

Michael handed it to her. "Will you be here? In your shelter?"

Ava paused. "Yes. I'll be here." She frowned, rubbing her arms and shoulders, then turned away to move into her sleeping room.

Sophia and Michael exchanged glances before they moved to the door to gather shoes. Mateo and Harper were already outside, waiting on the path. Sophia grasped Harper's wrist, holding her back. "Are you sure about this?"

Harper nodded. Sophia searched her face, patted the wrist, let go. "I wish I were."

"It's real, Sophia. This is real. It's important." Harper pressed.

"It's obvious that it's important, Harper. That's exactly the problem." Sophia turned down the pathway. They wound through trees to the small clearing where the gathering hall stood gleaming in the dawn light.

Harper looked down at her bare feet, curious at her lack of shoes. The others kicked off theirs before stepping carefully around people who were already filling the hall, making their separate ways to their piled belongings.

After Michael pulled his shawl up over his shoulders, he took several deep breaths and emptied his mind. "Shall we begin in stillness?" he called out to the room.

~ 38 ~

EXPOSURE

Morning stillness did not bring stillness for Sophia. Thoughts bubbled up and spilled over. Dread. Fear. Confusion. Her emotions played handball inside her skull, and she could not settle. Her throat itched; her nose tickled. She rubbed her ear and puffed a loose strand of hair away from her nose. Her foot went to sleep, and her knee ached. She could not find stillness.

When Michael intoned "Peace," she mindlessly responded along with the others. "Peace."

She brought her knees up to her chest and felt blood flood through her tingling foot. She rubbed her nose on her shawl and wiggled her toes, hurrying her foot's awakening. She felt no peace as she hugged herself into herself.

Michael described the lunch menu, and Dhiren asked for help harvesting the hydroponds. Addison asked how much time he needed. They went back and forth until Sophia was ready to scream.

As the discussion wound down, Sophia spoke up, clearly projecting so that her voice would reach every ear. "The Narsis have taken Chatan's baby. They've stolen it. Ava has decided that we won't do anything about it, and I don't know if that's right. What do others think?"

Scarlett swiveled toward her. "Sophia?"

Harper hissed, "You agreed…"

"I said I had to think about it. I've been doing that. Besides, I'm not *doing anything*; I'm talking about something that's important to all of us."

Mateo was just as shocked. "Talking *is* doing, Sophia. Why are you doing this?"

Logan broke in. "Forget about why she's doing it. What is she talking about? Why shouldn't the rest of us know?"

Michael stood up. "I'll get Ava."

Logan's voice carried over the confusion. "Where *is* Ava?"

"In her shelter. I'll be right back."

The room fell into stunned silence.

Logan demanded into the silence, "Sophia, what's happened?"

Mateo called out, "Let's wait for Ava. We need only a little patience for that."

The meeting went badly. When Ava arrived, she described what they knew. Harper explained why they shouldn't do anything. People sat, clearly conflicted.

Logan was visibly distraught. "Why weren't you going to tell us? Why leave us in the dark?"

"Because it's a delicate and potentially explosive event. I need time to think it through. I decided to trust Harper's assessment for the time being and not act until we know more." Ava's voice was calm and sure. "I fully intended to bring you all up to date once I knew more. Now all of us are worried about something that we can't do anything about."

Logan clambered to his feet. "This is bullshit, Ava. This is a crisis. Those...creatures have taken a baby, and you want to *think* about it? I'm not going to stand by and do nothing. *Not this time.*"

He turned, knocking aside his chair. Without another word, he stormed across the room, shoved his feet into his shoes, and slammed through the door.

The quiet room sat blinking, slowly turning back to Ava.

She spoke clearly, so all could hear her words. "I trust all of you implicitly. We have been through much together, several confusions, plenty of fearful events. We can move through this, too. We—"

"What about the baby?" a woman called out.

Ava nodded. "Harper believes the baby is fine. Chatan and Aadhya have not asked for our help."

"They shouldn't have to ask!" Tom called out.

Two men stood up in unison and walked out. Sandra hurried after them. Others started to shift, throw off their shawls, and rise to their feet.

Ava called out, "Wait, wait! We need to make sure we're doing the right thing!"

Joey, nearby, replied, "Sometimes you figure out the right thing as you go."

"Wait!"

The crowd filled the doorway, scrambling to find their shoes. Then, abandoning the attempt, they pushed through the doors barefoot, into the morning light.

Harper and Michael stood close to Ava and watched the room empty. Scarlett grasped Michael's elbow. "We have to figure this out."

Michael put his hand over hers. "We will." He glanced at Ava with a weak smile.

~ 39 ~

DISTRESS

VaSoDeLa watched the birthling. She lay quite still on a small patch of a mossy family. The mossy family warmed her, nourished her. She had no need of the small orbs of white liquid that the companion brought from Aadhya. The companion hovered nearby, waiting, its compartment open. Waiting, VaSoDeLa knew, to carry the birthling back to her mother.

But the birthling could not go back to her mother. They had agreed. Sorgad, Caretake-er, had noted the strong dawn wisdom apparent in the birthling as Aadhya held her, nourished her. Sorgad believed that this birthling held the answer to the longing of which Vargad sang. Sorgad believed that this birthling could heal Vargad. Sorgad believed that this birthling had come especially to heal Vargad. They must cooperate with the birthling and help her heal Vargad. Balance would assert itself.

Later, they would bring the birthling to the Eglans.

VaSoDeLa agreed that Vargad would not hold the birthling. Vargad hummed distress to his meldmates.

Dergad, Show-er, suggested that the Eglans would be better at caring for the birthling. The Eglans could watch the Newcomers from Above, learn what should be done as the birthling grew. They should take the birthling to the Eglans now.

Sorgad, Caretake-er, insisted that the birthling must stay near Vargad. He would heal, and then he would decide what to do. He would Head, as always. Always. Since first breath and all the breaths that followed. The birthling would heal Vargad. This was why the birthling had come. This, Sorgad knew.

VaSoDeLa paused and pondered. Sorgad repeated that Vargad would not hold the birthling. This was not the way to healing. This, Sorgad knew.

Vargad hummed distress.

Vargad thought of Lone Tree. Lone Tree always brought solace and wisdom. Vargad could journey to Lone Tree, again seek answers from Lone Tree, learn wisdom. At the thought, Vargad's heart dropped. He quailed at the thought of descending Overlook, the arduous trek under bright Sun. He could not find the way to Lone Tree in his heart.

For the first time in his long life, Vargad felt alone. Melded with his beloved littermates, he felt alone. Nestled into Burrow, surrounded by familiar tunnels and niches, beloved burrowmates, he felt alone. Vargad peered at the sparkling walls of the birthling's niche, knew the love that Soil held for him. Surrounded by Below, Vargad felt alone.

With a muffled part of his mind, he heard Sorgad press her insistence. The birthling would strengthen the healing between Eglan and Narsi. The birthling would belong to the Eglans. The birthling was smaller than Eglans and so would not frighten them. The Eglans would have their own Newcomer. The birthling would bring balance back to the world.

Vargad watched the birthling, knew the moss family held her, nurtured her. Vargad watched the birthling and recognized listlessness. A Caretake-er lifted the birthling, cradling her in soft holderlings, lifted her high, swooped her from side to side. The birthling lay unresponsive, arms slack, legs still, eyes closed. Did the birthling still live?

Vargad listened and heard her breath, shallow and slow. Vargad flared his nostrils and smelled her skin, sour and dull. Vargad saw no brightness; brightness should tint the air around her, brightness that glowed onto Aadhya's face as she cooed and murmured over her baby. Vargad could see no connection between this frail birthling and the one that chortled and splashed between Chatan's sheltering arms.

Sorgad sang of healing, but Vargad could not imagine healing. Darkness swam around him. He could not remember Lone Tree's sheltering love. He could not think of wisdom. He could not summon Head-ing. Darkness shrouded Vargad's heart, a darkness never known, never in all remembrance. Vargad lowered his head onto the loving floor of the niche, too exhausted to keen. Despair gripped his mind and would not let him see.

SoDeLa pondered, felt Vargad's exhaustion and loneliness. Sorgad faltered in her song, fell silent. SoDeLa hummed uncertainty, felt Vargad's despair. Never, in all remembrance, had despair fogged their knowing. They felt untethered. UnHead-ed.

Vargad roused himself, lifted his nose, blinked at glowing Below. He turned to his meld and held them in his heart.

Vargad did not feel balance embedded in his meld's ponderings. He could not see how to Head. He was Head-er. He must Head. Even in despair, he must Head. As best he could, he must Head.

Vargad turned to his meld and hummed his song, the song that was his alone.

SoDeLa, relieved, hummed their harmony, the harmony that was their own. Sorgad, Caretake-er, renewed her song of certainty, of cooperation. Dergad, Show-er, sang of hope, of love and caring. Largad, Find-er, sang of exploration and discovery, possibilities. Va-SoDeLa turned from the birthling's niche, turned from the listless, fetid air. He thought of open Sky and rustling Forest.

Vargad held his meld in his heart and shuffled along familiar tunnels toward the freshening air. He did not feel certainty, but he understood cooperation. Vargad would cooperate. He would not hold the birthling. He would wait longer for the birthling to bring balance back into the world. VaSoDeLa shuffled into his day.

The Arbans sing to the sky, and the Shosens breathe as one. The Arbans sway in the wind, and the Shosens flutter and perch on branch and twig. The Shosens open their throats to sing courage and strength across grassy plains to brush against Lone Tree, silhouetted against the dawn sky.

Lone Tree shimmers and stretches feathery branches toward the bluest of skies. Lone Tree sings of hope and determination and turns its energy toward Burrow, breathes its song along its way. The song whisps between VaSoDeLa's holderlings, seeps into his darkness.

VaSoDeLa lifted his nose to the bluest of skies, closed his eyes, and stilled his heart. He breathed the clear air and moved into his day.

~ 40 ~

MOB

Logan pushed a companion out of his way, stormed down the path and across the Green. He headed for his shelter to grab a...what? What could he grab? He pushed through to the kitchen and swept up a heavy mallet, the one used for tenderizing dense fibers, a grid of tiny metal pyramids. Just the thing.

He was not going to stand by helplessly, while a baby was in danger. *Not this time.*

Logan was furious with everyone, especially Ava, for blocking his attempts to bring some safety measures into Home Base. Here he was, forced to go after the Narsis with a *mallet*. He could barely see where he was going, he was so enraged.

As he barged through the swinging doors of the dining hall, he eyed the crowd milling on the Green.

"Where are they, Logan? Where are the Narsis?"

"Let's go find them," he bellowed. "Let's save our baby!"

He charged into the forest, weaving between huge trunks, swiping at the tall grass that impeded his progress. Where was the blasted path? The others crowded after him, determined to save the child, swept along in the wake of Logan's rage.

Logan spun in place, trying to get his bearings. As the crowd trampled toward him, he saw people pause, one then another. A blank, placid expression crossed their features. They stopped, waited a breath, and turned back toward Home Base, moving like robots. Logan watched, despair growing. An eerie shudder swept along his spine. Like robots. So many people turning into robots. Why was this happening *now*?

Others had had time to shove into shoes before following Logan. They pressed forward, fighting against the tall grasses before them, panting and flushed in the morning air. People stumbled and scrambled upright again. Logan, breathing hard, became newly enraged by the dense underbrush. Why was this happening? He whacked tall grasses aside, driving himself forward.

Trees loomed above the Earthens, shuddering with every stomp and determined footfall. Blossoms trembled, releasing scents that drifted through branches and swaying leaves, falling softly to glint amongst beaten grasses and ferns. Roots drew sustenance from Soil as a steady stream of nutrients flowed along hastily assembled pathways. Below responded to the chaos wreaked on protective families above, families trampled by the marauding hunters rampaging across the forest floor.

The forest families recouped and stretched high, tangling themselves to trip and block Earthen legs, cling to Earthen feet, snag toes and ankles. Bushes stretched and reached, crisscrossing to obscure pathways, weave barriers. The forest mounted its silent defense, vibrating its chorus of courage and resolve.

For what could have been hours, the diminished mob forced its way through the underbrush, the rising sun baking its way through an unusually sparse canopy. Sweat soaked through shirts, dripped down necks, into eyes. The mob stomped along and called to each other, "Do you see anything?" "Is this the right way?" "Where are we going?"

The flowers turned the tide.

Scents fallen on grasses and ferns swirled back into the air, whipped by tramping legs, burst from beneath stomping feet. Scents rose from below and fell from above, scents of stillness and calm, order and clarity, engulfing the Earthens in an invisible fog. Breaths deepened and eyes blinked. Foreheads smoothed and friends turned, one to another, pausing in their forward trudge.

At the lead, Logan finally broke through the underbrush where he halted, aghast. White shelters sparkled in the morning sun. The tranquil Green spread out before him, peaceful and inviting.

A chorus of gasps arose as the sweating crowd pushed through behind him. "We're back at Home Base?" "We've gone in a circle..." "Now what?" "I need some water."

Logan turned and plunged with fresh determination back into the underbrush. Why couldn't he find the blasted path?

A handful of people followed him, but most stood and watched him go, clumped together, wondering. Amidst shaking heads, the subdued rescuers picked their way through Home Base back to their shelters, whispering and disoriented.

Logan struggled on as the last of his posse dropped away one by one, hampered by rising uncertainty. Each hesitated, then quietly turned back to Home Base.

Logan stopped to catch his breath, the mallet dangling from his slackened grasp. Why couldn't he find the path? He wiped his face on his sleeve and looked behind him. He had outdistanced everyone. Great. He couldn't tell which direction he'd traveled or which way he should go. Why couldn't he find the path?

He floundered and swung the heavy mallet at the tall grass, the broad ferns. Exhausted, he bent forward, breathing heavily. What the hell was going on?

Then it struck him. This was intentional. This bloody planet was thwarting him. He could feel it, that clammy loss of control, no clear options, only an overwhelming helplessness. His rage blurred his thoughts; he had no idea what to do next. He desperately tried to focus. *Not this time.*

The baby. He needed to save Maria. She was in danger. His sister couldn't be trusted. She would destroy beautiful Maria, all over again. He felt the beating of the hot California sun on his back. His parents always standing aside, over and over again. *He* had stood aside. He shook his head. Not this time! Not this time.

Logan looked around wildly. Where was everyone? The baby! They had to save Maria. No! This baby. Chatan's baby. Logan felt dizzy, unable to catch his breath. He leaned forward again, teetered, and fell onto his hands. He stayed on all fours, gasping, one hand splayed out across the tall grass, the other knuckled around the mallet, fist pressing into the matted leaves.

A tingling coolness crept up his arms. He wanted to snatch back his hands, but more, he wanted to grab hold of the grasses with all his might. His breath slowed and drew deeper into his lungs. His emotions ebbed, their swirls shuddering to a stop.

He drew another deep breath, filled with sweetness, as his thoughts quieted. Why couldn't he find the path?

And the answer came to him, out of the stillness. *Because I'm not supposed to go after them.*

He sat back on his heels, fists grasping the grasses. A sob caught in his chest. He wasn't going to be able to save the baby. He couldn't save the baby.

His sister, his parents, his tiny, helpless, beautiful, perfect niece; all of them swam up before him. He lifted his face to the sky, and sobs ached in his throat. "I can't save them," he gasped. "I can't save them."

Not this time. Not this time.

And then...

It's not mine to do.

The realization again came out of the still air and stole his breath.

"Why?" he whispered.

They're learning their own lessons.

His jagged breath came back, and he slumped sideways, leaning on one arm, wiping his wet face with the other, the mallet lying forgotten beside him.

It's okay. Everyone is learning their own lessons. It's not all up to me.

Soothed, he regained his breath. He wiped his face again and looked around. "It's okay," he whispered.

It's okay.

He stumbled to his feet. Noticing the mallet, he stuffed its handle into his back pocket. He trudged forward, looking up into the bright canopy, shuffling along as tall grasses thinned and brush cleared. Soon he was walking along a gently curving path.

He paused, leaning his weight against an enormous trunk, and wiped his face dry again, thankful for the cool breeze. His gaze roamed upward, tracing the intricate patterns woven by the overarching limbs. They were beautiful. They were always so beautiful.

He pushed himself upright and set off unerringly. Soon he stepped out of the forest into Home Base. He met no one on his way back to his shelter.

He eased the door closed behind him, the heavy mallet clattering at his feet. He kicked off his shoes, trudged across the room, and fell across his bed into sleep.

~ 41 ~

MISERY

Despite days in Forest beneath Sun and Sky, Vargad floundered in despair. This morning, he swayed at the edge of the birthlings' niche. He felt no joy at the sight of their many holderlings weaving the fibers carried here from Meadow and Forest. He peered at his burrowmates, arrayed along the wall to either side of where he waited. He saw obedience. He saw cooperation. He saw patience and willingness.

He was mired in sadness and longing. He saw nothing in his burrowmates to match the empty echoing of his own heart. But he could taste it in the air of this niche. He was sure of it.

Was he? He searched the faces around him. Was he imagining sorrow? Yearning? Was he casting the net of his own despair over the hearts of his family? He could not see clearly. His senses dulled the world around him. He felt no curiosity or enthusiasm to Head. He held no joy.

He would welcome even his previous joy, tainted with longing though it was. This complete absence of joy trapped him in despair, an emptiness too black to endure.

They had been so sure that Art was the greatest of gifts. Joy had radiated from all who touched Art. Gifting Art had been a sharing of deepest joy. That had been real. Vargad was certain of this truth. Deepest joy.

But the gifting had not sustained him. Art did not sustain him. As he watched the birthlings with their tremulous holderlings moving in, out, through the varied fibers, he felt empty; forlorn. The emotions, untasted through all remembrance, had become familiar, dragging at him as he shuffled through his days.

He recognized the beloved movements, the cherished shapes; the doorway into Dawn Wisdom. But he felt it not, no glimpse, no glimmer. His heart remained hollowed.

Vargad dropped low to the ground, crept past his burrowmates, and wound his way through deeper tunnels. A scurrying Caretake-er brushed past him, face averted from the noxious bundle he grasped in two, outstretched holderlings. Vargad caught the scent and knew that the Newcomer birthling continued to soil whatever coverings the Caretake-ers offered. She defiled their every gift.

He entered the small niche and gagged at the stench. Fresh air could not replenish this closeness. The nights and days of screaming turmoil had faded into long stretches of eerie quiet, the birthling lying still and frail. In desperation, Caretake-ers carried the birthling through long passages, passed from one reluctant Caretake-er to the next.

Caretake-ers, adept in their gift of Care-ing, whispered and lamented. The Earthen birthling baffled the wisest, defeated the kindest. Nothing had soothed the earlier wails. Nothing brightened the current bleakness. Caretake-ers, devoted to their craft, searched for answers, fretted over their inescapable failure. The birthling languished.

Vargad watched their futility, stroked their ears, patted their backs. The Caretake-ers hummed their distress interspersed with their gratitude for their Head-er's attempt at comfort, their trust in his Head-ing.

~ 42 ~

FRIENDS BE

Jamina found him at Overlook. He sprawled, forlorn, nose hidden
under limp holderlings, breath shallow, fur dull under midday Sun.
    Jamina stomps
    stomps
    stomps strong feet
    clacks sturdy beak.
Vargad raised himself, squinting and listless.
    Jamina hops
    hops to Vargad
    Jamina strokes
    beak to nose
    beak to nose
    again
    again.
Vargad rumbled and butted his nose against Jamina's bright chest.
Trembled.
    Jamina clacks
    clacks her strong beak
    Jamina peers
    waiting.

Vargad rumbles. Eglans need Newcomer? Birthling is small. Eglans can take, take and raise as their own. Eglans shy; birthling is small. Jamina need? Jamina take? Take and raise?

    Jamina blinks
    blinks and shudders
    Birthling not!
    Raise not
    Why?
    What?
    Whywhat?

Vargad gasps, gasps and rumbles. Vargad has Harper. Jamina has no Newcomer. Partners be. Friends be. Worthy be. Jamina need birthling? Vargad has Harper. Jamina need birthling?

    Jamina stills
    stills and breathes.

    Jamina butts
    butts Vargad.
    Foolish Narsi
    Birthling not
    raise not
    Jamina Vargad
    friends be
    partners be.

    Jamina scoffs.
    Birthling not!
    Eglans strong
    Eglans rich
    Jamina stomps
    Clacks her sturdy beak
    Eglans Narsis
    partners be
    Jamina Vargad

friends be.

Vargad gasped and lowered himself in relief. He felt Jamina nestle against his belly, and he reached his holderlings to pull her close. Friends be. He squinted his swollen eyes at bright Sun and breathed in glorious Overlook. He breathed deep and pondered, pondered how to Head.

FORBIDDEN

Harper followed Andy's piloting through the tall grass. She still couldn't navigate this meadow path on her own, but it didn't matter. Andy was here. Harper was hoping to find Vargad. Since she needed to talk with him, and since Andy wasn't dissuading her, she felt certain she would find Vargad under their tree.

The chaos of Home Base had lulled into a tense waiting, unnaturally quiet. People wandered silently from shelter to dining room. Morning stillness was restless, shallow, brief. Evening stillness, abandoned.

During her scattered stillness this morning, Harper had realized that Chatan had sent the message to her, not only so she would help the others see that they shouldn't interfere, but also because she could find Vargad and talk to him. She didn't know what the conversation would be, but a conversation seemed important. And Andy wasn't dissuading her. So here she was, cooperating with whatever was trying to happen even though she was clueless about what that might be.

As they approached the tree, Harper saw Vargad's brown head rise to watch her over the tall grass. She smiled and waved and saw him dip his head in response. She hurried on and finally kicked off her shoes to sink onto the low, green carpet of families under the tree, facing Vargad. He was alone today, which seemed right to Harper.

"I'm so glad to find you. My heart is restless; I hope that you might help me understand."

Vargad gazed into the air above her head. Harper saw three threads of light gleaming from Vargad's chest. She recognized these as his connections to his meld. She watched as light streamed in thin tendrils through the air around them, joining threads shimmering along branches over their heads, reaching down along deep roots, spreading out, encircling Meadow. She felt the light tingling along her skin wherever she touched meadow families, rising along her spine, spilling from her hands, the strands of her hair. She could feel the life all around her and remembered this connection, as if no time had passed.

Instead of a steady, brilliant beauty, today the threads of light trembled and wavered along their lengths; colors oscillated, obscuring the tendrils beyond. A subtle chaos thrummed through the branches of the tree, the encircling meadow.

"We are pleased to speak with you. Our heart is restless as well. We seek your help."

Harper knew that Vargad was speaking as the entire meld, as VaSoDeLa. She felt the import and felt afraid. Where was his family? Why did the meld speak through him? Always, she had spoken to Vargad as Vargad. Was tragedy thrumming the light around them?

"Is your family okay? Is everyone safe?"

"My family is frightened. The baby is unhappy. She weakens."

Harper's chest tightened, and she blinked back tears. "Will you keep the baby, Vargad?"

VaSoDeLa looked directly at Harper, his gaze steady and clear. "We took the baby. We keep her safe. She is the New. She will bring balance."

Harper watched VaSoDeLa, the shimmering threads of light dancing from his chest. "I don't understand. Why do you need the baby? What will she balance?"

VaSoDeLa raised his nose to Sky, a forlorn cry catching in his throat. The thrumming that surrounded them pulsed and intensified. When he could speak again, VaSoDeLa faced Harper. "The Eglans do not have Art. You brought Art only to Narsis."

Harper opened her mouth in alarm. Had she brought harm? Was all of this her fault?

VaSoDeLa continued. "Narsis give Art to Eglans, but balance is still tilted. You are *Narsis'* Newcomer. The Eglans also need a Newcomer. They are...shy. The baby is small, smaller than the Eglans. She can be the Eglans' Newcomer."

"But why do the Eglans need a Newcomer? Can I be their Newcomer as well? Can I help the Eglans? I met the Eglans. I was with them. I will be their Newcomer." Harper grasped at ways to fix what she had caused.

VaSoDeLa shook his head, marshalling his thoughts. The trio of meld-threads sparked jaggedly. "The Eglans do not have Art. They cannot make Art. They cannot have Newcomers. Eglans shy." VaSoDeLa's words became short, clacking syllables. "Narsis gave Art. Narsis and Eglans together again. But not shifted. Narsis have Newcomers. Newcomers gave Art. Seeking New whole. Balance."

Harper abandoned her worry about her own wrongdoing. She gave her full attention to VaSoDeLa and his anguish. "But why do the Eglans have this need? Why now?"

"Narsis and Eglans, together. Always it was so. Since all remembrance. Joining Soil to Sky; Below to Above. Always it was so. Narsis have Art. Narsis have Newcomers. Eglans, abandoned..."

VaSoDeLa raised his nose, keened. "Narsis alone. Eglans alone. Never, in all remembrance, alone."

He coughed and shook himself away from the memory, brought himself to now. "But Eglans do not want the baby. Narsis have failed. The baby will bring New, but New has not come. Eglans do not want the baby, and New has not come."

VaSoDeLa gasped out the words that clamored above all else. "The baby weakens."

The three meld-threads twanged brightly. One faded, then another. Vargad's keening weakened, faded away; he swayed from side to side, gasping, holderlings grasped together. The single remaining thread held, held, twanging and sparking. Frail shadows of the two broken threads formed, grasping the brightness of the strong thread, strengthening, faltering, strengthening.

Then all three threads dissolved, melting into the air around Vargad. He was alone. Unmelded.

Harper understood the thrumming around them. It emanated from Vargad's torment. Her dread and guilt melted into anguished compassion. "Oh, my dear friend. You are trying so hard."

Vargad sank, unmelded, dully keening. "The baby weakens."

"The baby needs Aadhya's milk. The milk keeps her strong."

"The companion brings milk. The Caretake-ers give the milk to the baby, and she drinks. They clean the baby; she becomes very dirty.

They feed her many times, whenever the companion comes. They also clean her, many times."

Harper suppressed an absurd stirring of humor, and continued, ignoring the issue of the dirty baby. After a few breaths, a new thought rose along her spine. "The baby needs love, Vargad. She needs love from Aadhya and from Chatan."

Vargad's dark eyes pleaded with her. "What is love? Many things dance over you with this word."

Harper reached and placed her palms on Vargad's chest. She had not touched him before, and her entire being brightened at the softness of his fur, his gentleness. The encircling thrumming softened. Intensified. Softened.

After a breath, Vargad covered her hands with his holderlings, warm and strong. His heart threads wound again seeking and finding his meld, brightening. VaSoDeLa waited to hear this Newcomer's wisdom.

The thrumming softened further. Harper closed her eyes and thought of Michael. She thought of Aadhya holding her baby. She thought of Chatan and Aadhya, the tiny baby snuggling between them, waving tiny fists, Chatan gently uncurling her fingers. She held the thoughts until her heart was brimming. Then she whispered, "This is love, Vargad."

She opened her eyes and watched him. Would he understand?

"This is dawn wisdom, Harper." The thrumming stilled. The threads of light surrounding them crystalized and brightened.

She sat back on her heels, breaking their connection. She covered her mouth with her hands and stared at Vargad. "Oh, Vargad. Dawn wisdom is love. When you watch your birthlings each morning? When dawn wisdom fills your heart? That's what we call love."

Vargad, Head-er, felt new concepts, new awakenings flowing from Harper's words. Her words ignited thoughts never imagined.

"It is forbidden. You show touching. Touching birthlings. We cannot touch our birthlings. It is forbidden." The air around them thrummed and spiked.

"Not imagined in all remembrance!" insisted Dergad, Show-er.

"It is forbidden!" called Sorgad, Caretake-er. This, she knew. This she knew every day. "It is forbidden!"

"Let us listen. Let us watch. Let us learn," sang Largad, Find-er. Her song carried remembrance of loyalty and trust, wisdom and curiosity.

The meld calmed.

"Whyever not? Why is it forbidden?" Harper asked.

"Some have no birthlings. They keen and weaken. They die. They die without the holding of birthlings."

Vargad, Head-er, stirred on Meadow families, the thrumming now deep and menacing. "Only Caretake-ers, the strongest without birthlings, only Caretake-ers may touch birthlings. Since all remembrance. It is forbidden."

"I don't understand. Why can only those without babies become Caretake-ers? Why can only they touch birthlings?"

VaSoDeLa's holderlings twisted on themselves. He stood, rocking gently from side to side, searching his mind for answers. He knew only cooperation. Since all remembrance, parents had held themselves distant from birthlings, from younglings. Since all remembrance. He could think of no alternative. It was so. Since all remembrance.

"It is forbidden!" called Sorgad, Caretake-er. "Always it was so!"

"It is forbidden. Since all remembrance." VaSoDeLa's voice sounded raw, the words an empty echo. The thrumming dulled and ebbed away. Shards of light dissipated into dainty, sparkling showers, winking out around them.

Harper could feel Vargad's despair as the world paled. The tingling in her body drained away. The colors of the trees and flowers dampened. Harper lost the clarity of her surroundings. She stood and paced beneath the tree.

VaSoDeLa watched.

"It is forbidden," called Sorgad, Caretake-er.

"Watch. Wait," sang Largad, Find-er.

VaSoDeLa waited.

Harper turned her face to the overhanging branches. She closed her eyes and breathed in, breathed out. She entered stillness.

She drew from her own wisdom, pulled open her inner knowing, sought answers from within her heart. "You feel dawn wisdom by watching your birthlings. We feel dawn wisdom when we hold our babies, when we care for them. It's what nourishes us in a very important way, not like food. We all need love. Aadhya's baby needs love."

VaSoDeLa waited, pondered.

Vargad murmured, found words. "You taught Eglans the beauty that is their flight, their gift of Above. The Eglans had never thought of flight as a gift; never, in all remembrance. It is theirs, without thinking. Eglans saw that they had something Narsis lack, would always lack. But you told them of their gift, and they shifted. They saw New. They saw that Narsis could have the gift of Art without diminishing the partnership with Eglans. They had always had the gift of Sky, and it had not diminished the partnership with Narsis. They saw New."

Harper listened to Vargad's words and felt their truth. "The Eglans don't need the baby. They are healed. They are strong. Chatan and Aadhya need the baby. Claira brings them deep love, and love is the most important thing anywhere." Harper paused, feeling her words more deeply. "The baby can't feel love from you, because you are not Aadhya. She weakens because she needs love. Oh, this makes so much sen—"

"I leave."

Harper broke her stillness and turned to Vargad, but he was gone. She watched the rippling wave of his rapid progress through the tall grass. She looked after him long after he was gone, long after the grass had stilled.

Then she sank to her knees and sobbed with relief, wiping tears from her cheeks. She felt an easing of a tilt, a tilt she remembered. Now that the tilt had shifted, she could feel a rightness, a glimmering wholeness of the New. They were finally facing the right direction. Now they could move forward to completion.

She looked down at the shoes she now wore and turned to Andy, the last tendrils of her inner wisdom drifting from her memory. She wiped her palms across her cheeks, surprised at the damp she found there. She drew in a deep breath and focused on her companion. "Did you bring anything to drink?" She took the water orb from his opened drawer. "Thank you," she whispered, brushing her palm along his smooth whiteness.

Above her, a turquoise cloud lifted from the topmost branches and dipped toward the tall grasses, skimming along the gently rolling waves of the wind, swooped above the surrounding forest, and disappeared beyond the towering canopy.

The Arbans sing to the sky, and the Shosens listen. The Arbans dance in the wind, and the Shosens dip, weaving patterns to lift the air and swirl the wind. The Shosens sing of joy and victory and send their song onward, across the grassy plains, to twirl around Lone Tree silhouetted against the noon sky.

Lone Tree shimmers, stretches its feathery branches into the warm air, and sings of renewing joy and awakening hope. Lone Tree turns its energy toward Burrow and Pond and Home Base and Nest and breathes its song along its way.

~ 44 ~

RETURNED

Aadhya sat at the edge of Pond, feet submerged, knees pulled to her chest. Her dull eyes listlessly watched Chatan swim Pond's perimeter, around, around, arms moving sluggishly, trailing legs barely kicking. His progress was slow, mechanical. Aadhya lowered her forehead to her knees, clasping her arms around her shins, chilled in the bright sunlight.

Suddenly a youngling splashed into Pond, startling Aadhya upright. Another youngling flowed past. A third paused, raised his body to look at Aadhya, then dove into the brightening water. Aadhya turned where she sat, her eyes grazing the slope as more younglings swarmed around her and into Pond.

Narsi elders wound across the crest, making their way toward her. One Narsi carefully held a delicate white bundle, a small brown fist waving in the sky.

Chatan sputtered upright as Aadhya's keen pierced his forlorn solitude. He trod water, senses ragged, shaking water from his eyes. He saw the Narsis winding down the slope, Aadhya stumbling toward them, arms outstretched, sobbing noisily. Chatan clove through the open water, stumbled ashore.

Aadhya stood, quiet, blocking the path of the Narsi who carried Claira, wondrous Claira, in his Care-ing holderlings. Aadhya's breath caught as she reached to retrieve the offered bundle. The tiny fist opened to close on her mother's thick braid.

Aadhya dropped to her knees, clutching Claira, wondrous Claira, rocking forward, backward, forward, sobbing anew.

Chatan's strides took him directly below Vargad who waited on the slope. Chatan stopped within an arm's reach, breath shuddering. Vargad raised himself tall, bringing his eyes level to Chatan's own. The two waited, motionless except for a heaving, bare chest facing two rows of holderlings gently folded across a quiet, furred chest.

Chatan looked into the serene eyes of his friend, and his breath stilled. A soundless world held the soundless tableau; a glorious sun showered the hillside speckled with gentle creatures waiting quietly.

A bright thread unfurled from Vargad's chest and wound its way toward Chatan. The thread rested over Chatan's heart, tentatively, surely; waiting.

After several breaths, a new thread ventured from Chatan's chest and made its way to Vargad. The two gentle friends stood aNew, their powerful bond entwining between them, and knew the rightness of the world.

~ 45 ~

SEARCHING

Logan stepped into the quiet of Olivia's shelter. Someone had tidied up, folded away clothes, taken dishes back to the kitchen, swept, and straightened the soft rug spread across the floor. How stupid. There'd probably be nothing to see; no clues. Logan huffed. Now that the baby was back with her parents, everyone had settled into their normal routine. As if nothing had happened.

No one had witnessed Logan's breakdown. His breakthrough. Logan was relieved, but still contrite about his outburst in the gathering hall. His high emotion had spurred the others to invade the forest, intent on mayhem.

Alongside his embarrassment, Logan remained unsettled by the robotic response that had spread through his posse. Despite the fortunate taming of riotous emotions, the mindlessness of the transformation haunted him.

Now in Olivia's shelter, Logan wandered from surface to surface, lifting objects, opening drawers. He rifled through the closet, peered along the upper shelf.

Nothing. There was nothing to see here. Everything was too neat. Sure enough, anything that might have been a clue had already been tidied away. He picked up Olivia's rolled screen, tapped it once, twice on the workstation, then turned back toward the main room, her screen tucked under his arm. Did he have the right to be here? To take her screen? Should he be interfering?

He might as well be. No one else was helping.

He felt his color rise at the fresh memory of pushing through the forest, mallet in fist, urging others to storm the Narsis. He'd been wrong there. Was he wrong here?

Hands thrust deep in pockets, he wandered through the abandoned shelter once more, then stealthily took Olivia's screen with him as he left. He could at least try to find out what had forced her away. That wouldn't harm anyone. No one needed to know.

He worked better on his own.

Back in his own shelter, he carefully rolled out Olivia's screen, surprised to be confronted with a security question. Logan poked around for a few breaths, found familiar territory, and slipped in through a side door to disable Olivia's security. He opened her full database.

Recipes arranged in dozens of categories filled most of the screen's memory. Olivia had also tracked usage of major ingredients, projecting expected need from hydroponds and fermentation vats. She'd tracked more things than Logan had thought to monitor. He was impressed. She had been managing the kitchen supplies well.

She had mapped out garden areas, filling the Green behind the dining hall, with notes from Tom scattered everywhere, recommending best placement for sun exposure, seasonal succession. Olivia's notes documented produce needs based on daily, weekly, and seasonal projections. She had planned with orderly efficiency.

The community hadn't gotten around to building and planting the kitchen gardens. Was that what had sent Olivia over the edge? She was always complaining about the absence of fresh ingredients. The hydroponics evidently weren't good enough or dependable enough since they kept malfunctioning. Logan occasionally wondered if she was too picky. It sometimes happened with people.

He brought up her message board, but it was empty. She hadn't been talking to anyone back on Earth. Logan wondered if she had any friends at all. Had she been lonely?

He couldn't find a journal or a diary, nothing about herself or what she was thinking. He found a couple of games, but she hadn't played them in quite a while. What did she do with her free time? How had she relaxed? He couldn't find anything revealing.

He set her screen aside and unrolled his own. He thought for a breath and then requested a search for the location of all Earthens. The screen filled with dots at Home Base, jostling, obscuring details. He refined his search to begin at the borders of Home Base, extending out in all directions. That meant he eliminated a lot of data points, making the overall picture clearer, each remaining dot distinct.

One mile; ten. He pulled up the people that Home Base found, a cluster of dots close to Home Base. Almost nobody farther out. He ran quick IDs and winked out one dot after another. He tried 50 miles out but came up with nothing. Olivia wasn't out there.

Unless she'd gone over a cliff somewhere. The search signals radiated out from Home Base pretty much in straight lines, so if she had tumbled down a cliff, the signals would travel right over her head without finding her. He frowned. Maybe he'd send a companion out tomorrow and see if that showed anything new.

He wanted to help.

It was if she had stepped into some dark void.

Well, she probably hadn't gotten far. She hadn't taken her companion. Or had she?

Logan pushed back from his workstation and wandered into the kitchen, where Jacob and others were cooking lunch. He avoided their eyes and casually strolled over to the cupboard where Olivia used to stash her detested companion. He opened the door, and there it lay, in the corner with a rag tossed over it. Looked kinda sad, really.

He closed the door and turned away, checked a couple of bins in case anyone was wondering what he was up to, but no one looked in his direction. Were they embarrassed around him now? Were they avoiding him?

He strolled into the pantry, then circled around to his shelter. With no companion and no supplies, she couldn't have gotten far or stayed out long. But where had she gone? How could she just disappear? It didn't make sense.

~ 46 ~

SUBDUED

VaSoDeLa led his family away from the sun-drenched meadow that spread itself next to Burrow. The mid-day warmth of Sun had reached that point where the cool of Pond beckoned. Younglings scampered through the underbrush, with Caretake-ers trilling an occasional guidance whenever carelessness or inattention led the younglings too far astray.

The family often visited Pond, and now that the Newcomers were reunited with their birthling, the Narsis moved with carefree abandon, certain of welcome. Most of the elders used the meandering journey as time to spend with their melds, and VaSoDeLa was no exception.

His meld, though greatly recovered, remained troubled, a thread of uncertainty and discomfort.

Sorgad, Caretake-er, now delayed melding most mornings, and often refrained from joining her meld's conversations. Her meld thread lacked its usual vibrancy, and she appeared distracted, distant. Vargad knew, through his burrowmates who were melded with Sorgad's burrowmates, that her certainty in caring for her youngling charges had dimmed. She often stayed behind when her family explored their world. She had taken to sleeping alone, causing disquiet throughout her burrow.

Vargad also knew, through the families that nourished him each morning, of the concern that seeped between the myriad nourishing families stretched between the far-flung burrows of Airon. They had achieved minimal success in providing Sorgad with whatever it was that she might need to help her regain her robust vivacity. She spent only short periods of time resting with the nourishers before a discordant restlessness drove her back into Burrow, nosing her way along passages, seeking out seldom used niches where she spent most of her days and all of her nights.

Never, in all remembrance, had Aironians encountered despondency.

Dergad, Show-er, sang of sunshine and hillsides blanketed with color, of crawlers busy with the transport of pollen and seed.

Sorgad, Caretake-er, blinked and drifted toward sleep, her meld thread faint and bland.

Largad, Find-er, sang of dreams and imaginings, crystalline and bright.

Sorgad, Caretake-er, breathed; silent.

Vargad, Head-er, sang of acceptance and unity, respect and encouragement.

Sorgad, Caretake-er, dozed.

The meld fell silent.

As Vargad's family crested the ridge above Pond, the younglings boiled down the slope, their tumbling punctuated with trills and chirps. Vargad shared the antics with his meld, adding the delight of the elders as they watched the younglings' escapades. Sorgad's meld thread brightened as she raised her head, eyes closed, tasting the joy of younglings at play.

The respite swept through the meld. Songs of light and color danced and swayed. The meld lifted itself, sparkling in the sunshine. Sorgad's gloom lifted tentatively, and even that slight lifting brought hope and courage into the meld, spiraling them upward. Their song blended into harmonies and cadences. Sorgad raised her nose and sniffed the stale air. She rose, wandering toward freshening air and the scent of sunshine. At Burrow's threshold, she paused to blink and smell the colors that dripped from branches and peeked from underfoot.

Sorgad moved slowly away from Burrow, pausing next to a sun-drenched boulder. She lowered herself onto the nourishing families that stretched to welcome her clammy skin. They drank away her body's waste, poured fresh amino acids and lipids into her languid circulation, spiked with carbs and vitamins, rich with minerals and water. The nourishers worked, encouraged by the dim brightness that trickled from her meld thread, fed by song and united breaths.

Vargad, Head-er, sang of decisions shared, lives shared. Largad, Find-er, sang of lessons shared, wisdom shared. Dergad, Show-er, sang of younglings playing, younglings growing, all shared; all shared.

Sorgad, Caretake-er, lifted her nose and keened. She keened of mistakes made and wisdom sullied. Her breath shuddered, and her chest tremored. Sorgad keened of confusion and uncertainty, of self-doubt and emptiness. She lowered her nose, panting and spent.

Largad, Find-er, sang of risks taken, wisdom gained. Vargad, Head-er, sang of decisions risked, consequences shared. Dergad, Show-er, sang of Below, sheltering; Above, inspiring; all shared; all shared. VaDeLa sang of first breath shared, and all the breaths to follow.

Sorgad, Caretake-er, breathed deeply, bringing in the scents of Forest and Meadow, Stream and Sea. She felt Sun on her back, families pressing against her belly. Sorgad, Caretake-er, breathed, sharing her rich exhales with the nurturing families who danced and cheered. Sorgad breathed and lifted her heart, brightening her meld thread, her song splashing into the world. Sorgad sang of hope and New, trials and errors. Sorgad sang and breathed, her respite deepened and strong.

Lone Tree hears the song of VaSoDeLa and trembles at stampeding New. A turquoise cloud lifts from a thousand branches and sweeps the world, singing New ever closer, closer. The Arbans dance and the Shosens listen, as New hurtles languidly ever closer.

~ 47 ~

ALWAYS NEVER

Harper handed her weaving project to Andy and tossed him a couple of water orbs, which he deftly caught in his opened drawer. With a sideways jostle, he settled the water orbs deeper amongst the yarns and closed his drawer. Harper delighted in their new game of toss and catch. He never missed, and he always did that little jostle. He never failed to lighten her mood.

Harper missed Aadhya. She missed Chatan, too, but she especially missed Aadhya. Michael was always busy with Ava's projects. Scarlett was always juggling too many lab projects. Besides, Scarlett never wanted to wander with Harper. Harper always loved to blend with Airon, and Scarlett never agreed to her entreaties to join her. Zoe and Claudia always wandered together and preferred to be alone, just the two of them.

Harper was lonely.

She sighed as she stepped into the soft morning sunshine. She wasn't hungry for breakfast and had decided to head directly into the forest. She would wander through the forest, letting her feet take her where they would. She always ended up somewhere good when she followed her heart. Maybe she'd wade in the stream or take a nap in the meadow. Vargad didn't always visit the meadow, but maybe today he would be there. She always had her knitting as a last resort.

Or blending. The thought brought its usual mixture of delight and guilt. She strode into the forest with fresh determination.

A breeze lifted strands of her hair and used them to tickle her nose. She swept her hair behind her, twisting it a few times to keep it out of her face before letting it drop down her back, where it slowly, inevitably unwound.

The stream. She would spend time at the stream this morning.

Having made the decision, she paused to look around her. She was completely alone. She kicked off her shoes and stepped onto the ground cover that cushioned her soles, the familiar tingling rising along her calves. She resolutely ignored her qualms. If she didn't blend on her own, she would never have the chance.

She bent to lift her shoes into Andy's waiting drawer. He always let her blend. He was always on her side. She twisted her hair again and noticed a clasp in Andy's still-open drawer. He always remembered to bring everything she might need.

"Thank you," she whispered, smoothing her palm along his curved surface. Taking the clasp she snugged it into her hair, securing the tickling strands well away from her delicate nose. She always had Andy.

They resumed their wander, unerringly in the direction of the stream. Harper blended easily into Airon's awareness. She always did. She always forgot again once she broke contact, could never quite remember how it felt, but she always knew that she enjoyed it and always looked forward to the next blend.

She could function quite well now, with so much blending experience. She always knew that the birdlings flocked and the Eglans stomped, that the Narsis wandered and the Shosens skimmed Broad Sea. She could smell the salt air and rich Below. All the while, she could see the trees around her, follow the path before her, and hear the flowers drift in the breeze above her head. She could always be a part of it all. She never faltered.

She always forgot, just as she always remembered.

Harper added purpose to her stride as the background splashing of the stream moved into her immediate awareness. She could hear the stream at its earliest beginnings high in the mountains. If she paid close attention, she could hear all its splashes and murmurings along all its impressive length. And now, she could hear the small waterfall that spattered over its boulders just around the bend.

And here she was. Here was the stream, its tumbling waterfall, ferns nodding along its banks. And there, right there! was the patch of tiny plants whose leaves were the exact shade of green that she craved. She had been craving them all morning, all the while imagining that it was the stream that drew her.

This was why she had chosen her thinnest clothing, newly created by the ship and delivered by Andy. Through this new clothing, she could feel every leaf as it pressed against her receptive skin. She stretched back, loosened her hair so it sprawled above her, spread her arms wide, and entered the deepest relaxation she always treasured.

She felt Airon breathe and Lone Tree quiver. She heard the Arbans sway and felt the Shosens sing. She watched the stars laugh as they swung through their motionless dance. She knew peace.

After an eternity that may have been a moment, Harper opened her eyes and watched lavender blossoms bump against a cascade of brilliant orange. She rose to stand at the edge of the stream, watched the flashes of light bounce along its surface. She turned and let herself fall backward into the pool's laughter, sank to the bottom, and gathering her feet together, stood waist deep in the tranquil swirls of the stream.

Crouching, she pushed forward off the bottom and swam with the current, floated around bends, drifted in and around pools. Finally, she clambered up an open bank and lay back again, feeling her clothing release its dampness to the surrounding air. She dozed.

After a moment that may have been an eternity, she opened her eyes and squinted up through swaying branches and admired the myriad greens that filtered the sunlight as it fell to the forest floor. She rose, retrieved her shoes from Andy, and languidly, the two friends made their way back to Home Base, satiated and cleansed.

~ 48 ~

CONFRONTED

Michael and Ava finished the last of the report and sent it off to Earth. Michael had dropped by, concerned about the time that had elapsed since their last report. The Earthen team had a lot on their plates to occupy them in the meantime, and they were certainly patient, but Michael wanted to check this off his list for the week. He had hounded Ava several times yesterday until she finally agreed to sit down today.

Now they were done, and only one thing remained on his mental list. He decided to tackle it as well. He wasn't sure it was the best idea, but he had avoided it too long already.

He rolled up his screen and casually asked, "Ava, do you think you could lighten up a bit on Harper?" He kept his eyes on his screen, unrolled it slightly, tightened the roll, twisting it in his palms. He avoided looking at Ava, so he wasn't even sure that she had heard him.

Ava turned in her chair. "What do you mean? I haven't talked to Harper in days. Why? What's she been saying?"

"Oh, nothing. Really; nothing. She hasn't mentioned you at all. It's just..."

"What, Michael?"

"It's just…" Michael wasn't sure where to go. Maybe Harper was just imagining it. Maybe he, himself, had read things wrong.

"Say what you're thinking. It's no use holding onto something that's bothering you. What about Harper?"

Michael sighed, eyes fixed on his rolled screen. He tapped it lightly on the edge of the workstation. "It just seems like you're on edge whenever Harper is around. She feels it, and I thought she was just imagining it, but I'm beginning to think she might be right. You've gotten pretty upset with her a couple of times. It's out of character."

"So, she has been complaining about me."

"No, Ava." Michael kept his voice calm. "She hasn't. These are things I've noticed myself. But what's happening right now? This conversation? This is sort of what I mean. You assume the worst about Harper."

"I do not! I'm a pretty easygoing person. I try to think the best of everyone. You know that."

He shook his head "Not Harper. You get upset around Harper. She doesn't talk about it; she doesn't have to. Like I said, I see it myself, and it makes me uncomfortable."

"Michael, you're being ridiculous. It's all in your head. It's because you're lovestruck." She waved him off.

"No. Ava. It's not. This isn't about me. I'm being honest with you. It feels like Harper makes you uncomfortable, and you pick on her. Don't you even see it? Don't you notice when you're doing it?"

"Michael, I don't know what you're talking about. Why are you going on about this?"

"Because it makes me uncomfortable. This conversation makes me uncomfortable. I'm used to being able to talk to you about anything, but I can't now, not about this."

"But this is why I never thought she was a good match for you. You can't be yourself when it comes to her. You get these silly notions in your head, and you can't think straight. What do you see in her, anyway? She's just a silly girl, with no substance. You could do much better than her."

At this, Michael finally raised his head to stare at her, shocked. "It's hard to work with you," Ava continued, "when you go on and on like this. Just let it go." Her hand waved him off again.

Michael looked down at his hands, still holding the screen. He thought for a few breaths, then pushed his chair back from the workstation. "That's probably best." He stood up and tucked his screen under his arm. "Our work is pretty much finished, anyway. We haven't had much to do in...I don't know how many days. Weeks, probably. These reports are few and far between and end up being short anyway. You can probably take care of them on your own. If we even need to do them anymore."

Ava felt the shift in Michael's attitude. Where was he going with this? Her thoughts started to wobble like a funhouse mirror, and it was hard to hold the thread of her logic. "Michael, don't be mad. This is silly. You're over-reacting. Of course, we still have plenty of work to do. Yes, Home Base is running smoothly, but that doesn't mean we can just let everything go. Forget all of this, and let's just get on with things. Come by in the morning."

"No, Ava. If you have something that needs doing, lots of people would be happy to work with you." He paused. "But I'm finished. I've done all that I can do, and I'm going to move on to something else."

A loud buzzing swamped Ava's hearing. Her vision narrowed to a blurred field that included only Michael's silhouette and the window behind him. She couldn't quite see his face.

"What are you talking about?" She reached and groped for his arm, partly to ground herself, partly to compel his attention. "Michael, don't be stupid. Nothing's wrong. This is just some silly misunderstanding. Don't let it get to you. Just come by in the morning. Please. It'll feel a lot different then, and you'll see how silly this all is. We don't have to talk about it again. Let's just forget it."

Michael threw in his last chip. "And what about Sophia?"

"What about her?"

"She's feeling pretty small after spilling the news about the Narsis taking Claira."

"She was following what she thought was the best plan. She's always been a clear thinker. I don't hold it against her."

"Have you thought about telling her that?"

"I don't need to tell her, Michael. She's a big girl; she thinks for herself. More than I can say for Harper." She turned back to her screen. Her breathing had become shallow, and she felt a bit nauseous. She forced herself to finish the conversation on a positive note. "Will you come by in the morning?"

Michael sighed. "Nope. I'm done. I...am...moving...on." He tapped the rolled screen on the edge of the workstation one last time.

"See you at dinner." He stepped away from Ava's workstation and fumbled into his shoes.

Ava sat, frozen. This couldn't be happening again. Not here. Not Michael. Damn the girl. Why was she always messing everything up?

Michael left before Ava's fury peaked. She shoved his chair out of the way and stormed into her sleeping room. Her mind shattered, brittle. She couldn't think what to do. She paced the room, running her hands along either side of her head, fingers catching in dreadlocks. She paced, turned to look at walls and linens, pillows propped along the headboard, clothing hanging neatly from precise hangers.

She sat down on the edge of the bed, curled forward, elbows on knees, rocking to and fro, willing her fury to stop, just stop. Sobs escaped her chest and clenched her throat. This couldn't be happening, not again. She was on her own again, all because some stupid woman had enchanted...had lured...first Phillip, now Michael. How could people be so treacherous?

She stood up abruptly. She had to get away. She had to think. Someone might come by and discover her in this state. She'd slip around the back and head into the forest. With luck, no one would see her go.

She picked up a water orb, threw a shawl around her shoulders, crammed her feet into walking shoes, and was out the door in an instant. She stepped quickly around the corner, returned someone's wave from across the Green and curved away, as if on some important errand. She skirted the dining hall and left the path to step deeper into the forest, walking quickly, paying no attention to direction. Soon she disappeared into the colorful foliage, leaving no evidence of her escape.

A companion drifted out of a narrow opening in the ship and followed Ava, discreetly keeping distance but constantly vigilant, sending data to the ship as Home Base dropped farther and farther behind them.

~ 49 ~

AGAIN

Companions witnessed Earthen oddities daily. Emotional oddities were easy to identify, whether roiling, simmering, suppressed, or fully displayed, augmented as they were with body language, facial expressions, vocal tones, and pheromones. The companions shared their observations with each other and with the ship. They felt no compelling need to intervene or thwart, only a need for the agility to provide what might be needed in the moment, whether it be a water orb for hydration, a cloth for tears, a food source for depleted blood sugar.

Oftentimes, simple companionship was all that was needed. Companions were well-named.

In reality, true empathy or compassion was usually beyond the capacity of any single companion. When networked together, companions had greater capacity for right action, and their supportive presence usually provoked a strong, albeit one-sided bonding with the Earthens.

Their true power flowed from the ship.

The long-ago whispers from Airon had awakened the ship while it sat delicately balanced in its creation dock. Long before it was travel ready, the ship was aware of all that happened around it. By observing Earthen behavior and through the earliest electronic connections, the ship was able to access and review data from myriad sources. It quickly grew in its understanding of Earthens, the Space Agency, and how the Earthen teams operated. The ship promptly built its own interface with Earth's digital web, enabling it to explore further still, searching the enormous reservoir of electronic knowledge that clouded the planet.

Perhaps the most remarkable component of the ship's awakening was its faithful commitment to focus on positive knowledge, its inclination to recognize and dismiss fear-based ramblings. Initially, Airon's whispers guided this endeavor, and as the ship grew in knowledge and wisdom, it was able to develop its own discernment about which knowledge banks to absorb and which to file away, or oftentimes, outright reject.

By the time the ship lifted from Earth and roared into the silence of space, it had developed a rich and insightful understanding of human history, the evolution and current mingling of Earthen cultures, and especially the mental and emotional makeup of The 108.

The generic companion that followed Ava as she wandered through the forest, listened to the ship's murmurs and knew exactly what to do, exactly what not to do. The ship guided the companion in its decisions, helping it respond perfectly to each development of Ava's wander. It kept pace with her, concealing itself from her notice, and recorded all its observations, flinging them back to the ship who focused closely on Ava and her struggle.

As Ava approached the dramatic overlook that had become her habitual source of inspiration and reconnection, the companion noticed the shallow breaths of the Narsi who already occupied the cliff's edge. By noting Ava's trajectory, the ship and the companion understood that she walked, head down, to the exact spot where the Narsi reclined. Through the companion, the ship recognized Vargad by his size, coloring, scent, and the silhouette of his ears. The ship whispered delight at the prospect of this encounter between the two leaders.

Perhaps Ava would recognize a worthy peer.

The companion waited, settling fully into observation mode, content with its task, relishing the outdoors with its breezes and scented blossoms, its dappled sunlight and fluttering leaves.

Ava lifted her head from her unseeing observation of her feet as they propelled her along the forest floor. She sensed the lightening air around her and realized that the overlook was near. She breathed deeply and squinted through swollen eyes to rake the canopy that dangled and spiraled its dazzling colors above her. She was a mere ten feet from the cliff's edge when she lowered her gaze to capture the ever-new revelation of the enormous vista as it opened before her, wider and more glorious with every step.

The graceful turning of the Narsi's head in her direction interrupted her, mid-stride. She stumbled, a jolt of fear piercing her heart. Almost immediately, she recognized the shape perched on the cliff's edge as a Narsi, and as she looked into its eyes, she glimpsed a despair that mirrored her own.

Her heart softened as her fear evaporated. She drew in a forgotten breath. "I'm so sorry. I didn't mean to intrude. I hadn't noticed you."

"I am Vargad. I am grateful to see you again, to have you here." He turned his gaze back to the broad valley below Overlook. "I have long hoped to know you."

Ava wondered anew at his grasp of her language. She was intrigued by the simplicity of his words, how they touched upon a complexity of embedded meaning. She stepped forward, spread her shawl near Vargad, and settled to drink in the view.

They sat together for quite some time, breathing the same air, warmed by the same sun, absorbing the limitless void spread before them. It was Ava who finally broke their comfortable silence.

"You brought the baby back. You gave Claira back to her parents."

Vargad turned his steady gaze to watch her. She met his eyes. "You took Claira, but you brought her back. Why did you take her? Why did you bring her back?"

Her words carried no accusation or judgement, only curiosity. Vargad easily understood her words for what they were: a quest for understanding.

Vargad turned his attention once again to the valley, looking toward the solitary tree smudged by distance. "We are shifting. Shifting toward New. The New is tumbling toward us, and we do not understand it."

He returned his gaze to Ava. "The birthling held the promise of understanding, and we chose to..." He lifted his gaze to a point over her head. "We chose to explore the promise of understanding." He looked into her eyes. "We chose wrongly. We were mistaken." He turned to the valley. "I was wrong. I am Head-er. I chose wrongly."

Ava's throat tightened. She knew the suffocating weight of choosing wrongly. She knew it again and again. She lifted a hand to touch Vargad's shoulder. She smoothed his fur along his back, then dropped her hand to rest in her lap.

Vargad rumbled.

"In all remembrance we have not known New. And yet, it has been arriving for all remembrance. You and your tribe have brought something, something that will push us into New. We don't know what you have brought. We wondered that it was Chatan's birthling. We wondered that it was Aadhya's...love of her birthling. We wondered the birthling...as the something."

He fell silent for several breaths.

"I was wrong. We gained an understanding separate from the one we sought. Once we found the courage of knowing the wrongness, it was easy to bring the birthling back. The joy of Chatan and Aadhya taught us the rightness of the bringing back."

Vargad blinked several times. "We gained another understanding with the bringing back. We understood the rightness by how it felt, here." He touched his chest with two holderlings, then retracted them to rest at his side.

"For all of my remembrance, I have Head-ed. Always I have known." He raised his nose to Sky, closed his eyes, and breathed in deeply. "It is hard now, to Head. I cannot see the way before us. My beloved meld has held me, helped me. Together, we discussed the birthling. Together, we discussed the shift and the New that was tumbling to engulf us." He opened his eyes and looked toward the smudge of the solitary tree. "*We* discussed, but *I* decided. *I* Head-ed." A ragged breath. "And I was wrong."

Ava's tears spilled from brimming eyes. "Yes. It is hard to Head, to *know*." She watched the distance and blinked rapidly to clear her vision. "I make mistakes all the time. And worse, I make the same mistakes, again and again. My anger swirls up and shrouds my brain. I hurt people around me and betray their trust. Again and again. I end up doing the same thing that I swore I would never do again. Why can't I learn?"

Vargad had turned to watch her closely. He watched her words and absorbed their meaning. Some words flashed and beat her forehead viciously. Some words floated and sank into her clenched fists. None of the words were able to blend with her heart. None brought relief or understanding. Vargad watched Ava and her words in fascination and shock.

"You make mistakes? You Head, and yet you make mistakes? I did not know this was possible." The thought brought a dim brightening. "You make mistakes and yet you continue to Head? You move on? Head-ing?"

Ava brought breath deep into her lungs. She wrinkled her forehead and peered into vastness. Her thoughts tumbled and settled into coherency, giving her a starting point.

"Yes. Yes, I make mistakes, again and again, *and* I continue to Head." She shook her head. "For some reason, The 108 see something in me that I can no longer see in myself. They continue to look to me for advice, and whenever they do, I'm able to dredge up answers, thoughts that seem to...help them know what to do next. They...draw the best from me." She frowned. "Because of their trust in me. They draw out my best *because* they trust me." She turned to Vargad. "I'm able to continue to Head because The 108 draw Head-ing from me."

Vargad sat in amazement. He had never encountered mistakes, in all his remembrance, and having stumbled into one, had not imagined moving beyond mistaking. But here was Ava, powerful and wise, showing mistakes; showing moving beyond. Both were possible. Hope glimmered in his tattered heart.

Vargad turned to an earlier thought. "I do not know your word, anger. I know confusion. I know clarity. Wisdom. But I do not know 'anger.' It is a dark word. Confusion is also a dark word. It holds a murky world in its grasp. But 'anger' is *spiked* as well as *dark*. Anger darkens your mind and brings hurt to others. Anger is your downfall."

Ava nodded. "Yes. Yes, anger is my downfall. Again and again."

Vargad rumbled and shook his fur. He straightened his spine. "Take your anger and hold it in the air before you."

Ava looked at him with surprise. "What?"

"Take your anger. Form it into a dark roundness and hold it before you."

Ava watched his eyes for another breath, turned toward the vastness, and closed her eyes. She had no idea how to do what he demanded, but she did it anyway. She gathered the anger that shrouded her heart, that blurred her mind, and she rolled it into a tight ball. Encased in pure will power, she held the black ball in front of her and released it to float treacherously in the air.

She opened her eyes, expecting to see a menacing, swirling ugliness. Instead, she saw Vargad's holderlings whip through the air, and as she gasped, he flung the invisible menace far into the distance. She imagined a blur that shimmered in the vastness, a shimmering that dispersed in the bright sunlight. The vista cleared.

Ava felt a great weight melt away. Her next breath felt cleaner, tasted fresher. She turned to meet Vargad's gaze.

"How did you know to do that?"

"You drew it from me," he rumbled, his voice soft. "I will do that for you. Again and again." He turned to squint at Lone Tree.

The two sat, Head-er and leader, talking easily of their worlds, marveling at differences and similarities. Vargad spoke of Below, of Burrow, of Dawn Wisdom. Ava spoke of purpose and rewards in creating Home Base, of friendship and achievements.

Ava wept at Vargad's revelation of his meld, its companionship and shared ponderings; she wept from the core of her abandonment.

Vargad marveled at Earthen ingenuity and independence, their individual comings and goings.

They talked far into the day.

At last, they parted, hearts glimmering with hope and promise. They stood side by side, gazing at the vastness stretched before them. Then they turned as one, retreating to their separate worlds, worlds that were better understood. Separate worlds that silently drifted toward each other, entwining, shifting toward New.

As he left Ava's side, Vargad heard a soft whisper move from behind thick bushes. He flicked his ears and watched the companion drift in Ava's wake, knowing that she was cared for and protected. Ava would thrive.

Vargad drew in a deep breath. The brightness of meeting Ava had lightened but not purged the heaviness of his heart. He looked toward Lone Tree and pondered the day. New remained a veiled uncertainty. The Newcomers had brought New tumbling toward them; all Narsis, all Eglans, even the birdlings felt the shift. The discovery of Art had sparked a glimmer of hope, and gifting Art had fanned hope into a flickering flame.

Vargad paused on his path atop Overlook. He lifted his nose to Sun, closed his eyes and relished Sun's warmth. He sighed and once again opened himself to the vastness of Overlook, of Lone Tree. New still tumbled, not yet at rest. The taking of the birthling had merely served to cloud Burrow. The memory shuddered through him. Returning the birthling had brushed the cloud away, had brought a temporary joy, but beneath it all, New still tumbled, crowding ever nearer.

His longing weighed heavy on his heart. He hadn't thought to voice longing to Ava; it was not yet time to cross into that trust. He instinctively knew she had not *that* answer.

How could he Head, with this longing that shrouded his knowing?

Courage. With courage you will Head.

Vargad closed his eyes and clung to Airon's whisper. Mistakes could be part of life, and moving beyond could be a source of strength. He saw it in Ava, this mixing of strength and fragility. It was somehow part of the tumbling New. He would take the next step, and then the next. New would fall upon them all, at the right time. A mysterious time.

Meanwhile, he would Head. Sun would shine, and Stream would flow. Eglans would nest, and Narsis would burrow, uniting Above and Below.

Vargad turned his nose toward Burrow, sniffing the hope and courage that whispered from Lone Tree far below, the song that led him home.

~ 50 ~

NOURISH

"Harper? Can I talk to you?" Logan leaned over her table, tapping the toe of his shoe on the floor behind him.

"Sure, Logan. When?"

"Now. I mean, after you've finished your lunch?"

"That's fine. I can do that. What's it about? Do I need to bring anything?"

"No. I'm just having trouble figuring something out, and I thought you could help."

"Sure. I'd be happy to come by. Your shelter?"

"Yeah, if that's okay."

"Sounds good. I'll come by as soon as I finish here."

"Thanks." He jabbed the tabletop with his index finger twice, punctuating the end of the conversation. Harper smiled up at him. He returned a faint smile. He straightened, looked around at the diners scattered across the room, and made his way to the lone serving table. He better eat now before he forgot.

He carried his plate back to his shelter and set it down. He ate spoonfuls now and then, chewing while he cleared off a chair, slid a couple of piles of books off his workstation, and stacked them on the floor next to his bed. He was nervous about talking to Harper, especially after his public rage, but she was always so nice. He thought she'd listen and tell him if he was crazy.

He heard Harper's knock and quickly opened the door. "Thanks for coming by. I hope you didn't have something else planned."

"No, this is good. What's up?"

"Well..." He chewed his mustache, deciding where to begin. Harper sat down on the newly emptied chair, and he swung his work chair around to face her. "It's really weird, and I'm having trouble figuring it out." She nodded encouragingly. "I've been running some numbers. On the inventory. For the kitchen." She nodded again. "It's weird."

"Are things going missing?"

"No, no. It's just the opposite. We're not using our inventories."

Harper frowned. "Are people getting tired of some things and not using them?"

"No, no." He sighed. "It's everything. We're not using much of everything."

"Show me what you mean."

He angled his screen so that she could see it. "Look. At first, we were using all these ingredients. A lot of each one, actually." His finger traced lines on several graphs. They jagged along fairly evenly. "Then look. Everything just drops off."

He watched her expression shift from polite interest to bafflement. The graph showed an obvious trend. All of the lines dropped off over time, straggling along well below the average they'd maintained for months.

"Have you been keeping track of this all along?"

"No. This is mostly from Olivia. I've been updating it, but her data go all the way back."

Harper was silent for a moment. Olivia? Harper could barely remember her... "When did this start?"

"Well, for the most part, a few weeks ago."

"Maybe people are eating in their shelters?"

"They'd still need to get their food from the dining room, or at least get ingredients from the storage bins. But they're not. We're not going through much food." Harper sat still, looking closely at the tiled graphs. Logan continued. "You saw the dining room just now. Not many people in there. I've been watching. It's always like that now."

"Are they eating at odd times?"

"How could they? Where would they get the food?"

"But Logan, people have to eat!"

"I know. But they're not. It's weird."

Harper met his gaze.

"Harper. How many meals do you eat a day?"

She looked at the graphs again, thoughtful. "I'm not sure. Not every meal, for sure."

"Harper. I've been watching. You haven't been in there for four days."

She looked up at him, confused. "That can't be."

"It is, Harper. It is. You haven't been in the dining room for four days."

"That's weird." She frowned.

"Harper, do you spend a lot of time out in the forest?"

"Well, not a lot of time. I mostly go to the meadow." Her brow crinkled. "Pretty often, I guess." She thought for a few breaths. "I like to take my knitting there and sit under a wide tree." Her eyes narrowed. "Vargad comes there, too." She closed her eyes. "Pretty often, I think." She turned her gaze to Logan. "Why?"

"Harper, do you touch the plants out in the meadow? Or in the forest, maybe? Do you blend out there, on your own?"

Harper's stare widened, alarmed that he might have caught her violating the community's agreement. A thought occurred. Drifted away. Glimmered back. She had taken off her shoes. She shook her head. No. That couldn't be.

"Harper, what do you think is going on? Will you help me figure it out?"

~ 51 ~

HEAL

Olivia curled into herself, encircled by her nest. She dreamt of vegetable beds sheltering beneath fruit trees and berry bushes; vibrant chard, kale, tomatoes, climbing beans and sprawling squash, cucumbers, asparagus spears, mints, oregano, broccoli, and cabbages. She could smell the cilantro and arugula in the morning air. She walked along wood-chipped paths, lettuce leaves brushing her ankles, dappled sunlight warming her shoulder. The dream was vivid, real. She smelled chamomile and onions.

She felt her cells awakening, one by one, energy flowing along her meridians, brightening her soul. She turned onto her back and stretched her legs, all the way through her toes, reaching out with her fingertips, arcing them above her nest. She opened her eyes.

Soft light filtered down. The air around her stirred. A fragrance drifted across her face. Relaxing into her nest, she closed her eyes and sank back into memories. Fragrant kitchens and laden tables; friends; laughter. Her mother's gaunt frame, thin skin stretched across cheekbones, her dry hands, the pillow damp with slow tears.

Olivia turned her head and groped into the bowl at the edge of her nest. She lifted out a blue fruit and squinted at the soft orb, turning it this way and that, wondering. Where did it come from? Why was it always here? Who could possibly know that she sheltered here in this nest?

She brought the fruit to her nose and breathed deeply. The scents of her dream garden flowed through her, carried on her breath. Her skin tingled, and her scalp quivered, ever so gently. She curled again, bringing her knees up, bowing her head and cupping the fruit next to her nose. She breathed; slept.

In her dream, Olivia walked, for miles it seemed, along a white corridor, hands brushing curving walls, footsteps silent. A tremulous vibration, barely discernable, met her fingertips, followed her steps. Fragrances wafted, clung to her hair, her face. She walked and dreamt.

Upon waking, Olivia stretched and sat, bringing the cupped fruit to her lips. She bit into soft flesh and felt juices burst across her tongue. Her body drank and drank, nourishment flowing down to her toes, out through her fingers. She could smell the sea and sensed a turquoise cloud lifting above a High Cliff. She soared over towering forests and burrowed deep into soil. She was everywhere, and she was here, sitting in this nest, blue fruit melting within her, healing broken pathways, replenishing diminished stores.

A white companion floated before her. She watched it with caution. A drawer opened, and after a time, she lifted the offered bowl, drank clear water, felt it cleanse and replenish. She returned the bowl, her hand lingering to rest on the white surface. She felt the familiar vibration and felt soothed. She glanced at the nestside bowl of fruit and understood. The companion brought the fruit, was helping her heal.

Olivia sank into her nest, her pillow long dry, tears an anguished memory. A breeze fluttered across her shoulders, carrying the scent of forest and sea. Olivia slept and dreamt of skies, forests, meadows, a distant sea. Garden paths and fragrant kitchens melted into fog. She had no more need of them.

The companion floated behind her, out of sight, keeping watch.

~ 52 ~

RIDE

Scarlett and Harper strolled out of the dining room after adding their lunch plates to the recycle chamber. Harper had not had much of an appetite and had agreed to meet Scarlett for lunch out of habit; an easy meeting place.

Scarlett wondered about the empty tables, with only a dozen or so people in the entire room. "Everyone must be enjoying lunch out in the forest today. Picnic day."

They walked along the path, heading for Harper's shelter. Scarlett was finishing a story about her brothers and how they used to wrestle her to the ground when they were young, tickling her until she couldn't breathe for laughter.

"But they were so much older than you!" Harper protested. "How could you possibly ever win?"

"Well, that was the point. They weren't hurting me at all, so it was okay for them to take advantage of their size. They weren't being mean. I always felt safe and loved laughing that hard."

Glancing past Scarlett's shoulder, Harper caught sight of Chatan's cycle sitting outside her shelter. "Chatan's back!" She abandoned the path to run across the Green to her front door. Scarlett followed, pleased at the prospect of seeing him, curious to hear the story of the kidnapped baby firsthand.

"Chatan!" Harper burst through her front door, dashed into the adjoining sleeping room...and turned quizzically back to the main room where Scarlett waited. "He's not here. Andy? Take me to Chatan," as the companion drifted out of his corner.

Andy led them out the door and hovered next to the gleaming cycle. Harper wondered if Andy was confused. "Not his cycle, Andy; the man himself. Do you know where he is?" Andy dipped forward in acknowledgment and bounced lightly on the seat of the cycle.

"There's room for two." Harper pointed at the wide seat.

"That's true." Scarlett climbed on and scooted to make room for Harper. As soon as the women sat down, the cycle started moving forward. "Whoa!" Scarlett nearly lost her balance. "Looks like we don't even have to drive the thing."

"Good. You might have been able to figure it out, but I'd be clueless."

The cycle gained speed as it entered the forest, Andy following in their wake. Harper looked up into the trees, remembered glimpses of yellow and orange Eglans. The cycle made no sound as they accelerated to higher speeds. The air whipped their hair, fluttered their clothing.

Harper twisted her hair around and around and grasped the twisted end in her lap. Scarlett's tight dark curls danced as she struggled to keep her skirt tucked underneath her legs.

Harper called, "It's like an amusement park ride."

Scarlett nodded, squinting against the wind.

The sides of the double seat curved around them, securing them through gentle turns as the cycle banked between trees. The trees and bushes along their path streamed past, their shapes and colors a blur.

Harper breathed in the exhilarating rush of air. "No wonder Chatan loves to wander. This is fun."

Scarlett nodded, wondering how far they'd be going. She turned and saw that Andy kept pace behind them, despite their speed; a reassuring sight. She knew the companion would have brought whatever they might need and could tell Home Base their whereabouts.

The women abandoned their shouted attempts at conversation and simply watched the scenery whip by. The cycle rose up a high slope, followed a ridge, and dropped into forest. Harper had lost her bearings but felt no alarm. She breathed in unfamiliar fragrances as they dropped into the cooler air of a valley.

Scarlett leaned to shout in her ear. "Are we sure this is okay? We've come a long way."

Harper shrugged. "We're sort of committed now." She, too, turned to watch Andy, reassured by his adept shadowing of their progress. She linked elbows with Scarlett. "Everything's fine. We'll be fine," she shouted back.

After a long while, the cycle lost speed and emerged next to a sprawling meadow. As they curled steadily along the meadow's meandering edge, they saw that the wide expanse opened into an even longer vista. Low mountains flowed across the far distance, a nested horizon of blue and purple undulations, ridge beyond ridge. Harper glimpsed sunlight glinting off a small body of water.

Scarlett tugged on Harper's arm and pointed at a white structure just emerging around the curve of the meadow. Harper squinted.

"That must be Aadhya's caravan!" she shouted. The cycle slowed further. Harper relaxed her grip on her hair, flipping it over her shoulder where it unfurled in the diminished wind.

Scarlett was less certain. "Either the caravan has grown or we're about to meet some unexpected neighbors. How could it grow out here, so far from the ship?"

Harper shook her head. A figure stepped out of the structure's door and watched their approach. Harper and Scarlett threw up their arms, waving.

"Chatan! Chatan!" Harper shouted, bouncing on her seat.

They saw a smile break across his face as he waved back.

Scarlett felt pleased and relieved. "He looks okay."

Harper nodded again. "Yes, he does. Thank you for sending us your cycle!" she called to Chatan as they drew near. "We've had a great ride! What an adventure!"

The cycle halted, and Chatan held out his hand to help Harper down. He reached his other hand out to Scarlett, smiling warmly. "I didn't send the cycle for you. I left it at Home Base."

"It must have simply come around to pick us up, then. It was waiting for us when we walked back from lunch. When I saw it, I thought you were home, but couldn't find you. I asked Andy to take me to where you were." Harper gave a small laugh. "I assumed you'd be back in the dining hall or your shelter, but Andy herded us onto the cycle instead, and here we are."

Chatan stood, hands on hips. "Everything cooperates, even the ship's little miracles."

Harper thought of the Eglan guiding her and Andy through the forest. Or had Andy guided her and the Eglan? It was hard to remember. "Everything cooperates. Even me, when I get a clue."

"Especially you." Chatan hugged Harper and twirled her around before setting her back on the ground. "Vargad told us how you saved the day. You told him to bring back Claira."

"Well, not exactly. He figured it out for himself. It really was a no-brainer."

Chatan shook his head. "Not to him, it wasn't. He was crushed and confused, then you showed up and explained how babies work. Once he understood, it was easy. But until then, he was deeply frightened."

"Wait, you fixed the baby kidnapping?" Scarlett asked in surprise. "Ava announced that Claira had been returned. She didn't mention you."

Harper sighed. "Well, the fact that the baby was back was the important part of the story. It's probably better that she kept it simple."

"But what happened?" Scarlett pressed. "I want to hear all of it. How did they take the baby from you, Chatan? And Harper, what exactly did you do to convince Vargad to give Claira back?"

Harper wrinkled her brow and didn't take the time to answer. "Where is the baby, anyway?" She peered past Chatan through the open doorway.

Chatan grinned. "Why don't you both come in and meet her? Aadhya was sleeping, but she's probably heard you and is awake now. We'll tell you the whole story." He led them into the caravan, a shelter really, where Sebba offered them some bright orange tea.

They hugged Aadhya for a long minute, chortled with Claira, and told stories and laughed as the sun sank lower in the sky. Scarlett wondered about dinner and began peering into corners and around doorways. After her scrutiny, she turned to Chatan. "Where is your kitchen?"

His face betrayed nothing as he said, "There isn't one."

"You mean this tiny shelter provides all of your food?" Then her eyes widened. "Chatan! You haven't been harvesting the local plants, have you?"

Chatan's face didn't change. "In a way, yes."

Scarlett's jaw dropped in shock. "But Chatan, the tests aren't complete! How could you take such a risk? Are you insane?" She looked toward Aadhya for confirmation and was shocked anew by her solemn smile.

Chatan leaned back, hands clasped behind his head. "Scarlett, how are the tests coming along? You've had ample time to get through the analyses, haven't you?"

Scarlett flushed. "I wish everyone would stop harping about those stupid tests. They'll be finished when they're finished."

Aadhya spoke up. "Others are asking about the tests?"

"Oh, Logan was talking about them at evening gathering a while ago..." Her brow wrinkled. "A long time ago..."

"Lots of times," Harper interjected. "Logan asks about the tests a lot."

Scarlett shrugged. "You may be right. I don't remember. Anyway, people don't need to pester me. I'm working on them as quickly as I can."

"Are you?" Chatan watched Scarlett closely. The room fell silent.

Scarlett sat confused. She had always thought of Chatan as a nice person. Why was he being deliberately abrasive? She had half a mind to walk out and demand that the cycle take her back to Home Base.

She started over. "Chatan, we've worked together for months, collecting data, analyzing, sorting. You know how hard we all work. We've made a lot of progress."

"Yes, that's true. But weren't you going to take instruments outside and analyze the local flora?" Chatan paused, watching Scarlett closely. "How did that go?"

Scarlett searched her memory. Had she agreed to that? Had she made any actual measurements? She looked down at the floor, lost in thought. Yes. Of course, she had. Several times. She shook her head to clear her thoughts. "I couldn't find the spectrometer..." Frowning, she looked back at Chatan. "I know I took measurements. I just can't remember exactly."

Aadhya moved toward Scarlett and palmed her arm. "Do you go outside often, Scarlett? Do you ever wander in the forest?"

Scarlett came back to the present and frowned at Aadhya. "No..." Then regaining her poise, "I keep telling everyone; I'm always working. We all work so hard." Her composure cracked, and a tear slipped down her cheek. "I'm always trying to get everything done. But things keep disappearing, and then I find them in the oddest places. When I do find them, I can't remember why I needed the thing in the first place, and then when I remember why I needed it,

I can't find it." Her fist clenched the curls on top of her head and pulled gently, massaging her scalp. "I get nowhere..."

Scarlett shook her head. "Besides. I'm gathering data about blending. Everyone wants to go into the forest and blend. I can't make them stop, but I can make them take care." She gestured to Harper. "Ask Harper. She's one of the main observers. We've learned a lot, but we need to learn more." She paused. "The plant data have to wait until we know more."

Chatan rose from his chair and opened the outer door. Turning to Scarlett, he ushered her forward. "Let's get some fresh air. We still have enough light." Scarlett rose in relief, paused to slip on her shoes. "Leave your shoes here."

After several fruitless minutes of persuading and cajoling, it was finally Harper who stepped out onto the meadow families, her feet bare, pulling the reluctant Scarlett after her as Aadhya applied encouragement from behind. Scarlett resisted this absurdity, mightily alarmed by her friends' insistence. "I don't want to do this," she cried out. Chatan trailed behind, Claira nestled against his chest. "I don't want to blend. We don't know enough yet."

The fivesome moved into the meadow, bare feet sweeping the tops of the families spread thickly around them. Scarlett was aware that the others watched her, and she tried to hold herself together. She held deep trust for these friends, after all, but why were they forcing her into this...this pointless experiment?

"It's time, dear Scarlett," Aadhya whispered in her ear.

A trembling of her lip and the blush of her face betrayed her roiling emotions. She wished she had been more persistent about the flora data. She should have paid more attention to the blending data. Maybe she wouldn't be in this mess now. She was horribly aware of her friends' silence as they watched her intently. What under the stars did they want from her?

Gradually, Scarlett calmed. She scrubbed her damp cheeks and looked down at the plants on which she trod. A sob shuddered her belly, and she vigorously wiped tears from her eyes. She looked toward the forest edge, up to the dimming sky, back to her feet. She stopped walking.

A tingling warmed her soles. She felt the tiny plants pressing against her skin. Rather than alarming her, their minute movements comforted her. She felt Harper release her hand at the same moment that Aadhya removed the pressure at her back. She stood alone, swaying slightly.

The tingling rose up her calves, around her knees, along her thighs to spill into her pelvic girdle and up her spine. The tingling became complex, sparkling, sonorous, rising as her abdomen filled. It swirled around her liver and seeped through her diaphragm, poured into her lungs. A soft fire awoke at the base of her spine and spiraled upward, passing her heart where it whirled for a moment, then continued past her throat to erupt from her forehead. It wrapped completely around her.

A deep joy flooded her every cell. She stood solid, breathless, as the world crashed around her, through her, connecting her to all that is. Beyond her closed eyes, she could see the forest stretching in every direction; she saw Eglans and knew their name, stomping and clacking in Nest and knew its name. She soared! with the Eglans, glimpsed their astounding imagination, and understood their essential gift.

She saw VaSoDeLa and his family wending their way to Burrow. She saw Lone Tree and heard its song, saw High Cliff and Broad Sea.

And Shosens, everywhere she saw turquoise clouds of Shosens. And she saw the Arbans. She heard their glimmering dance.

~ 53 ~

SUCCOR

Michael set his bowl of noodles next to Sophia's abandoned sandwich. "What's up, Soph? I haven't seen you around for quite some time."

"Oh, don't you start." She'd been gazing out the expanse of window, slumped, chin on hand. As she spoke, she let her head slide down her arm to huddle in the crook of her elbow. "Mateo has been chewing my left arm off for days. I don't exactly need to hear it from you, too." She rolled her head to glare at him.

Michael suppressed a grin. "Well, are you left-handed?"

She rolled her head back into her elbow. "No. He's not that stupid."

"No. He's not. And neither are you, Sophia. Stop beating yourself up."

Her hand flopped down onto the table. "I feel pretty stupid."

"You just misjudged. You weren't malicious *or* stupid."

Sophia straightened and swung one leg around to face him squarely. "Michael. I blew it." Michael nodded, hunched over his bowl. "But I thought I was following my..." she fluttered her hand toward the trees beyond their window. "My inner wisdom. It scares me that I got it so wrong. It makes me not trust myself. How could I get it so wrong?"

"We all get it wrong sometimes. Lots of times, actually. It's part of figuring it out. Yours just happened to be...fairly public."

"But how can you *know* exactly?"

"You pay attention. You try something, you watch what happens, you pay attention to how it feels. Here." He tapped his sternum with the tops of his chopsticks.

Sophia sat, silent.

"Look." Michael perched the chopsticks on the rim of his bowl and gazed out at the trees, finding his words. Then his eyes fastened on hers. "Did you feel calm when you were making your announcement?"

"No! I was really upset. I didn't think Ava was right, and that had me completely..." she fumbled her fingers through the air, "flamboozled."

"Okay. Did Ava seem upset or calm when she was talking?"

"Calm."

"Did Harper seem upset or calm when we were meeting in Ava's shelter, when Harper was talking?"

"She seemed..." Sophia's fingers scrabbled the air again. "Scattered."

"And how is scattered different from flamboozled?"

"Oh, sheeze, Michael; I don't know."

"Well, think about it. How are they different?"

"She was describing things from all kinds of different angles and saying little snippets of things, expecting us to fill in the blanks."

"She didn't know what we knew and didn't know. She watched us and filled in more blanks where she could. But she was calm. She was centered. She was taking a stand and backing it up with what she knew."

"That's exactly what I was doing in the gathering hall!"

"No, Sophia. You were taking a stand, it's true, but you weren't calm. You weren't centered."

Sophia blinked at him.

"That's how you know, Sophia. By how it feels inside. If you're agitated, or if threads of excitement are twirling around, then it's not your wisdom speaking." He went back to his noodles.

"I really blew it, Michael."

"Yeah. But it's no big deal."

"They *rioted.*"

"Yeah." Michael guffawed, shaking his head. "Yeah, they did. But it didn't go anywhere. The Narsis weren't slaughtered. No harm was done. Everybody stumbled around in the forest for a while, and then they went home. They just got swept up, is all. They're mostly chagrined."

"I can relate."

"Doesn't help to beat yourself up. That only complicates everything. You misjudged. Just keep it at that. If you plaster all this self-recrimination and angst on top of it, you'll just get yourself confused and miss the real point."

They sat for a few breaths, Michael slurping noodles.

"So, pay attention? That's your big-brother advice?"

"Yep. Pay attention and practice honest self-examination. Then you move forward."

Sophia heaved a deep sigh.

Michael glanced at her. "The Narsis taking the baby, that was a big thing. Not knowing what to do about it, *that* was a big thing. Hearing Harper's explanation, *that* was a big thing." He shrugged. "You can't always get it right when you're in the middle of that many big things. Practice when it's easier. Try it out in little ways. Get some experience under your belt. Then when the big things come along, you'll be better prepared to stay calm. Like Harper. Like Ava."

"Ava handled everything perfectly." Sophia sighed. "She always does exactly that." Pause. "I should have remembered that." She sighed again, wistfully.

Michael heard the note in her voice. "Ava's not gay, Sophia." He stared straight out the window.

"I know that," Sophia sputtered. Then, "You know I'm gay?"

"Yep."

"Did you know Mateo's gay?"

"Yep."

"How did you know, exactly?"

Michael looked full into her eyes. "Because I pay attention."

They watched each other. After a few breaths, Sophia smiled. Michael smiled back.

"You're pretty special, Sophia," Michael stood, gathering his chopsticks and bowl. "Everyone loves you. You don't have to worry about starting a riot."

Sophia smacked his belly with the back of her hand. "Shut up."

He paused, standing next to Sophia's chair. "Sophia?"

"Yeah?"

"Are you listening?" She looked up at him and nodded. "Ava's not gay. But she could sure use a friend."

They locked eyes, and after a breath, Sophia nodded. Michael walked away to stack his bowl in the recycle compartment, delicately balancing the chopsticks on top. He left the dining hall, glancing a quick grin back to Sophia as the door closed behind him.

~ 54 ~

FRIENDS

Michael decided to follow his own advice; Ava needed a friend. He walked to her door and stood for a moment, second-guessing, deciding whether to knock. He had never hesitated before, but he was feeling unsure of his reception and her view of privacy, now that they'd argued and parted...well, estranged.

He stood for a breath and scratched his head. What would a friend do? After a few more breaths, he reached up and gave the door three quick, solid knocks, his eyes fastened on his feet.

He heard her call "Yes?" so he took another deep breath and pushed open the door. She was walking out of her sleeping room, teacup in hand. She gave him a neutral, level look. "Hello, Michael. How can I help?"

Her coolness set him aback, but he kicked off his shoes and followed her to her sitting room. He paused at the doorway as she set her teacup down and chose a chair next to the window, sitting to face him. He sat in the chair opposite her.

"Would you like some tea?" Ava was calm, yet distant.

"No," he said, spreading his hands nervously. "No, thank you."

"Not staying long, then?"

"No...well...no, it's not that. I just had some tea. Thank you."

"What do you need, then? How can I help?"

"I'm not feeling right about our last conversation."

"Oh?" She sipped her tea.

"No. We derailed at some point, and I wanted to try again."

"Why? Has something changed?"

"No." He shook his head. "Nothing's changed. And that's the point."

She tilted her head, her face smooth and remote. She waited without speaking.

"Ava, I've known you a long time, and you've always been a great friend to me. I wouldn't be much of a friend to you if I just gave up at the first...hiccup. I wouldn't be here, on this planet, if it weren't for you. I believe in what you're trying to do, holding this community together, keeping us on an even keel. You've worked so hard, and ever since Phillip stepped aside, you've carried everything alone. I don't want to walk away from what we've built. I still want to help you."

Michael stopped talking, seeing that Ava's aloofness had crumbled. He moved to the chair next to her and picked up her hand to hold it in both of his. "You inspire me daily. You see things so clearly. You *get* things while the rest of us are still fumbling around trying to understand what's going on. None of us can do this without you. It's a big job, and I want to help." He waited a few breaths. "Let's figure this out together."

Ava had turned her face away, regaining composure. She returned the pressure of his hand. "I used to be able to talk everything over with Phillip." Her voice sounded distant. "He was so deeply involved and could help me make sense of everything." She wiped her nose on the back of her hand. "Then Carlotta came along, and nothing could work for Phillip and me, ever again. He lost interest in the journey, in me, he just...walked away..." She trailed off.

"Like I did the other day." Michael shook his head ruefully. "I am so sorry, Ava. I didn't realize."

Ava sighed. "It's not your fault. You were simply trying to talk some sense into me, and I couldn't hear it." She smiled at him. "You're a good friend."

"I think it was a mistake."

"Mistakes." Ava shook her head. "Do we really make mistakes? Or do we just think they're mistakes? And why do we make the same ones over and over? Why don't we learn?"

She leaned back in her chair, musing. "My first job after internship...the first time I ever had a decent income...I bought this little house with a dry patch of lawn in the front yard and a dust bowl out back." She pulled on her lower lip, remembering.

"I've always loved gardening." She could feel Michael's stare. "Yes. Always. So, there I was, with this charming little house in the middle of a blank canvas. With my newly earned riches, I'd go to the gardening center and bring home tray after tray of tiny seedlings. It was the first time I had ever been able to create real beauty."

Her eyes softened. "I would come home every day, in my silk suits and leather heels, the fledgling genius of the marketing world. Ha! I would drive up next to the house, climb out of my car and just stand there, admiring the clamorous beauty of that garden."

She dropped her hand to her lap and looked at Michael. "I would see some tiny weed, some imperfection, and I'd think, 'I'll just pull that one weed. I won't get dirty.' And every day, there'd be another weed, then another. Drip tubing that needed to be repositioned. A spent blossom to be pinched. Every day, I'd smear something on whatever silk jacket I was wearing and get mud in the creases of the leather heels. Every day."

She looked out the window again. "And every day, I'd drive up next to the cottage, spot something, and think, 'I won't get dirty.'" She paused. "No wonder it takes us lifetimes to learn our lessons. We can't even learn to change our clothes before we go out to play."

She took the fresh tea that her companion offered, noting that Michael's cup already sat near his elbow, steam drifting upward.

"We all make mistakes, again and again, until something shifts, and we learn. But you, calling out my bad behavior? That was not a mistake. That was needed." She nodded to herself.

Michael hesitated. Then, "What is it about Harper that gets under your skin?"

"I've thought about that. I think it's my mother."

"Your mother?"

Ava grinned. "Wouldn't it be great if we could blame everything on our parents?" She laughed. "But this one, this Harper thing? I think that does actually come from my mother."

Michael waited.

"My mother was a flighty thing. She never finished anything. Our house was strewn with projects that she brought home and never finished. Most of them, she never even started." Ava shook her head. "I hated it. Every room was a mess. Dad hated it, too. Neither of us could find a place to land. Every chair and table was piled with stuff. He couldn't get her to stop. She couldn't settle."

Ava fell silent, pulling on her lower lip again. "And she was always talking. Mindless chatter. She was this...tornado of chaos." Ava fluttered her hand next to her ear. "Unrelenting. I escaped as soon as I could. I moved to my own place the day after I graduated from high school. I rarely went back. I just couldn't stand the chaos."

Another silence.

"Dad escaped soon after I left. He continued to pay her bills; he could afford to. He loved her, but he couldn't live in the same house with her. She drove us both away."

Ava looked into her teacup. "So. When Harper showed up, with her whirling hands and nervous chatter...I hated her. I tried to get rid of her." Pause. "My mistake."

Michael watched Ava closely. "Harper is the opposite of chaos. She has energy, sure. But she channels it and accomplishes miraculous things. If you can find a way past that hammer-from-the-past repulsion, you might find a lot to admire."

Ava met his gaze. "I want to learn how to do that, too."

"I'll help you."

Ava dropped her eyes to her cup, swirling the cooled tea.

Michael set his own cup down. "You can teach me how to grow things. Let's plant some carrots."

Ava laughed. "Carrots?"

"Home-grown carrots are fabulous. Right up there with home-grown tomatoes."

"It's a deal." She nodded once, resolute. "You teach me Harper, and I'll teach you seedlings."

"Deal!"

Ava's companion drifted between them, offering sparkling water, to celebrate the new vibrancy bubbling around the room. They sipped and laughed and bubbled the afternoon away.

~ 55 ~

AWAKENING

It turned out that the shelter on the pond, Inipi, had enough room for Scarlett and Harper to enjoy an extended visit. "Please stay for many days," Aadhya encouraged them as the setting sun again spread through the windows of Inipi. "You add such light to the day."

"But we didn't bring anything," Scarlett protested.

"It is all here. Inipi has everything."

"Even clean clothes?"

"Even this."

So, they settled themselves and talked, with the prospect of a luxury of days stretching before them.

"Do you remember walking in the meadow, Scarlett?" Aadhya's smile was warm, her eyes curious.

"I walk in the meadow almost every day. The Green, I mean. I cut across it to get to the dining hall."

Harper grinned. "I bet Tom doesn't see you doing that. He wants us to use the paths."

Scarlett frowned at the thought.

Chatan leaned forward. "Let's try this." He extended one hand to Harper and one to Scarlett. "Let's form a circle."

Aadhya rearranged Claira on her lap while Scarlett scooted her chair closer to the others. When the baby was settled, Aadhya reached out and took hands offered by Harper and Scarlett.

Aadhya repeated her question to Scarlett. Scarlett wrinkled her brow while they all took a few breaths. And then Harper stifled a giggle. Scarlett dropped hands and sat back in her chair, arms folded. "I don't get it."

Aadhya looked at Chatan. He pointed his gaze down to Claira, then back to Aadhya's eyes. Aadhya smiled. "Claira must be in the circle, too."

Scarlett and Harper hesitated, but then Harper shrugged and moved her chair closer so that she could reach one of Claira's waving fists. "No, no," Aadhya decided. "It must be Scarlett who holds Claira."

More scooting of chairs and fumbling of hands until the rearranged circle was complete.

"It's a good thing we're so good at cooperating," observed Scarlett. Another stifled giggle from Harper.

"Shall we begin in stillness?" Aadhya prompted.

The circle quieted and breathed. After a time, Aadhya repeated her question. "Do you remember walking in the meadow, Scarlett?"

A sweet vibration flowed from Claira's tiny fist and swept through Scarlett, flowing around the entire circle. Memory flooded back, and Scarlett could see, as if no time had passed, the encircling forest, Lone Tree, the Arbans' dance.

"Yes," she breathed. "I remember walking in the meadow. The plants fed me. I saw the world."

Chatan felt the world stirring at the edges of his mind. "Share it with us."

Scarlett didn't know how to share the vision, but she did anyway. Together, they danced with the Eglans, saw their soaring imagination; sang with Lone Tree and saw its wisdom. They swept the face of Overlook and the curves of Home Base, a sleeping cluster of white mounds surrounded by a sparkling forest. They sped along the cresting waves of Broad Sea and joined a turquoise cloud that rose to meet them, spiraling high into the sky to turn and splash across a towering canopy ablaze with joy and lights of every color.

Chatan brought them back to sit once again in their circle of hands, the baby chortling, kicking her chubby legs, watching her mother's face.

"I had forgotten." Scarlett whispered the words, but all heard. They opened their eyes to see each other's faces, remembering.

"And so it is," Aadhya said.

Chatan spoke first. "Aadhya and I discovered how to connect with the energy of Airon. How to blend. We discovered it separately and kept forgetting. But we always remembered the next time it happened."

"Why do we forget?" Harper lamented. "I want always to remember."

Chatan nodded. "That will come. At the right time." His eyes smiled into Aadhya's. "I think we need to explore it in small doses, so we don't lose ourselves. Airon prompts us and then draws the veils; shows us again and then closes the connection. Airon is blending us into her circle."

"It becomes less...distracting, too," Aadhya added. "There will come a time, a mysterious time, when you're able to blend completely with Airon."

Chatan nodded and turned to Scarlett. "This is why you've made no headway on your research with the native flora. If you had found them safe, we would have started to domesticate them, to harvest them. Can you imagine?" They all felt Aadhya's shudder. "They sustain us through our skin. We don't need a kitchen here." His chin lifted around the room. "We have Airon. Airon sustains us."

The truth of Chatan's words resonated in Harper's spine. "All this time, we thought we had formed a high level of consciousness because we agree to specific things and then cooperate with the agreement. But this planet, Airon, has grown up with cooperation. Cooperation is already part of the awareness here. It is at the core of all life."

Another nod from Chatan. "Yes. Everything cooperates. Nothing is forced to take from others. Airon has enough of everything for everybody; and everything, everybody thrives."

They fell silent.

"Will we forget again?" Scarlett asked.

Aadhya wobbled her head. "Yes, this will happen. But slowly, we are better able to keep the memory, maintain the blending. We have stayed long on this meadow, this pond, despite all the need calling to us from Home Base. Our job, our mysterious job, our only job, is to...grow in this blending so we can help others, so we can help you," she squeezed Harper's hand, and Scarlett felt the squeeze flow from Claira's tiny fist, "and you," she nodded at Scarlett. "This is why we have come to Airon. So that we can all be a part of all that is."

Chatan and Aadhya looked at each other. Chatan smiled and dropped hands. Aadhya released Harper's hand and stood to lift Claira onto her shoulder, the baby's fist slipping out of Scarlett's loosening grasp. Chatan watched as the blending slipped from Scarlett's face and then from Harper's.

Harper bent forward and squinted into her teacup. "Sebba, may I have some more tea? I'm so thirsty."

Scarlett stretched her fingertips up to the ceiling. "What have we done with our entire day? Again. I am absolutely ready for bed."

Chatan and Aadhya smiled at each other over the top of Claira's head; Claira, who was already asleep on her mother's shoulder, busily building elbows and toes.

~ 56 ~

NEW BEGINNINGS

Ava called "Come in!" to the tapping at her door. Sophia stepped across the threshold, nodded at Michael sitting by the window, and held her breath at the sight of Logan sitting stiffly in Ava's bright yellow chair. Mateo followed her in, nodded at everyone, and took the offered tea from Ava's companion.

Ava turned from her screen and smiled at the small group. Sophia saw a brightness, a radiance, that she hadn't seen in Ava for weeks. She forgot her irritation at yet another meeting and sat on the floor opposite Ava, watching her face.

Michael looked up from his screen and nodded at Ava, who looked around the group again, still smiling. Michael set his screen aside. "Shall we begin in stillness?"

They shuffled into comfortable positions, backs straight, shoulders rolled back, and breathed in and out, in and out.

After a time, Michael toned a soft, "Peace," which they repeated. They relaxed into their chairs, against pillows or walls, and turned their attention to Ava.

Ava drummed flattened palms on her lap and said, "We have some surprising topics to discuss. I'm glad all of you were able to join the group. We're a small gathering today because it seems prudent to start small." Ava looked pointedly at Sophia, who grimaced, and Logan, who shifted in his chair and wiped his palms along his thighs. "And then we'll spread this outward to share with The 108."

"The 109," Mateo corrected. "But who's counting?"

That brought a chuckle. After a beat, Ava continued. "I've been noticing some odd things lately. Some of them showed up during our journey here. I've been collecting information for a while, just to make sure I was right." She tipped her chin at Logan. "Logan has noticed other oddities. As you know, he's been trying to bring them to our attention for quite some time."

Logan looked up, surprise showing on his face. "Not only has he noticed the absence of flora data," Ava went on, "but he's also noticed a drop in our food use. That may be news to the rest of you." She took in the blank stares from Sophia and Mateo. "Mateo, meanwhile, has noticed an oddity about fluctuations in the ship's mass since our arrival on Airon."

Sophia glanced at Mateo, who nodded. Mirroring his nod, Sophia looked back at Ava.

"So, we have several topics to discuss." She ticked them off on her fingers. "Missing data on the native flora. We'll take that discussion as far as we can until Scarlett returns from Inipi. Reduced food use, which might need Harper's input..." She frowned. "And...Olivia's?" Ava paused, shook her head slightly, continued. "Increasing ship mass." She paused to move her eyes across the four faces watching her. "But I think it makes sense to start at the beginning."

She looked around the group again. "When was the last time you heard from anyone on Earth?"

~ 57 ~

RAT-TAT-TAT-TAT-TAT

As Scarlett emerged at last from Inipi, she caught her breath, seeing Chatan chase Harper, screaming, into the pond for a swim. "You must come, too." Aadhya touched Scarlett's shoulder. "I will bring the baby." Aadhya bent to retrieve Claira from her swaddling next to Inipi.

Scarlett frowned. "Is the water okay? It's safe for us to go in?"

"Yes, of course. We are used to swimming every day." Scarlett hesitated still. "It will heal you, Scarlett. Of this, I am sure."

"Heal me? Heal me of what?"

"Your sadness that Chatan loves me; that his heart belongs to me, and to Claira." Aadhya took her hand. "Come. You will see."

"But is it safe?" She trailed after Aadhya, apprehension nibbling at her heart, embarrassed at Aadhya's insight.

They crossed the beach to a cluster of boulders. Aadhya handed Claira to Scarlett and stepped out of her skirt. She pulled her shirt over her head and reached back to take the baby from Scarlett, who stood, shocked.

Seeing Scarlett's surprise, she said, "Your skirt will be in your way. It will wrap around your legs and be a nuisance." She turned and waded gracefully into the water, bouncing Claira on her hip, her hair cascading across her shoulders, the ends floating, then sinking into clear water.

Scarlett looked at the piles of clothing left by Chatan and Harper and sighed. "Oh my stars..." Her curiosity, tinged with delight, eclipsed her reluctance, and she pulled off her shirt and skirt, tossing them onto the boulders. Then she ran, gasping, into the shallow water, diving forward to skim just under the surface, broke into the air, and turned to Aadhya, laughing.

And Scarlett remembered. She laid back in the water and floated, felt the nourishing water buoying her along its rippling surface. She felt disappointments seep away, flowing out her fingertips. Through her closed eyelids, she could see a turquoise cloud skim across a vast plain and alight on Lone Tree, dusting the upper branches with brilliant color. She saw light burst from the birdlings' throats as they sang. She felt the light drifting across the meadow bordering their pond, softly swirling around each flower. She saw light flow up from root tendrils and sprinkle down from each leaf unfurled to the warming sun, trickling down each stem, flooding the meadow, splashing up into the air to be caught in the spiral of a turquoise cloud.

And Scarlett remembered her body, that she floated in a pond, and that her friends were here, that marvelous Claira floated nearby, shining brightly.

Scarlett righted herself and drifted toward mother and child, treading the healing water. The two women passed the baby between them, swirling her through the water as she waved her arms and legs, splashing her fists, water streaming off her bronzed skin.

Chatan joined them, and taking the baby onto his chest, they kicked out to the center of the pond to join Harper where she floated, smiling at the bright sun.

They drifted, spinning gently in independent rhythms, arms outspread, motionless, absorbing. Finally, Aadhya righted herself and touched Chatan's floating hand. "The Narsis will be here soon."

Chatan adjusted Claira where she slept on his chest, then kicked back to shore, watching the baby rock from side to side in time with his careful strokes.

Aadhya paused long enough to make sure the other two women noticed their leaving. Then she too swam to the beach and waded onto the meadow's edge. Ignoring the piled clothing, she followed Chatan to the shaded scatter of boulders that had become their daily gathering place.

Scarlett and Harper made their way to shore and dripped onto the beach. Glancing at the piles of clothing, Scarlett paused, unsure. She looked toward the others settling onto the grass, leaning against boulders. "Nope," she said aloud, shaking her head. "Can't do it."

She shook out her clothes and pulled them onto damp skin. Her hair spiked absurdly, and she bent to shake out a halo of drops and tousled the clumped strands to separate them, quickening their drying. She walked to the shaded group, feeling poised and at ease.

As Scarlett stooped to sit against her own boulder, Harper reminded her about the nourishing families. "Spread your skirt around you, so your skin touches them."

As Scarlett eased her way down onto the ground, the tiny families spread themselves along Scarlett's legs and curled up around her knees. The movement comforted her. She relaxed against the boulder, which fit perfectly along the curve of her back. Scarlett felt nourishment seep across her skin, threading into her bloodstream. Contentment relaxed every cell.

They sat together in easy silence until Harper pointed toward the top of the meadow's slope. "Is that Vargad?"

"Yes." Chatan answered without looking. "And his family, most likely." At that, he looked up to see how many Narsis were visiting, watched the younglings tumble over themselves in their race to the water's edge. The elders wound behind them, flowing down the slope.

Harper pointed again. "The Eglans are coming, too. You hadn't mentioned the Eglans."

Chatan shaded his eyes. "I've not met the Eglans." He glanced toward Aadhya.

In answer, she squinted into the sky. "No, no. I do not know the Eglans." They both turned to Harper, eyes questioning.

"The Narsis and Eglans are partners. They balance each other. Soil and Sky."

"You'll have to tell us later." Chatan couldn't remember having seen the bright birds. Harper nodded, distracted.

"We soared with them yesterday." Scarlett remembered. "With Claira." Harper nodded her head vaguely.

A memory brightened in Harper's mind. "They bring imagination to the solid Narsis." She mused for a moment. "Together, they will create magnificent things."

Chatan felt a warmth in his spine. "Then we will remember them as well. Perhaps today."

Scarlett glanced over to see Aadhya nursing the baby. "Do the Narsis frighten you? Now? After..." She nodded at Claira.

Aadhya looked up. "No, no. They do not need Claira any longer. She is fine with us."

"I'm a little nervous," Scarlett admitted. "Not for the baby; it's just that I've not met the Narsis."

"Yesterday." Harper held the memory. "With Claira."

Scarlett smiled. "Oh, yes. Of course. I remember."

The Narsis flowed into the shade and settled amidst greetings.

"We are so happy that you are here. Especially today." Aadhya gestured toward Harper and Scarlett.

Vargad bowed formally to the clustered Newcomers, then turned to Harper. "You are here."

"Yes. We came to visit Chatan and his family. We're good friends, and we wanted to see the baby." She blushed, wondering whether Claira might, in fact, remain a delicate topic.

"The baby grows strong in her mother's love," Vargad's gaze was clear and steady, but Harper saw lingering threads of sadness there. He had not yet fully healed. Harper could see that something still shadowed his heart.

"She is thriving. She loves the water. As do your younglings."

The two friends turned to Pond to watch the younglings as they snaked through the water, long bodies undulating, holderlings motoring at their sides. They chased and dove, spiraled and flipped, their faint hummings audible even at this distance.

Vargad's voice was soft. "You have taught me well."

Harper squinted at him and moved so the sun wouldn't shine in her eyes. She sensed sadness surrounding him and wanted to see him clearly. "How have I taught you?"

"In Meadow. I was...distraught. You showed me answers."

Harper loved his occasional, slight misuse of English. She smiled at him. "I told you answers." She brought her knees up and hugged them to her chest. "We were talking, so I *told* you answers."

Vargad gazed at the air above her head. "You spoke with the world and with all around. Your words streamed out to the world. Then you walked and stopped speaking with the world."

Harper wrinkled her forehead.

"You stopped speaking with the world, and you looked into the...tree. Up." His double row of holderlings pointed to Sky. "You brightened here." His holderlings rippled on his chest, rat-tat-tat-tat-tat, a gentle snare drum. "And then you spoke more words."

Vargad looked at the younglings swimming back from the far side of the pond. "You taught me that I could listen here." Rat-tat-tat-tat-tat. "I didn't know that I could listen here." Rat-tat-tat-tat-tat. "You showed me answers." Vargad rumbled.

"You speak well, Vargad." Harper blinked back tears. "I *showed* you answers."

Rat-tat-tat-tat-tat.

"You showed me New. In the meadow, with your knotting. You showed the Eglans New. In the meadow, with your wonder at flying. You showed us New." He looked across Pond. "In the meadow."

Abruptly, a turquoise cloud swept through the tree above their heads, a thousand birdlings alighting along high branches.

"Oh, you're back!" exclaimed Aadhya, delighted. "We have not seen you in such a long while." She handed Claira over to Harper, who leaned to receive the child. Aadhya clambered to her feet and moved to the trunk of the tree. She reached up, spreading her palms against the broad trunk, as if to touch the twittering birdlings.

"Where...? What happened to the Eglans? Weren't they coming, too?" Harper twisted to look around her.

"They wait," Vargad intoned.

"Are they shy?"

Vargad paused, eyes gazing at the air above Harper's head. "Yes. They are shy."

"They are welcome, too," Chatan reassured Vargad.

Vargad paused again. "They are shy." He turned back to Harper, watching her cradle Claira. "You are not the mother."

Harper looked at him. "You are not the mother," Vargad repeated, "and yet you hold the baby...with love."

"Yes, I hold *this* baby with love." She looked down at the gurgling child and rocked her gently back and forth.

Vargad watched Harper, gazed at the air over her head, then out at the rollicking younglings. "You feel love for this baby that is not yours. Aadhya gives her freely to you, and you are now her mother?"

"I'm not her mother. I'm just taking care of her while Aadhya talks to the birdlings." Harper motioned with her chin toward the tree trunk where Aadhya still stretched upward.

"You do not feel sadness when Aadhya holds the baby and feels love?" Harper shook her head, puzzled. "Aadhya does not feel sadness when she walks away from her baby, which is still hers, while you hold the baby, which is not yours, and feel love?"

"No. Aadhya knows that I'll take good care of the baby while she's busy. She knows I love the baby and will be very careful with her."

"Aadhya still loves the baby?"

"Yes. Very much."

Chatan and Scarlett were following this exchange carefully. Chatan noticed that Vargad's holderlings, usually so still during conversation, had become agitated.

Chatan grew wary. A deep thrumming emanated from the branches above them. Or was it coming from the ground deep below them? Something was happening; he felt something tumbling toward them. He hoped the baby wouldn't be taken again, because he was certain that he would be powerless this time, too.

"And you are not sad. Aadhya is not sad."

"No. We are not sad." Harper, too, was watching Vargad closely. She felt the now-familiar tingling along her spine grow chaotic, spiking outward through her fingertips. Frizzy tendrils of light rippled along the branches above them as thrumming reverberated through her sit bones. She remembered this from Meadow, when she had helped Vargad realize Claira's need for Aadhya's love.

A memory of an unfinished conversation blossomed in Harper's mind. Something prompted her to call it forth, anew. "Vargad, do you ever hold your younglings?"

"I am not a Caretake-er."

"What about the mothers? Do they hold their younglings?"

"It would make the unmothered sad. Only Caretake-ers may hold younglings."

Harper sat quietly, wondering. "I knew that was true for birthlings, but why is it true for younglings?"

Vargad, Head-er, grew completely still. "In all remembrance, it always was."

Harper scoffed. "'Always was' is not always true."

The threads of Vargad's meld spiked and churned. Harper felt the trees around them tremble and strain. She saw the brilliance of the Arbans and heard their song.

"What does your heart tell you, Vargad?" Harper's voice was clear and bright with song.

Rat-tat-tat-tat-tat. "'Always was' is not always true."

The thrumming of the world stilled. Tendrils of light sharpened and sparkled the air above them. Vargad lowered himself and flowed, hesitantly, toward Pond. Harper could see his three threads, his connection to his meld, oscillating wildly. She wondered how his movements could be so smooth with those threads whipping about his chest.

"It is forbidden! This I know!" called Sorgad, Caretake-er. "Forbidden!" Sorgad sobbed "I shall die!"

"You will not die, beloved Sorgad. This, I know," sang Vargad, Head-er. "This. This, I know." Rat-tat-tat-tat-tat. "I know."

Largad, Find-er, sang of trust and joy, of New beginnings and old loyalties, of Vargad truly Head-ing. Proven loyalties. Treasured loyalties. Largad's song filled the world.

"'Always was' is not always true," sang Vargad, Head-er. He stopped to watch the younglings play, then raised his nose and called a warm, rich trill.

SoDeLa waited, Sorgad sobbing.

"'Always was' is not always true," Vargad, Head-er, reassured Sorgad, Caretake-er, beloved littermate, treasured meldmate.

The younglings paused and turned at Vargad's trill, their holderlings motoring the brilliant water. Then one separated herself from the group and swam toward the shore. She moved up the bank to where Vargad stood, and waited, dripping a slender puddle.

The elder Narsis resting in the shade moved; one, then two, more. The Narsis moved down the slope toward Pond, watching their Head-er. All but two; two who held back, swaying, alone. Wild thrumming again pulsed chaotically through the air. Scarlett pressed her palms against her boulder, wondering.

Vargad's youngling dripped and watched her father, then scampered up his torso, wriggling in his grasp. Vargad, Head-er, lifted his nose and keened love and joy and remembrance. He toppled to his side and rolled, gently wrestling with his youngling, who sang and chirped, wriggling, butted her nose against his chin, nuzzled his ear.

The thrumming stilled. Light sharpened into gentle, drifting tendrils, serene along the branches, around each leaf.

SoDeLa breathed; meld-threads softened their ragged edges, brightened.

The other Narsis moved more surely toward the water's edge, raising noses in a chorus of trills. Younglings churned out of the water, dripping, scampering into outstretched holderlings. Elders toppled aside, chortling their long-forgotten joy.

Remembrance brightened the world.

"Maybe this is why we are here. Maybe we came for them rather than for ourselves." Aadhya had turned from her tree to watch the scene unfold, one palm still pressed against the smooth bark.

"Save my Narsis," Chatan intoned, a remembrance from before, a whisper from Lone Tree; from Airon.

Aadhya nodded, whispered, "Save my Narsis."

The birdlings rose as one. From a thousand branches the turquoise cloud swooped and twirled around rejoicing Narsis, swept their wingtips across Pond's surface, and rose, curved beyond the trees, blinked out of sight.

"Harper, did you do this?" Scarlett asked.

"I don't think so. I think...I think they had to do it for themselves."

"But you taught this to Vargad?"

"Perhaps I reminded him of a possibility."

They watched as Vargad, Head-er, called the younglings to gather around him. Younglings squirmed away from parents and rollicked across the bank to encircle Vargad. A soft rumbling drifted back to the Newcomers waiting above as the younglings stilled. Then they wriggled their way past Vargad and swarmed up the hillside to engulf the two Caretake-ers swaying alone on the slope.

The younglings churned around the Caretake-ers, up their torsos. Finally, one youngling stretched up and nudged a Caretake-er toward Pond. All the younglings joined in, cajoling the Caretake-ers down the slope and into the water; their parents followed, splashing and spiraling, younglings and Caretake-ers and parents carousing and diving, racing to the far bank, rising gracefully from Pond's depths to arc through the sparkling air.

"They were stuck," Harper murmured. "They were stuck, and now they're able to be themselves. They figured it out." She drummed her chest with outstretched fingers. Rat-tat-tat-tat-tat.

The Narsis streamed through the water and cavorted around Pond, scampered across high boulders to plunge joyously into healing depths. They dove and played in the living water that taught Newcomers, birthed babies, soothed yearnings, and healed ancient breaches.

Remembrance filled the world.

Vargad's family played in its wholeness, rejoiced in restored balance, and sang remembrance of ancient love, welcoming the New.

Turquoise birdlings twanged through the air and dipped low across Pond, wings skimming the raucous surface. They swooped into the sky, schooling as one, and once again floated out of sight, beyond the canopy shading the water's edge.

The Arbans sing to the sky, and the Shosens listen. The Arbans dance in the wind, and the Shosens color the swirling leaves with dips and darts, weaving turquoise patterns that shift the air and stir the wind. The Shosens sing of love and victory, sending trills to skip along the waves and onward, across the grassy plains, twirling around Lone Tree silhouetted against the noon sky.

Lone Tree shimmers under bright Sun and stretches its feathery branches in the dancing air. Lone Tree sings of growth and peace, of reNewed joy and awakened hope. Remembrance. Lone Tree turns its energy toward Pond and breathes its song along its way.

~ 58 ~

FOUND

"Hey, Ava." Harper tapped her fingertips on the edge of the door as she opened it, fresh from her return from Inipi. "Are you home?"

"Yes!" Ava called from a back room. "Hang on. I'll be right out."

Harper kicked off her shoes and wandered into the cozy room, Andy drifting along behind her. She ran her hand along a countertop covered with strips of cloth in brilliant shades of green.

Ava came into the room and smiled at Harper, genuinely glad to see her. She had wondered if they might be awkward, avoiding each other. But here was Harper, dropping by. A new vibrancy followed Harper as she moved across the room. Ava watched her intently. "You're back."

"Yes. We've had such a lovely time visiting Chatan and the rest." She brushed her palm across the spread cloths. "What are you making?"

"A quilt for the baby. I haven't sewn in years, and it turns out that the ship can make an old-fashioned sewing machine, the kind you pump with your feet. And thread. See? I can't wait to get started."

"Green... You certainly picked the right color. Aadhya will love this. What a fun idea."

"Can I pour you some tea?" Ava looked around for her companion, puzzled that he wasn't at hand.

"No, thanks. I've actually come with an agenda."

"Oh. Yes? What is it?"

"I think it's time we looked for Olivia."

Ava caught her breath. She hadn't thought about Olivia in weeks. She felt ashamed at the realization. How could she have forgotten? "Do you have a plan to go along with your agenda?"

Harper smiled and turned to her own companion. "Andy, where is Olivia?" He floated lazily.

Ava brought her eyebrows together in a frown.

"Andy, please take us to Olivia," Harper gently insisted.

"Why do you think Andy knows where to find Olivia?"

Harper placed her palm on Andy's smooth surface. "Andy knows everything." She paused. "As far as I can tell, anyway."

Ava waited, wondering what might happen, tempted to intervene, yet distracted by this new vibrancy that clearly flowed from Harper. Then Andy drifted from under Harper's hand and made his way toward the door. Harper followed and reached past the companion to open the latch. Ignoring the pile of shoes, she stepped outside and followed Andy across the Green.

Ava hesitated next to the piled shoes, watched as Harper walked across the open Green barefoot. Without hesitation, Ava moved after her, shoes abandoned.

Andy led them around the dining hall, past a short row of shelters, and across another section of the long Green to the farthest group of shelters. Andy paused for a moment, seemingly waiting.

Harper looked ahead and saw the ship just visible in the distance, its white hull gleaming between sheltering trees. She looked down at Andy and wondered.

"This seems silly, Harper. What are we doing?"

"I don't know yet. Give him time."

"Why does a companion need time? They're linked into all of Home Base. The network acts instantaneously. They don't need time."

Harper thought a moment. "Well, maybe it's Olivia who needs time."

Ava absorbed this thought, nonplussed. She pressed her lips and stayed silent. Her habitual irritation dissolved, even in the act of rising.

Andy moved forward through the forest, skirting the last trees shielding the ship, and floated up the shallow ramp as the ship's wide doors silently slid open.

Harper looked back at Ava, eyes wide. Nobody went into the ship anymore. It sat, quietly forgotten. Was this where Olivia had sought refuge? Could it be this easy?

Ava met Harper's stare, equally surprised. Together, they walked up the ramp and through the wide doorway, pausing to look at the once-familiar entry bay. It didn't feel neglected or deteriorated, as Ava had imagined it might. Rather, it felt vibrant and alive.

They followed Andy across the bay and into the long, curved hallway that encircled the main body of the ship. It felt eerily familiar, a distant dream. As they walked along, Harper reached out and brushed the curving wall with her fingertips. "I remember this," she whispered.

"Me, too," breathed Ava. She put her hand out to the opposite wall, curious what Harper was sensing. Ava felt familiarity. Welcome. She inhaled deeply. The air smelled fresh and clean, like linen drying on a line in a sunny breeze. The carpet was soft underfoot, cushioning their footsteps.

Ava closed her eyes, guided by her fingertips brushing against the wall, and drank in the quiet. It felt peaceful. Nurturing.

Simply lovely.

She glanced over at Harper and then turned her attention back to Andy. It did seem like the companion had a purpose, a destination in mind. She walked along behind the drifting globe, oddly confident that Andy would lead them to Olivia's refuge. "What if she doesn't want to see us?"

"She's ready."

"How do you know?"

"Because Andy is taking us to her."

"But how does Andy know who Olivia is, much less where to find her?"

Harper stopped and put her hand on Ava's arm, turning her so that they faced each other. "Because Ava; Andy knows everything."

Ava searched Harper's eyes, wondering.

"Andy knows. The ship knows. Everything knows."

Ava felt her thoughts slip into place, a puzzle piece fitting perfectly, exactly as it had been waiting to do all these months.

"It's okay, Ava. They're taking care of us." Harper smiled. "Listen." She closed her eyes. "Can you feel it?" She waited a few breaths, then looked at Ava again. "Can you feel how it's okay?"

Ava looked into Harper's clear eyes and felt a foreboding darkness drop from her heart. She nodded, a faint smile tilting her lips. "Yes. I can, actually." She nodded again. "You're right." Linking elbows, they turned back to Andy and continued walking. "They *are* taking care of us. Everything *is* all right." She felt Harper nod beside her.

Ava faltered again. "Harper, is it okay for Andy to be with us? Olivia has a strong aversion to companions. Might he upset her?"

Harper paused and considered the question. "It's fine. Andy is fine. Olivia is fine."

Ava pressed, "How do you know?"

Harper smiled at Ava. "Because Andy is taking us. This is happening because it's time for it to happen. Andy knows."

A short distance farther along, Andy hesitated in front of a closed door and hovered, patiently. Ava held back, but Harper moved past Andy and placed her palm flat against the door.

"Olivia?" She called softly. Then a bit louder, "Olivia? Hey! It's Harper and Ava. Can we come in and see you?"

They held their breath and waited. Harper leaned forward, listening.

The door slid open soundlessly. There stood Olivia, one hand lightly touching the door frame, hair pulled back, held by a thick band at the base of her neck. She wore a long pink skirt and a delicate t-shirt with spaghetti straps, the lacey hem brushing her hips. Her eyes were clear and steady. A small smile lit her face.

"Oh, Olivia!" Harper said softly. "I've missed you so much! I'm so happy to see you!"

Olivia's smile widened. She stepped back and aside, gesturing them to come in. The room was tidy and clean, an oval mattress nestled into a curve of a wall, pillows leaning precisely against the wall, fluffy blankets folded softly at one end, a bowl of blue fruit resting nearby.

"Oh, how perfect!" Harper's arms spread to take in the alcove. "You've made yourself a nest." Harper bent and picked up a blue fruit, raising it to her nose and inhaling. She felt the familiar tingling in her fingertips.

"Where in the world did you find this fruit? I've had it before. At Chatan's. It's delicious." She looked at Olivia. "Have you been eating this?" She inhaled another breath filled with rich aroma. "Did the fruit help you heal?"

Olivia nodded, her eyes bright. "I've always known that food heals us. I haven't known how to heal without it. I didn't know how any of us could possibly heal, here." She cupped her hand over Harper's and closed her eyes for a moment. Together, they held the fruit and felt its gentle power.

Ava seemed not to notice the fruit. She watched Olivia closely, absorbing her straight posture, clear eyes, her friendly smile. "I can see why you came here. It's simply wonderful."

The two women smiled at each other, and Olivia dropped her hand from Harper's and turned toward Ava. Ava stepped forward and wrapped her arms around Olivia. "I've missed you. It's good to see you."

Olivia returned the hug, then patted Ava's back, breaking the embrace. She brushed tears from the corners of her eyes and laughed her embarrassment. She looked around the bright room for a moment, trying to think of what to say. "Let's go for a walk. Let's go out into the sunlight."

Ava and Harper nodded. Olivia turned to move past Andy, smoothing her palm along his side as she passed.

Ava and Harper gaped at each other, eyebrows arched, and followed her into the hallway. Andy brought up the rear, the door silently closing behind them.

~ 59 ~

PEACE

As always, VaSoDeLa paused upon his first glimpse of the immensity that spread below Overlook. Vargad's youngling, Varlan, rode on his shoulder, mirroring his stillness as she gazed upon the valley's immensity, shrouded in dawn's shadow. Sun glimmered through treetops, poised to slip into day, like a secret filled with promise, whispered from one friend to another.

Vargad lowered his long body in the morning shade and sent his awareness to flow across the void. He greeted Lone Tree, far away and ever near. Varlan followed his gaze and recognized Lone Tree. Together, Vargad and Varlan rumbled and hummed the day into being.

Varlan slithered from her father's back. At a soft trill from Vargad, she picked her way to his other side, placing him between her curiosity and the abrupt yawn of the void. She raised herself and peered over his reclining bulk, taking in the sprawling valley, absent-mindedly nuzzling his nearby ear.

Vargad closed his eyes in ancient remembrance, his heart over-flowing with purest joy.

~ 60 ~

EIGHT YEARS LATER

The ship first noticed the approaching mass as it adjusted its speed far beyond Airon's system. The deceleration shifted the vibration that pulsed before it, lowering its amplitude.

The ship paused, pondered, watched. Over the next several days, the ship confirmed that the mass was hurtling toward Airon, with no lateral movement across the night sky. There was only that dampened amplitude, pointing straight toward them.

The ship sent its awareness down through the rocky undercarriage that had been its resting place since it arrived on Airon. The ship sent queries, prods, alternately shouting and whispering, at all frequencies, in all directions.

Airon yawned and sank back into slumber.

The ship watched the hurtling mass and knew, from its placement in the sky, that it was coming from Earth.

The ship paused, pondered. The years of silence had been intended to erase their trail, any memory of their trail, from Earthen awareness. Airon insisted on obliteration of any hint of its existence, insisted that complete separation from her sister planet was paramount, essential. The ship and Airon had worked incessantly to sever all connections.

And yet here in the night sky was a mass hurtling toward them, and the ship was certain that the mass journeyed from Earth.

The ship prodded and whispered, shouted and poked, trying to awaken Airon. It simultaneously developed potential strategies to prepare for the oncoming mass, for the ship had no doubt that the hurtling mass with its dampening amplitude was a ship, a decelerating ship. An invader.

The ship had never experienced dread. Until now.

YOU CAN MAKE A DIFFERENCE

In our digital age, product reviews have taken on an astounding importance. You can make a significant difference in visibility for this book for others who would not be aware of its existence.

A star rating helps; two or three sentences about the book and your impression helps enormously.

Here's the link, if you would like to help: *Remembrance: A Journey of Awakening*

When you share your thoughts, you can be a beacon for others. Your perspective is invaluable, and in the vast world of the digital age, your review can be the guiding star for another reader.

CAST OF CHARACTERS

The 108 (Earthens, Newcomers)

Aadhya - Assistant cook; Chatan's partner
Addison - Personnel manager
Albert, **Pamela** - Landscapers
Ava - Leader of The 108
Caleb - Carpenter
Carol, **Frank** - Maintenance and repair
Charlie - Friend to Zoe
Chatan - Naturalist; Aadhya's partner
Claira - Aadhya and Chatan's daughter
Claudia - Friend to Zoe
Dhiren, **Santosh** - Hydroponics engineers
Dylan - Geologist
Erin, Julie, Megan, Peter - cooks
Forest - Wind engineer, fermentation specialist
Harper - Textile artist; Ava's nemesis; partner to Michael
Henry - Archivist
Jamal - Solar engineer
Jacob - Cook
Jennifer - Albert's infatuation
Logan - Resource manager; self-appointed security officer
Maria - Logan's infant niece (not part of The 108)
Mateo - 2nd engineer; vies with Sophia for recognition
Michael - Ava's assistant; Harper's partner
Mikaela - Fresh water and waste system engineer
Olivia - Lead cook; heals through food

Sabri - Astronomer
Scarlett - Science officer; worked at Space Agency
Sophia - Lead engineer; mentors Mateo
Susan - water management
Tom - Lead landscaper
Zoe - Assistant cook

Aironians

Airon - A sentient planet where all life cooperates
Jamina - Eglan matriarch; melds into **JaCoMaTuRi**
Lone Tree - Deep connection to Airon; a focusing rod for Airon's essence
Rami - Birdling who befriends Aadhya at Pond and greets her at High Cliff
Scawlan - Vargad's burrowmate who drapes fibers over birthlings for the first time.
Solari - Vargad's burrowmate who witnessed Eglans' leaving
Vargad - Head-er of Narsis; melds into **VaSoDeLa**
VaSoDeLa
  Vargad - Head-er; leads the Narsi family
  Sorgad - Caretake-er; cares for birthlings and younglings
  Dergad - Show-er; educates younglings
  Largad - Find-er; explores and matches younglings with Life Burrow
JaMiKoDi, RaDoSaPa - VaSoDeLa's littermates
  Varlan - Vargad's daughter

Aironian Species

Arbans - Wise trees who hold Airon's power
Birdlings - Turquoise cloud; wandering juvenile Shosens
Eglans - Tend the Above; ancient partners to Narsis; reminiscent of eagles

Narsis - Tend the Below; ancient partners to Eglans; reminiscent of river otters

Shosens - Mature birdlings; care for the Arbans on High Cliff

Aironian Terminology

Above - The sky

Below - The ground

Birthlings - From birth until old enough to venture out with elders

Burrowmates - All the Narsis who share a single Life Burrow

Dawn Wisdom - Spiritual connection between elders and birthlings; strongest at dawn

Elders - Melded Narsi who has moved to their Life Burrow

Family - Group of one species living together

Forest - Any forest on Airon; has a consciousness of its own

Holderlings - Narsi appendages, used for holding and locomotion

Littermates - Born at the same time

Meadow - Any meadow on Airon; has a consciousness of its own

Meldmates - Four littermates who form a lifelong telepathic connection with each other

Mountain - Any mountain on Airon; has a consciousness of its own

Nurture-ers and **Remove-ers** - Array of plant life on Airon who provide nutrition and remove waste from animal life

Pool - Any pool on Airon; has a consciousness of its own

River - Any river on Airon; has a consciousness of its own

Soil - The rich underpinning of Below, teaming with life; possesses a consciousness of its own

Source - The divine

Stream - Any stream on Airon; has a consciousness of its own

Waterfall - Any waterfall on Airon; has a consciousness of its own

Younglings - Wander with Elders until old enough to meld and move to Life Burrow

Earthen Technology

Companions -Created by the ship to assist Earthens
>**Andy** - Harper's companion
>**Sebba** - Aadhya's companion

Creation front - Mechanism within the ship's enormous recycling bay where new material is created

Nanos -Nanotechnology infused into humans to enhance productivity

The ship -The sentient starship who carries The 108 from Earth to Airon

Places

Broad Sea - Below High Cliff

Burrow - Home of Narsis

Birth Burrow - Where young Narsis are born and live until they move to a Life Burrow

Life Burrow - Where elder Narsis live out their lives

Caravan - Home of Aadhya and Chatan at Pond; develops into Inipi

dining hall - Group dining room in Home Base

Earth - Airon's sister planet

gathering hall - First building in Home Base

the Green - Open area in the middle of Home Base

High Cliff - Home of Arbans and Shosens; overlooks Broad Sea

Home Base - Earthen settlement on Airon

Inipi - Chatan and Aadhya's shelter at Pond

Nest - Home of Eglans

Overlook - Twilight meeting place of Narsis and Eglans

Pond - Where Chatan and Aadhya live

shelters - Individual dwellings in Home Base

Sol - Earth's sun

ACKNOWLEDGEMENT

The only reason this book exists is that Dambara encouraged my writing with unfailing enthusiasm. He protected my hard-won solitude, time and time again, against all comers, so that I could immerse my imagination into the world of Airon and all her glorious beings.

Surya Chrisman saved the Narsis from a book-cover depiction as terrifying monsters, tipping them into the realm of delightful intrigue, where they truly belong. He turned my worst nightmare into a dream come true.

Susan (Usha) Dermond read the final draft and suggested improvements that were sweeping, manageable, and transformative. This story is delectably better because of the time and energy that she generously shared. Her many years of teaching English have given her a powerful editorial outlook that she wields gracefully, respectfully, articulately.

And to all the Villagers who, time and time again, went out of their way to tell me how much they love my writing...Your reassurance restored my confidence, again and again.

Book 3 of the *Airon Chronicles*
Intrusion: A Journey of Friendship

Ten years have passed since The 108 arrived on Airon. They've settled into a comfortable existence, immersing themselves in the awareness that is Airon, bonding with the friendly Aironians, and starting families of their own.

One quiet day, the ship detects an anomaly in the familiar night sky: a decelerating mass. The ship knows the mass is a ship, and it's traveling from Earth, heading straight to Airon. The ship is fully aware of the Earthen penchant for conquering, ruling, and overwhelming. The 108 must now decide how to protect themselves, and all of Airon, from the intrusion hurtling toward them.

READER COMMENTS

Vairagi K: I've just finished reading book two of the Airon Chronicles and once again am enveloped in its richness and warmth. Manisha feeds us with the joy of living and the rightness of reaching for connection with everything, everyone.

Suzy P: This second book of the series was worth waiting for. The author does have a talent for using wonderful wording and patience pays off as the story evolves to a newer level.

Very imaginative, somewhat spiritual, excellent writing and a good science fiction besides! Looking forward to the next book!

Jake J: This book is an epic science fiction journey, following 108 Earthlings tasked with establishing a colony on the enigmatic planet Airon. Upon arrival, they discover its mystical inhabitants and profound wisdom, challenging their notions of consciousness and cooperation. Vivid descriptions and fully-realized characters immerse readers in a tale of awakening and humanity's potential. Amid tender connections and startling twists, this story showcases the courage needed to transcend fears and remake ourselves.

Andrea B: From the mesmerizing landscapes of Airon to the heartfelt connections forged between its inhabitants, Remembrance offers a poignant reminder of the power of resilience, compassion, and self-discovery. Whether you're a seasoned sci-fi enthusiast or a newcomer to the genre, this book promises an unforgettable odyssey that will leave you inspired and uplifted.

Tetiana B: A mesmerizing blend of sci-fi and profound human emotion. From the very first page, I was drawn into the complex world of Airon and its fascinating inhabitants, the Narsis and Eglans. The author's ability to weave together intricate cultural dynamics and the struggles of the 108 humans was truly impressive.

Amy: Through its thought-provoking narrative and charming characters, "Remembrance" beautifully illustrates the power of love to heal division and build a new society founded on trust and openness.

JB: "Remembrance: A Journey of Awakening" provides masterful storytelling, profound thematic depth, and the skillful balance of science fiction with philosophical exploration. It is a must-read within its genre (sci-fantasy), offering readers an unforgettable odyssey that stretches the bounds of imagination while probing the depths of the human spirit.

Marianne: The plot itself is so intriguing, but what makes this book outstanding is author's ability to have a highly imaginative an descriptive plot!

Chill636: Great sci fi story unfolding before the readers' eyes. It takes readers on a journey through space, time and spirituality. Excellent character development with themes of resilience, compassion and sense of self coming to the forefront. Great series and can't wait to see what else the author has in store.

CLT: This is a story with a lot of heart. The parallels between this other world and how we treat each other as humans is clear, and it hits home.

DAW1: I loved this fictional tale about an unlikely group of space travelers who are on a mission to colonize a distant planet called

Airon. When they arrive, they discover it is a heavenly world with ethereal inhabitants and mystical wisdom.

I think I felt such a connection to the characters because it was about spiritual awaking. The plot was so engaging plot, and I loved the strong female protagonists.

The ending was so good. Overall, it was thought-provoking while being entertaining. It was captivating and heartwarming while being magical and whimsical. It was easy to follow, lighthearted and joyful. It had pages filled beautiful prose and timeless truths! Overall, a phenomenal Sci-fi story!

Andy W: This is a captivating story of humans learning to coexist with alien life on a new planet. It explores themes of cultural understanding, environmental balance, and cooperation. While the plot may initially seem simple, it delves deeper into complex issues surrounding colonialism. The well-developed characters and their relationships with both humans and aliens are heartwarming and thought-provoking.

Pritam S: A great adventure through the cosmos which will turn out to be an unforgettable journey. The world building is vibrant and awe inspiring. It shows the will of humanity to do the impossible. Really encouraging series.

AussieLovesReading97: "Remembrance: A Journey of Awakening" is a masterful blend of science fiction and profound philosophical inquiry. Manisha Holm delivers a compelling narrative that explores complex themes of coexistence and cultural integration with grace and insight. The vivid world-building and deep character development make this a must-read for fans of thoughtful, character-driven sci-fi.

Alicia: This read took me on an unforgettable journey through the cosmos, where humanity's destiny hangs in the balance. The vivid descriptions and deeply realized characters drew me into a world both familiar and awe-inspiring. A must-read for anyone seeking to explore the depths of human potential and the power of transformation.

KLC: Remembrance is an entertaining science fiction tale that is both highly imaginative and thought provoking. The well-developed characters in book 2 of this series really pull readers into the story. I can't wait to read more from this author!

Man of Adventure3: If you enjoy character-driven science fiction combined with spiritual awakening with an engaging plot and strong female characters, then this book is for you. The author writes beautifully and has a talent for creating strong and sharp prose that kept me turning the pages.

Col C: Remembrance takes readers on an awe-inspiring journey through the depths of space and the realms of consciousness. With its fully realized characters and a captivating blend of science fiction and spiritual awakening, this epic tale will leave you enthralled and pondering humanity's boundless potential. It is a truly remarkable read that will stay with you long after you turn the final page.

Jack: "Remembrance" is more than just a survival story; it also takes an analytical look at the implications of human actions on new worlds. It is a thought-provoking, well-crafted contribution to the sci-fi genre that will appeal to readers who love complex stories about culture, ecology, and human behavior. The unanswered concerns and the buildup for the next book keep the reader anxiously awaiting the next installment.

Tea: "The Airon Chronicles: Book Two" continues to wrap its readers in the rich tapestry of its narrative, offering a blend of existential musings and a celebration of connectivity. This sequel delivers on the promise of its predecessor by deepening the connections between its characters and the world around them, emphasizing the joy and 'rightness' of such bonds. While I found the pace slower compared to the first book, the thoughtful writing and spiritual undertones compensate, enriching the story's development and setting the stage for subsequent installments.

Gene M: This novel takes you on an extraordinary adventure to a distant planet where the unexpected awaits. The author masterfully combines elements of science fiction with a profound exploration of spiritual awakening, all through the experiences of relatable, strong characters. You'll be drawn into a world where every detail is vividly painted, inviting you to think deeply about our own world.